ATTAGIRLS

Based on a true story

by

Paul Olavesen-Stabb

AETHERIS

First edition 2021 United Kingdom

Aetheris Publishing Ltd
3 Shottery Brook Office Park
Stratford-upon-Avon
Warwickshire CV37 9NR
England

www.aetheris.co.uk

ISBN: 978-1-5272-8942-0

To Marianne, Nadine and Victoria

Front cover photograph taken by the author at the site of the RAF Bomber crash of 2nd June 1943 at Broadway Tower in the Cotswolds, England.

Aircraft A.W. Whitley Z6639, of No 24 O.T.U from RAF Honeybourne, Worcestershire crashed while on operational training killing all members of the five-person crew.

In memory of:

FLT/SGT H.G. Hagen (Pilot R.C.A.F.)
SGT R.S. Phillips (NAV RAF)
FLT/SGT D.H. Kelly (B.A. R.C.A.F)
SGT D.A. Marriott (W.A.G. RAF V.R.)
SGT G.E. Ekins (A.G. RAF V.R.)

We will remember them.

Foreword

by Minnie Churchill DL

Lord Beaverbrook, World War II Minister of Aircraft Production, gave an appropriate tribute at the closing ceremony disbanding the ATA at White Waltham on 30 November 1945:

> *"Without the ATA, the days and nights of the Battle of Britain would have been conducted under conditions quite different from the actual events. They carried out the delivery of aircraft from the factories to the RAF, thus relieving countless numbers of RAF pilots for duty in the battle. Just as the Battle of Britain is the accomplishment and achievement of the RAF, likewise it can be declared that the ATA sustained and supported them in the battle. They were soldiers fighting in the struggle just as completely as if they had been engaged on the battlefront".*

The ATA delivered 309,011 aircraft of 147 types, including 57,286 Spitfires and Seafires; 29,401 Hurricanes; nearly 25,000 Lancasters, Halifaxes and Stirlings; 171,934 single engine and 110,636 twin engine; and nearly 1,000 flying boats. 742,614 hours were flown covering over 18,000,000 miles. At the height of the war over 550 male and over 127 female pilots were operational and there were 154 fatalities.

All of this remarkable service was the brainchild of my father, Gerard d'Erlanger, later knighted, a British banker and an early director of British Airways. As Commodore he commanded the ATA throughout the war and gathered together a wonderful selection of both men and women pilots. His words tell it all:

"These men and women are Ferry Pilots. A.T.A. officially stands for 'Air Transport Auxiliary' but by nickname it has many other labels: 'Ancient and Tattered Airmen' is one; 'All Terrified Airmen' is another; 'Anywhere to anywhere' is the description I favour as describing most aptly what our initials stand for; since our job is, with or without notice, promptly to fly any of His Majesty's aircraft from any point of origin to any destination".

Acknowledgements

by Paul Olavesen-Stabb

First and foremost, I should like to thank Graham Rose, the son of the heroine of this book - ATA pilot Molly Rose, and the current Chairman of the Air Transport Auxiliary Association (ATAA). Since hearing the incredible story of his mother, I have been inspired by Graham's encouragement, ideas, knowledge and particularly to the original sources pertaining to his mother's life and work at the ATA, much of which has been used in the writing of this book. Without Graham's thoughtful guidance and patience, the book would not have accurately told the story of his mother.

I am also extremely grateful to the following people for their contributions: RAF Squadron Leader (RTD) Andrew Rawcliffe, my business partner at Aetheris Films, with whom I co-wrote the original motion picture screenplay of *Attagirls*; Richard Poad, Chairman of the Maidenhead Heritage Centre who kindly wrote the Introduction to this book; John Webster, Secretary of the Air Transport Auxiliary Association who provided a great deal of technical information and who was kind enough to allow Andy and I an in-depth look into the archives of the ATA; the RAF Club on Piccadilly in London for unlimited access to the RAF Club Library; and to the Battle of Britain Memorial Flight (BBMF) for their in-depth details of the Lancaster bomber, Supermarine Spitfire, Hawker Hurricane and several other WWII aircraft.

I should like to extend a special thanks to Minnie Churchill for penning the Foreword to this book and for sharing her invaluable memories of her father Baron Gerard John Regis Leo d'Erlanger, founder and Commodore of the ATA.

Introduction

by Richard Poad MBE
Chairman, Maidenhead Heritage Centre and ATA Museum

Until relatively recently Air Transport Auxiliary (ATA) was one of the forgotten stories of World War II, despite making an enormous contribution to victory by keeping the RAF and the Fleet Air Arm continuously supplied with serviceable aircraft. The idea of using civilian pilots as a kind of Territorial Air Force was put forward in 1938, when the Civil Air Guard was formed to offer subsidized flying training to people up to 50 years old. There were also many pilots who had learned to fly in the 1920's and 1930's who were either too old or unfit for RAF service but wanted to use their flying skills in some way in the impending conflict. At the outbreak of war, ATA came into being as an autonomous subsidiary of the airline British Airways (later BOAC). Gerard d'Erlanger, a director of British Airways was put in charge of arranging the recruitment, flight testing and organisation of male pilots aged between 28 and 50 with a minimum of 250 flying hours. He moved quickly and the first group of pilots signed up on September 11th, ready to be loaned to the RAF provided they passed some rapid training at RAF Upavon.

ATA's "Ancient and Tattered Airmen", though widely experienced, were either too old or unfit for active service, some having served with the Royal Flying Corps in World War I. There was even a retired admiral, while Charles Dutton and Stewart Keith-Jopp both had only one arm: this handicap did not stop them flying aircraft such as the Spitfire and the Typhoon.

For the first 6 months, ATA pilots based at Whitchurch supported the RAF's existing ferry pools at Bristol Filton and Hucknall near Derby. In February 1940 ATA established its headquarters at White Waltham near

Maidenhead in Berkshire and took over from service pilots the routine task of ferrying RAF and RN warplanes between factories, maintenance units and front-line squadrons. ATA expanded rapidly and credit for turning a piece of British improvisation into a well-oiled machine must go to Commodore Gerard d'Erlanger.

The first 8 women joined ATA on New Year's Day 1940, recruited into this man's world by Pauline Gower, who had made a living giving joy rides with a flying circus. The women all had over 600 flying hours but despite their experience were restricted to flying non-operational types of plane, such as trainers or communications aircraft. They were also paid 20% less than the men, which was typical of the times. On 19 July 1941 Winnie Crossley was the first woman to be checked out on a Hurricane fighter, and from then on the sky was the limit. Out of a total of around 1250 pilots and flight engineers employed by ATA, 168 were women including the famous trail-blazing pilot Amy Johnson and 4 female flight engineers. Janice Harrington took the job as she was too short to become a pilot. She was killed in an accident in a Mosquito and is buried in Maidenhead.

It is a myth that ATA pilots received no training. ATA had its own flying schools at Thame for initial flying training and White Waltham for advanced flying training and recurrent skills checks. In each class of aircraft pilots were trained on a generic type, for instance the Harvard for single-engined fighters for which there were no dual control versions. Pilots were allocated a classification according to the types of aircraft they had been cleared to fly. Yet sometimes they had never seen a particular aircraft type before.

Men and women came from all over the world to join ATA and there was even a royal prince from Siam. The largest contingent from Europe were 17 Poles, including three women who reached Britain after escaping via the Balkans and France. Flight Captain Klemens Dlugaszewski had years of experience with LOT Polish Airlines and had such an unpronounceable name that he was known as "Captain Double Whisky". Sir Freddie Laker, the buccaneering pioneer of cheap air travel was an ATA flight engineer based at White Waltham. John Gulson was awarded the George Medal for his part in the rescue of the crew of a Halifax bomber which crashed into the railway cutting at White Waltham in July 1944, with live bombs on board.

In the mature ATA pilots were based at 14 Ferry Pools as far apart as Hamble near Southampton and Lossiemouth near Inverness in Scotland.

Two of these Ferry Pools (Hamble and Cosford) had only women pilots, with female Commanding Officers: Margot Gore at Hamble and Marion Wilberforce at Cosford. Several were near aircraft factories which were priority targets for the Luftwaffe. The peak monthly output from the Spitfire factory at Castle Bromwich was 320 machines, so it was necessary to move aircraft away to relative safety as soon as they came off the production line.

ATA was much more than just its ferry pilots, who formed around one sixth of the total workforce. There were flying instructors, ground school instructors, ground engineers, crash rescue teams, met. officers, motor transport drivers, nurses and doctors, administration staff and so on; there were even Air Cadets and Sea Cadets employed as messengers and auxiliary crew members.

From late 1944, ATA's operations began to contract, with training reducing and ferry pools beginning to close. Finally only White Waltham remained. After a spectacular Air Pageant at the end of September 1945, the ATA base was closed on November 30th, though a handful of pilots continued to fly for 41 Group RAF until March the following year. In total 173 ATA aircrew had died in ATA service, including Amy Johnson. Poor weather, mechanical failure or accidents in training were the principal causes.

There are memorials in St Paul's Cathedral, London and at various airfields including White Waltham, Ringway, Ratcliffe, Whitchurch and Hamble. The largest group of ATA graves is at All Saints' Cemetery in Maidenhead, where 17 official war graves represent men and women of 5 different nationalities. However official British government recognition did not come until September 2008 when all surviving veterans were awarded a special Veterans Badge at a ceremony at 10 Downing Street in London. As Molly Rose, the heroine of this novel, said "Better late than never".

One

The closing bars of Edward Elgar's beautiful and enigmatic choral music *"Ave verum"* reverberate beneath the awe-inspiring and cavernous central dome of St Paul's Cathedral. The vast dome rises impressively two-hundred-and twenty-five feet above the nave, transepts and aisles, dwarfing the choir below; its members immaculately dressed in their white surplices and black robes. As the final bars of music fade, the choir, with bowed heads and hands clasped in front of them, pause before taking their seats, anticipating the ensuing silence.

The majority of those present are members of the Air Transport Auxiliary Association; formed by the descendants of pilots, engineers and ground crew of the Air Transport Auxiliary (ATA). Conceived at the outbreak of the Second World War, the ATA was a British civilian organisation which ferried warplanes between factories, maintenance units and front-line squadrons, freeing up RAF pilots to concentrate on a more combative role and thus making an enormous contribution to the Allied victory.

Although there are more than one hundred in the congregation, they seem almost lost amongst the vast columns supporting the eight spanning arches of the cathedral designed and built by Sir Christopher Wren nearly three centuries before. The dark clothing and sombre expressions of the congregation contrast starkly with the magnificent gilded cornices and ornately decorated English Baroque architecture, known famously as the Jewel of London.

Three elderly ladies are seated in the front pew, a few feet away from a bronze special memorial plaque mounted on the wall. At first glance there is nothing remarkable about the ladies; they are smartly dressed in dark

1

twin-set suits, silver-haired and bespectacled, sitting close together as if warding off the cold. But there is something about their presence and demeanour that sets them apart from the other members of the congregation. And it is not just the winged brooches that each wears on their lapel: there is radiance, an aura of calm steeliness about them which everyone else seems to feel, but to which the ladies themselves appear oblivious.

The silence in the cavernous space is suddenly broken by sharp echoing footsteps as a tall, smartly dressed RAF officer walks from his place towards the memorial plaque. His steely blue uniform is adorned with the rank of a Group Captain, and the gold braid across his right shoulder denotes that he holds the exalted position of a Queen's Equerry, an honour achieved by only a few carefully chosen officers. He walks in front of the seated congregation, each person craning to see him as he cuts a fine figure in his ceremonial attire. His left hand steadies the gilt sword slung on its gold belt, while in his right hand he carries a large wreath of red poppies. He approaches the memorial plaque, carefully lays his wreath, takes two steps back, and salutes. The small sounds of his actions drift high above the congregation; upwards into the Cathedral, into every corner of the vast space above, through the Whispering Gallery and up into the very top of the dome itself.

The three ladies remain motionless only a few feet away from the officer as he holds the salute, standing in silent tribute to those commemorated on the memorial plaque; "To the 173 men and women of the Air Transport Auxiliary who gave their lives in the allied cause between 1940 and 1945". After a short pause, he smartly drops the salute.

One of the ladies stirs from her own quiet reflection and reaches over to take the hand of her companion. Molly, a diminutive lady at over ninety years old, stands and walks unaided, her short silver hair stylishly swept back high above her brow, her brown eyes still bright and intelligent, sparkling with enthusiasm. She walks the short distance to join the officer in front of the memorial plaque. He gently acknowledges her with a smile, reaches for a second wreath and hands it to her. He moves away, his heels clicking loudly in the silence, leaving Molly standing alone.

She reads the inscription as she has done every year without fail since it was unveiled in 1950, a few years after the end of the war and the disbandment of the Air Transport Auxiliary. As Molly studies the plaque, she swallows hard and fights to contain her emotions. For a brief moment

2

her mind is a whirl of images and sounds… speeding aircraft against a mass of colour and action, echoing propellers, the droning hum of aircraft engines, the shouts of familiar voices interspersed with faces from long ago. Her head spins with euphoria as all the while the congregation watches her intently, silently oblivious to the tumult of scenes flashing inside her head.

She takes a steadying breath, composes herself, and steps forward to lay her wreath. She pauses for a few moments, stands back, and turns to walk to the lectern where her eldest son, Graham, waits patiently to assist her up the few steps. She climbs the steps, takes her position and shuffles her notes on the lectern. Once organised, she lifts her head and looks out over the congregation sitting expectantly and silently below her.

Molly gazes across the congregation, their dark clothes sombre against the solid grandeur and awe-inspiring backdrop of the Cathedral. Her two friends on the front row smile and nod encouragingly to her. She takes a deep breath and raises a hand to touch the golden-winged brooch and ceramic branch of lilies on her lapel, both of which were a gift from her beloved husband Bernard. Molly steadies herself and in a strong and clear voice begins to speak.

'Thank you friends and families for coming today to this glorious St Paul's Cathedral to remember those members of the Air Transport Auxiliary who are no longer with us. Those courageous souls – one and all - who served bravely in a time of great adversity. Many whom we knew and loved, and many of whom we lost. Those who, without any thought of self, gave their all; their dedication, and in many cases, their lives in the pursuit of peace and freedom.'

There is ten seconds of silence before Molly continues.

'There are not many of us left now. Some of my close friends…' she stops momentarily to acknowledge the two ladies on the front row '… Joy and Mary, are here today. But many are not – my lovely friends Margie, Diana, Lettice, Jackie…' she stops to catch her breath, fighting to control the quiver that has entered her voice, blinking hard before continuing. '… Irene, Jane, Margo … and so many more. So many.'

Joy and Mary, looking up at their friend, whom they first met more than sixty years before, hold hands and try without success to blink away their tears as the names conjure their own vivid memories.

'I remember it all as if it were yesterday. We were young and ready to do our duty for the country we love. We had wings on our tunics, and wings in our hearts – and we embraced and lived the motto of the incredible organisation we were part of – we were Eager for the Air.'

Molly stops talking and looks over the heads of the congregation, upwards to the magnificently decorated dome of the Cathedral. She stares nostalgically as the ornate ceiling fades to a cloudless blue sky. Molly is smiling.

Two

September 1940

A yellow and black de Havilland Tiger Moth biplane made slow and lugubrious turns between the clouds as if playing a gentle game of hide-and-seek with the sun's rays. The game continued for a few minutes as the little aircraft dodged in and out of the clouds, occasionally disappearing completely, its presence given away only by its engine noise.

The sky had the deep and intense colour of emerald-blue silk and was dotted with almost impossibly white cotton-candy clouds, their under-sides tinged with pink as the sun neared the end of its daily trajectory across the flat Cambridgeshire countryside. Losing its intensity and forming a perfectly round orange orb, the sun dropped gently towards the horizon, casting long shadows from farm buildings and tall trees across the patchwork of well-tended fields. It promised to be a beautiful evening with a spectacular sunset, but for now the view from the aircraft was gin-clear, showing the network of country lanes criss-crossing the fields as far as the eye could see. Glittering shards of light shimmered off the River Cam as it forged its meandering journey north east to join the Great Ouse near Ely, before carving its way towards Kings Lynn and its journey's end in the North Sea.

Appearing after a few seconds from a particularly large and fluffy cumulus, the propeller-driven two-seater began a series of graceful aerobatic manoeuvres, barrel rolling and swooping down towards the ground like a skimming swallow, seeming to drink in the beauty of the Cambridgeshire vista.

A young female pilot was at the controls, with leather flying helmet, goggles and a cream coloured scarf which was blowing haphazardly in the wind. As the evening sun showered her small round angelic face in a golden glow, she whooped with delight and was clearly cherishing the moment and the sights, sounds and smells that only a Tiger Moth can deliver. The aircraft changed speed, direction and attitude, occasionally as if the wind was somehow blowing it from behind, and at other times through clouds which billowed around the Perspex screen, threatening to obscure the forward view.

The pilot pulled the small aircraft towards the orange glow of the sun, climbing steeply and losing speed until the one-hundred-and-twenty horse-power engine could no longer compete with gravity. The seventy-five-inch single-pitch wooden propeller clawed at the air, desperately trying to keep forward momentum, before finally giving up, the aircraft almost stopping in mid-air and the pilot's scarf hanging limply as the airflow subsided. The pilot dexterously averted a full stall by quickly pushing the stick forward and opening the throttle. The engine reacted immediately, the propeller picked up revs and accelerated the aircraft to achieve airflow over its fabric wings, quickly restoring full flight. The scarf billowed rearwards once again and the Tiger Moth continued its progress.

As the pilot moved the control stick hard left, the movement was transmitted by cables through a series of bell-cranks, pulleys and levers to move the flying control surfaces on the lower wings, causing the left wing to drop suddenly. The pilot anticipated the movement, and quickly pulled the aircraft into a steep left-hand turn towards the ground and entered a series of vertical manoeuvres. The world turned sideways as it spun around the front of the aircraft, as if the biplane were stationary and a huge hand was rotating everything else. But the buffeting wind and g-forces pulling the pilot left and right were a strong reminder that the aeroplane was at the mercy of the laws of physics, and that constant attention and skill were required to keep it in the sky.

The air-test complete, the pilot levelled out and gently placed a palm of her hand on the dashboard of the aircraft and, for a brief moment, she felt as though they were as one entity - uniform in their love of the pure and simple freedom that is symbolic of flying into the blue unknown. She checked that the wings were straight and level against the horizon, checked the instruments and fuel gauge, and turned the aircraft to find one of the most notable land-marks in the area: Whitehill, an unmissable statuesque white manor house surrounded by parkland, and home of the Marshall family. The pilot smiled. If there was one thing that she loved as much as flying, it was being at home with her family. Having located the manor house, which almost glowed in the afternoon sun, the pilot dropped the nose of the aircraft, increased the revs, and headed straight for it.

Whitehill was set in twenty-five acres of private grounds which included formal gardens, apple orchards and tennis courts, and was typical of the opulent style of the Edwardian era. The elegant country house looked impressive from the outside, and was spacious and comfortable internally, providing ample space for its wealthy owners to live and entertain in style. Arriving along the gravel drive to a large turning circle in front of the house, visitors were welcomed through a large and impressive front entrance door to a broad and high central hallway and leading to a wide staircase. The opulent and colourful Edwardian-style drawing room was an essential space for social interaction and display, with an oak-panelled room symmetrically paired with an elegant dining room to the other side of the hall in a typical arrangement of neo-Classical domestic planning. Light sparkling from the crystal chandelier and a number of elegant oil paintings depicting country scenes graced the silk-papered walls. The beautifully oak-panelled drawing room, which was the beating heart of the house, was resplendent with several pieces of fine art and formal but comfortable antique furniture, fine fabrics and wall coverings. One of Turner's landscapes graced the prime position above the magnificent Adams fireplace. The furnishings were mainly cherry-wood and mahogany, sumptuously upholstered and covered in pretty orange and green fabrics sourced from Liberty of London. The semi-formal arrangement created a warm, comfortable and inviting drawing room and was symbolic of the well-established social hierarchies and distinctions of décor in an English country house and as frequented by the upper echelons of British society.

Devoid of the usual evening's activities, from quiet games of bridge and canasta to society cocktail parties, or more raucous celebrations with dancing set against a well-furnished stage, the afternoon mood was by contrast somewhat sombre and calm. Despite the warm weather, a fire gently crackled in the large hearth, spitting as the logs settled, and throwing out a subdued amber glow over which could be heard the sound of a radio playing 1940s music. The evening sun streamed through the high patio doors, casting its light around the room, and reflecting off several silver-framed photographs arranged on the side tables. In keeping with the remainder of the room, the photographs were carefully arranged, showing what appeared to be numerous members of the same family. In one large black and white image a mother and father stood before a huge elaborately decorated Christmas tree, surrounded by seven children, six girls and only one boy, the youngest a babe in arms, the tallest, the boy, almost the same height as his father. In this image, they are formally dressed, and staring from the photograph as if transfixed.

Other photographs depict more relaxed family members, some standing alongside aircraft, others beside expensive motor cars, the women in furs and hats, long cigarette holders in hand. The largest of the photographs is a soft-focus portrait of Rosemary Dimsdale, the current matriarch of Whitehill and bluestocking granddaughter of the 6th Lord Dimsdale - a strikingly elegant woman wearing a Parisian haute couture black evening gown. But the most noticeable photograph by far was displayed in an Art Nouveau-styled sterling silver frame made in the form of a latched country gate, showing a newly married couple posing casually in front of a charming village church, beaming with happiness. The bride is holding a pretty bouquet of roses and freesias and her short dark hair is stylishly swept back high above her brow, her brown eyes bright and intelligent, sparkling with enthusiasm and joy. Beside her stands a tall, handsome man, smiling shyly, and immaculately dressed in a Prince of Wales check double-breasted suit.

Through the high bay windows with wide open doors was an expansive view of a long and well-manicured lawn surrounded by an enthralling and quintessential English country estate. Abundant flower beds, box hedges and trimmed topiary provided a playground for a family of swallows who were chattering away in high-pitched peeps. In this magical Golden Hour, the last of the pale mauve blooms of the wisteria spread generously across the conservatory entrance, gradually and gently changed in hue as the sun descended.

In the drawing room, either side of the patio doors, two men were seated in high-backed armchairs, each engrossed in a broadsheet newspaper with the bold headlines "Hitler's Forces March Through Europe" and "Fears of German Invasion". The large newspapers were raised high to take advantage of the evening light, making it easier to read the tightly spaced print but obscuring the men's faces. However, it was evident that each was smartly dressed, one in a hand-made three-piece Harris tweed suit, with a cream polka-dot handkerchief in the top left-hand pocket. The other wore a British Army officer's No 1 khaki uniform complete with a highly polished Sam Browne leather belt. Neither spoke, keeping a companionable silence for several minutes, smoke drifting gently from behind each newspaper, the rich smell of tobacco mingling with the pungent wisteria perfume drifting through the open doors mixed with the late afternoon air.

The sound of a single-engine biplane punctuated the peace of the drawing room, and the eldest of the two men neatly folded his newspaper twice and carefully balanced his lightly smouldering briar pipe in a silver ash-tray on the table beside him, before both stood up and walked towards the patio. Arthur Marshall was the eldest of the two men, an extraordinarily stylish and rather handsome figure whose tailored suit marked him as a man of tradition and meticulous dress sense, and whose already rosy cheeks were glowing from the warmth of the fire and the traditional afternoon glass of Mortlach, his favourite single Speyside malt whisky. He was quiet, tactful and intensely patriotic, although with little interest in politics. At thirty-seven years of age, he retained the fine features of his youth and his thin, carefully combed moustache suited his classic profile perfectly. His athletic frame was that of a natural sportsman; he was an accomplished tennis player and cricketer, and excelled in athletics, selected for the 4x400 metre relay team as part of the British contingent at the 1924 Paris Olympic Games. On completing his engineering degree at Jesus College, Cambridge he took flying lessons at the Norfolk flying club, securing his pilot's license in 1928 when he purchased his own Gipsy Moth which he flew from the field behind the house, and only two years later he was awarded the title 'master instructor' by the Guild of Air Pilots.

As he passed the mirror, Arthur's blue-grey eyes briefly glanced at his reflection to ensure that his perfectly Windsor-knotted tie was straight. He paused for a brief moment and his eyes lowered to the black armband he wore in honour of his father David Marshall, who tragically died a few months earlier whilst riding one of his Arab horses on a country lane near the house. The Coroner's verdict was that he had suffered a sudden and severe stroke which caused him to lose consciousness and to lose control of his horse, which had stood protectively over his body until they were spotted.

After the initial shock, Arthur was only now beginning to come to terms with the event. His feelings of loss were tempered by the sudden responsibility of assuming the role of Chairman and Joint Managing Director of his father's business. The last few months had been hectic as his father's affairs were sorted but Arthur had eased into his role with superb diligence and focus, as he was wont to do. Filling his mind with work provided a welcome distraction, but as he glimpsed the armband briefly, Arthur felt a deep pang of grief.

As Arthur listened to the sound of the biplane approaching, he paused and thought about his father - a man whose life was dedicated to his business and to his family, and who had been the greatest influence on Arthur's early life, with his death signifying the end of an "adventurous partnership", as his father had often said. In 1909 David Marshall developed a modest car hire and garage business into Marshall of Cambridge, an internationally renowned aviation and engineering empire. He had worked his way up to become manager of the exclusive undergraduate Pitt Club in his early twenties before visiting Paris in 1906, where he gained the inspiration to establish a motor car hire company. When he returned to England, he began ferrying its wealthy undergraduate members. He expanded the business in the 1920s to include a car hire and garage business, selling Rolls-Royces and Daimlers, before diversifying into aviation. David's engineering and flying skills paired with his entrepreneurial flair led him to the realisation that there would be a sound future for aviation after the First World War, and it was against this background that in 1940, with the onset of war with Germany, that Marshall's was well placed to obtain government contracts to support the British war effort.

The company which Arthur was now overseeing dominated the industry, profiting from rearmament and wartime contracts. The aircraft repair division was run from huge servicing hangars at Cambridge, the building of which David Marshall supervised himself. The repair division handled a wide range of military aircraft, including Spitfires and Hurricanes, Flying Fortresses, Typhoons, Mosquitoes, and even Lancaster Bombers. The company also equipped Tiger Moth trainers with bomb racks to be used in the event of an invasion. In addition, the Marshall Flying School was one of the main centres for rapid training of RAF pilots and flying instructors.

His father's legacy was incredibly impressive, and Arthur reflected on how lucky he was to take over the reins and ensure that the business grew even further in the coming years. He snapped out of his thoughts, touched the armband and turned to continue towards the patio. However, his movement came to an abrupt halt as an announcement cut through the music on the radio. He stood motionless, listening intently.

'We interrupt this light programme to bring you an announcement from the Ministry of Aircraft Production. The Air Transport Auxiliary is expanding to help the Royal Air Force with aircraft ferry movements and deliveries and air-ambulance work; and is in need of pilots, ground-crew, engineers and administrative staff. Interested parties are requested to contact the Ministry in the first instance ...'

Arthur turned the radio volume down.

Standing next to Arthur was Bernard 'Bunny' Rose who was wearing the khaki uniform of a First Lieutenant in the 4th Royal County of London Yeomanry. Whilst outwardly epitomising the confident look of a typical British Army officer, Bernard portrayed an element of shyness and modesty. At twenty-three years-old, he was handsome and tall, well connected but not wealthy, and a man utterly committed to his profession. He was immaculately turned out, with short hair that shone in the sunlight, and his was the same handsome face that beamed out of the wedding photograph in its silver frame in pride of place on the side table. In real life he appeared less ebullient, and slightly less self-assured, and he felt an element of reservation in the presence of his brother-in-law, whom he held in the highest esteem.

Arthur turned to Bernard who had a hint of a smile on his face.

'I know that she is my sister and I am biased,' said Arthur, 'but I can't think of anyone better suited'.

'I know Arthur,' said Bernard, 'and I won't be able to stop her'.

'I know what my father would say if he were still alive. He would be all for it. He always did want everything for Molly that he wanted for himself'.

'I'm not quite sure how to feel about it,' said Bernard, 'would any man want his wife in such a dangerous situation?'

'My dear boy, as you well know, your wife - my sister, will not be happy unless she is pushing boundaries to their very limits, and testing herself in the process to confirm what she surely should already know - that she is through and through a Marshall'.

'Yes, quite,' said Bernard, a gradual smile of acknowledgement creeping across his face.

Both men walked through the large doors and onto the patio, gazing sky-wards. Bernard was worried that plans were about to change, as he had up to that point envisioned his wife being somewhat out of harm's way, but the thought of her being involved in aircraft ferry movements and deliveries sent a chill down his spine. He meditated on Arthur's words. He knew that they were true.

The sun was low on the horizon in glorious evening gold which irradiated the clouds with a deepening pink and orange as Arthur's wife Rosemary and two of his young sisters, Mary Cavendish and Brenda Marshall, appeared from different directions of the garden and joined the men on the patio. Rosemary and Arthur had been married for ten years, and she made him immensely happy, having been a great support through the recent loss of his father. Mary was twenty-six years of age and the taller of the two sisters. She was dressed in jodhpurs and boots with her hair tied and netted, and ready to try the new riding helmet which she had just received as a birthday gift from Arthur. Like all her siblings, Mary adored her brother Arthur, and sympathised with his struggle in not only assuming the complexities of running the family business, however also in taking over his late father's position as the head of the house. Their mother, Maude, died in 1930 when most of the children were still quite young, and Mary often thought how proud she would be of Arthur and the way he had handled everything.

Their brother had died of meningitis as a child, leaving Arthur as the only son. In the absence of their mother, Arthur's sisters Margery, Dorothy, Violet, Mary, Molly and the youngest, Brenda, were brought up by Violet, and the diverse and fun personalities of the six girls resulted in quite a lively household. The children had been fiercely competitive from a young age, with an inherent desire to take on any task with gusto and confidence, none wanting to be seen to fail in the eyes of their siblings. Their father had been the steadying hand at the tiller of his eclectic and rumbustious family who slowly came to terms with being orphans.

As the small group came together on the patio, Mary and Brenda were visibly excited as Mary stood on her toes and raised her arm high in the air to wave. Brenda, who was a good deal younger, and growing tall with the gangling limbs of a young adolescent, but with the exuberance of one even younger, was jumping up and down enthusiastically as the plane flew low over their heads, waggling its wings and with engine roaring. Brenda was perhaps the liveliest and most mischievous of all the sisters, and despite her young age, her British sarcasm and quick wit made her a feared adversary in any debate or argument. Like most of the family, she also loved aviation and anything to do with aircraft, and she was always ready to get involved at the factory whenever Arthur presented her with the opportunity.

All four watched as the aircraft circled low over the house, orchard, paddocks, and what was left of the former aerodrome; which had fallen into slight disrepair having recently relocated to larger premises at Cambridge Airport. The aircraft banked steeply into a perfect three-point landing on the huge lawn in front of the house and taxied towards the welcoming figures on the patio.

Bernard walked away from the group and towards the aircraft as it taxied to a standstill with the propeller gently turning. For a brief moment, he reminded himself how fortunate he was to be at that very point in time, given the uncertainty of all that loomed before him and the person he loved most in the world - the pilot seated in the Tiger Moth.

Bernard was the second child of three born to George William and Jessie Henrietta Rose. The tradition in the Rose family was for the names George William to be used one way, and then switched for the next generation. It was therefore breaking tradition for another name, Bernard, to be chosen as a first name – but then after "Bernard William George" was christened, he gained the nickname "Bunny" from the family.

Prior to the war, Bernard studied music as an undergraduate at St Catharine's College in Cambridge. His musical prowess quickly became apparent as a child, and immediately much of the family's financial resources were focussed on getting him the best education possible. His musical career began in earnest as a treble in the choir at Salisbury Cathedral in 1925 aged nine, and thereafter as a pupil at the Salisbury Cathedral Choir School. He completed his degree in September 1939 and started his career as a tutor in music at The Queen's College, Oxford.

With the declaration of War on 3rd September 1939, Bernard volunteered for service in the Army. Appearing before the selection board, he was told to await call up, and by 1940 he had joined the Northamptonshire Yeomanry, a tank regiment and a far cry from the hallowed spires of Oxford.

Bernard approached the biplane as the engine stalled and the prop stuttered to a stop. The pilot quickly unstrapped, jumped lithely from the tiny cockpit onto the wing, removing goggles and helmet to reveal curling auburn hair and bright laughing eyes, and a very pretty but decidedly grubby face. Bernard walked forward and took a deep breath, like a man in love with the only girl in the world.

Twenty-two-year-old Molly Rose was very much her father's daughter. In 1938, after schooling at Slepe Hall, St Ives, she was sent to Paris for six months to the finishing school of Mademoiselle Le Dieux. Despite Molly's polished education she exhibited a slightly mischievous and decidedly independent streak that nevertheless charmed those around her. Upon returning from Paris, having enjoyed flying as a passenger in Arthur's Gipsy Moth, it was unsurprising that on 1st June 1938 Molly gained her pilot's license. Her father suggested that she become an apprentice engineer in the hangars of the family business, to which Molly wholeheartedly and enthusiastically agreed. He would say: "It's important that an English lady should have good manners and deportment, but if you're going to be any use in the business, you need a proper trade behind you". With her usual good humour, Molly had willingly immersed herself in the world of engineering and aviation and since then had been flying at every opportunity.

Molly hopped down from the wing and her slender figure was, as always, hidden in baggy engineer's overalls with a scarf tied loosely around her neck and helmet in one hand. She was petite and pretty with a bright and vivacious smile and oozing charm. Her honest, forthright and determined manner coupled with a strong sense of curiosity had stood her in good stead to master the art of aviation engineering. Observing and listening with intent to everything around her, Molly was quick to learn and even quicker to turn her will into action. She embraced flying as if she were born for it.

Molly ran to embrace Bernard, with a mixture of excitement and adoration.

'Well, my hard work has paid off,' she said, 'I've played around with the trim controls and throttle and she handles like a dream; she is jolly well perfect.'

'You spend more time flying these kites than you do fixing them!' said Bernard, as he hugged Molly whilst at the same time trying to keep his immaculate jacket away from her oil-stained overalls.

'It's by far the best part of my job,' said Molly, brimming with pride, 'and it certainly beats stripping them down and pulling apart filthy engines. This one's going back to the RAF as a trainer aircraft. Anyway, you know that I love flying as much as you love being a musician.'

Bernard tried to smile as he took Molly by the hand, but his thoughts brooded on the radio announcement as they walked towards the house. He suddenly stopped and he put his hands on her shoulders, turning her towards him.

'Yes darling, but being a musician is a lot safer'. Bernard's frown quickly changed to a smile. 'Molly, listen; I've got some news', he paused as if struggling to find the right words, and then blurted it out, 'the Unit's got orders and I'm to report next week; our training is finished, and we're on our way. Not exactly sure where, but we'll be reinforcing the rest of the battalion on the front line. But it's not all bad news; I should be in line for a promotion to go with it.'

Molly's mood changed abruptly. Her brightness withdrew and the excited flush of her cheeks suddenly paled. She realised that she was about to come face-to-face with a reality that had been looming in the back of her mind for the past few months; and one which she had chosen not to give too much thought to until absolutely necessary. The moment she dreaded was now upon her, and she flashed back to the world turning sideways as she barrel-rolled out of the sky a few minutes earlier. Molly knew that her world was about to change forever.

'Oh Bunny, I do so hate this wretched war. We've just lost Daddy, and now you're going off too. Tell me that no matter what happens you won't do anything stupid and that you'll come back to me.'

Ignoring her stained overalls, Bernard put his arms around Molly in a warm embrace, tucked her head under his chin, and tried to be strong in not letting her see his deep concerns about the war and the events unfolding in Europe. Her soft wisps of hair smelled of gasoline and engine oil, but to him it was like breathing in the heady scent of the most expensive French perfume. He used all his strength to muster a smile and to assume an air of confidence; but his insides were churning, and the sound of gunfire could be heard like an overture to the miscellany of disturbing images in his mind. He quickly composed himself.

'But of course, we'll see Jerry off and I'll be home before you know it.'

Bernard bent a little so that he was at Molly's eye level as tears welled in her eyes.

'Please don't be too upset darling,' he said, 'we've all got to do our duty.'

'I know Bunny, yes, of course we do. And I have some news for you too; I was going to tell you later, but now is as good a time as any. The Air Transport Auxiliary have written to ask if I'd like to attend for an interview … as a pilot.'

Bernard smiled, but the words pierced his heart brutally and precisely. He continued his brave charade.

'That's a coincidence,' he said, 'I just heard an announcement on the radio, and I knew that it was only a matter of time. With your experience and ability, how could they turn you down? Now it's my turn to worry!' He reached out and grasped her arms looking straight into her beautiful eyes.

'I'll be a lot safer flying than you will be in the thick of it,' she said.

Bernard forced a grin, but then became serious.

'Do you know what you'll be flying? Surely it won't be combat aircraft?'

Molly saw the concern in Bernard's face, and she knew him well enough to see that he was worried. She put her arm through his and together they walked towards the family members waiting on the patio.

'Oh I doubt that very much,' said Molly, 'it'll be ferrying puddle-jumpers and transports I expect; stuff that the RAF fly-boys are too busy to do. Anyway, it's only an interview; I'm sure there will be plenty of men who will be chosen before me. But I do need to do something meaningful though; you know, to do my bit. And if that's by flying, I'll also be doing something I love.'

Bernard made a humming sound which he did when nervous, confirming what Molly had been thinking for the past few minutes. She dropped his arm and took a few quick steps forward before doing a three-hundred-and-sixty-degree twirl on the lawn with her arms wide open and a beaming smile. Her sweet face was caught by the golden aura of the moment and Bernard noticed the split-second reflection of the setting sun in Molly's eyes.

'Plus, I may look jolly dashing in ATA livery.'

Bernard could not help but to smile.

Three

Like most cities, Cambridge had transformed in the years following World War One, partly due to the advancements in aerial warfare. The city was surrounded by a multitude of military airfields and installations, where once peaceful neighbourhoods and in some cases green fields, were replaced with the grey and industrial fuel and ammunition depots and all the other factories and warehouses associated with the war effort. Like many other cities in Britain, an endless influx of personnel and military trucks delivering and collecting goods and equipment had descended upon this once quiet collection of quaint towns and villages, stripping away the tranquillity and, in some areas, turning the green to grey. As a result of this necessary and heightened activity and the rationing of petrol, Cambridge Train Station had become a central point for shipments and travel and an ongoing hub of activity for twenty-four hours a day. It was also a target for the Luftwaffe.

On a warm and cloudy September morning, an old steam train noisily shunted out of the station past a flurry of marching troops and military vehicles. Although unrefined and covered with grease and dust, there was something undeniably wonderful about this huge mechanical relic of a bygone age. Orders were shouted from Sergeant-Majors and station porters, and the noise echoed and bounced off the concrete walls and high over the heads of the crowd, enhancing what was already an air of frenetic activity. Like many other train stations, due to a shortage of staff as a result of conscription, the station had been declared an 'open station' meaning that barriers were no longer present and tickets were, subject to manpower, checked on the trains.

Through a security fence, and beyond the armed guards, could be seen piles of military provisions stacked high in boxes, some of which were leaning precariously to one side and on the brink of falling, as troops from several different regiments waited patiently to embark any one of the trains that loomed out of the gloom ready to depart. Another train was moving slowly as it lumbered into the station with immense majesty and a hiss of steam, smoke billowing around, thick and black as it ascended into the sky to do battle with the rays of the sun. A couple disembarked and pushed through the crowd of civilians, servicemen and women, many of whom were on their way to join regiments, squadrons, or any one of the variety of units preparing for or engaging in the war effort. Others were on the way home for a weekend pass or a few days of leave. Some in the station looked haunted, as though their lives and futures had been reduced to fragments by the trauma of war.

Two little girls stood in a daze clutching their teddy bears and dolls as they waited with a large group of children who had just left London for the countryside on an evacuation train. It was one of the saddest sights in the station, as the children were far too young to understand why they were being uprooted from their families and plunged into the unfamiliar surroundings of temporary homes.

Molly held Bernard's arm tightly as they bumped and weaved their way through the turmoil, as she had accompanied her husband to his embarkation station and, perhaps optimistically, had hoped that the experience would not be too upsetting, but the look in her eyes told a different story. The unusual heat did not help, as the heatwave made people uncomfortable and irritable, not least of all those in military uniform, and the intensity of the busy and overcrowded train station did nothing to ease the situation.

Molly wore a dark green floral summer dress with an open collar of white lace, and she had planned to look her best, in an effort to give Bernard an image to remember, but the rising temperature as they came closer to parting made her think that the best laid plans go to waste. The heat made Molly feel not quite as polished as she would have liked, but together with the delicate and elegant outfit, her eventual appearance was more beautiful than Bernard could remember ever seeing her, which was making it even more difficult for him to say goodbye.

He was dressed in uniform and was also struggling with the heat as he continually pulled at his collar, whilst trying to stay positive so as not to dampen what would be their last moments together for a while. His eyes were darting from left to right as he tried to locate a spot where their goodbyes would not be consumed amidst the confusion of the flowing crowd. Molly was clearly sad; all happiness had drained out of her at the thought of having to say goodbye to her beloved husband, but also disturbed by the overwhelming combination of heat and the overcrowded station. She regretted that they had not said their words somewhere else, quiet, serene, and in a place that would at least provide the opportunity for a less hectic memory. They moved towards the central concourse united in their silence, each holding back the words that were inevitable, words they had rehearsed over and over again in their minds during the past several days and which were now to be uttered and made real. Molly could already feel a burning in her throat.

As they reached the centre of the station, Bernard had resigned himself to the fact that this was as good a spot as any, when the crowd seemed to part in front of them in a 'Moses and the Red Sea' effect, and the tall, smart and supremely confident figure of Edward "Fruity" Egerton-Reed emerged and strode towards them. His striking appearance caused a number of heads to turn, both female and male, but he seemed oblivious to the heat and to the attention, quietly and calmly looking over the heads of the crowd. Like Bernard, he was also dressed in the uniform of First Lieutenant in the 4th Royal County of London Yeomanry and which looked as though it had just come off the tailor's peg, with gleaming buttons and buckle. His presence instantly lightened their mood.

At twenty-four years of age, Edward was six-feet tall with light brown hair, piercing blue eyes and a chiselled jawline; all of which should have, by the standards of most men of that stature, made him an over-confident or perhaps even a vain individual, however, he was not a man of those principles. Edward was by contrast modest and in some way inherently shy, despite having always been a heartthrob for a string of adoring young ladies, due to his kind and positive nature; a natural ability to listen; and most of all, his long-time love of only one girl.

Fruity, as he was known to his friends due to his father's successful Herefordshire-based apple cider farms, was a long-time friend of Bernard's, and had recently become engaged to his childhood sweetheart, who by coincidence was a contemporary of Molly's from her time in Paris.

'Bunny, old man. Chaos, what? I'll be glad when we get to the desert for a bit of sunshine.'

'Fruity,' said Bernard, thrilled to see his closest friend, 'there you are. I didn't think I'd be able to find you in all this hullabaloo, and what with all this heat, the whole place seems to be in disarray.'

'Yes, I know. Molly is easy to spot though. Quite one of the most beautiful girls in the entire station. Good to see you Molly'

Molly was smiling although she had become impervious over the years to what she often described as "The Natural Charms of Fruity".

'Lovely to see you too Fruity,' said Molly, 'and congratulations to you and Elisabeth on your engagement. Is Elisabeth not here?'

'Oh, thanks Molly, and yes Elisabeth is hopefully here … somewhere, but perhaps lost. We'll be centre-ailing the very moment I get back, and after we've given Jerry a good thrashing.'

'Yes, quite,' said Molly, hoping that both those statements would come true at the soonest, 'How wonderful. Well stay safe … oh, and please keep an eye on my husband.'

'Absolutely will,' said Edward.

Suddenly a voice from the crowd shouted "Fruity" and several people turned around to see who it was. Running towards Edward, who had lit up like a firefly, was the petite and pretty Elisabeth Hemsworth; her face beaming with excitement and arms outstretched as she leapt into Edward's arms and held him around the neck, as her feet swung a few inches off the ground.

Elisabeth was twenty-three-years-old, blonde and blue-eyed, with a fair complexion and a vivacious and alluring smile. She was wearing a white cotton summer dress and she had an oversized white bow in her hair which evoked the attire from an eighteenth-century fairy tale. It was a vision of loveliness as if a bright spotlight had shone down amidst the surrounding dullness of the station. Elisabeth's father was a member of Parliament and had used his connections to arrange for his daughter to undertake work at the War Office as a translator of German newspapers, as she was fluent in both French and German. It was a position which Elizabeth loved, not least because she could walk though St. James's Park every morning and evening to brighten up her journey to and from work.

Elisabeth released her grip on her fiancée, and turned her attention to Molly, opening her arms wide and giving her the warmest hug, in recognition of the affection that she felt for her "most trusted friend". Molly and Elisabeth adored each other and had been close since their heady days in France at the finishing school of Mademoiselle Le Dieux, and throughout their formative years. Their lives had been intertwined in a flurry of debutante balls and the Bright Young People, whose flair and defiance of the old ways burst into the century like a tornado, sweeping away the values, rigidity and stuffiness of the past. This period of flamboyance, brilliance and playfulness threw off the gloom of the First World War as the youth dedicated themselves to entertainment and immersion in the most imaginative and extravagant forms of self-indulgence. This had all come to a rigid halt upon the declaration of war, and the new-found freedom which had lasted for only two generations was swiftly curtailed. Both Molly and Elisabeth were acutely aware that a chapter in their lives was over, as war and the constant feeling of instability made their plans for family life seem like an age away.

'I'm so happy to hear about your engagement,' said Molly.

'Thank you,' said Elisabeth, 'I'm thrilled, and hopefully this beastly war won't drag on forever. Oh, and speaking of weddings,' she said smiling, 'there's something *very* special that I would like to ask you … later perhaps'. She touched Molly's arm and gave her a look which brightened up the otherwise sullen predicament of the morning.

The crowd had started to close in around the small group of four as they were being bumped into by passers-by, and at the risk of becoming dishevelled, Edward decided to quickly move on.

'Well it's all rather hectic here,' he said, 'time to go, I think. So, we'll leave you two lovebirds to your goodbyes and I'll see you, old man, at the barrier. Molly, take good care of yourself and cheerio for now.'

Elisabeth and Molly hugged again and then Edward and Elisabeth disappeared into the crowd as quickly as they had arrived. The void left by the ever-extravagant Edward Egerton-Reed and his high-spirited bride-to-be brought Bernard down to earth with a dull thud, as he realised that the moment he had been dreading for so long was looking him squarely in the face like an inescapable truth. He would need every last ounce of courage to say goodbye. With all the pending uncertainties and the dark shadows of war that lurked in every corner of every thought, Bernard was certain of only one thing - that he loved Molly more than life itself; and as he looked deeply into her watery eyes, he took great comfort in knowing that every fibre of that love was reciprocated.

'Well, this is it Molly. I suppose I must be off, I'm so very sad to leave you.'

'Fruity said the desert? Are you going to the desert, Bunny?'

Bernard gently took Molly's arm and led her to one side, away from the swaying crowd and to the relative calm of a doorway by the now-closed ticket office.

'Not so loud my darling - walls have ears and all that. He shouldn't have said anything. But yes, we're reinforcing the Desert Rats against Rommel's Africa Corps. We'll be smashing his strangle-hold in North Africa. It's what we've been training for, so please don't worry.'

'Of course I'll be worried. How can I not. I'll worry every waking moment. But I promise you two things: I'll think about you every day; and I'll do everything I can to help keep you safe. But you must make a promise to me Bunny. You must come back to me. Will you promise me that?'

'Of course my darling. But you'll be far too busy doing your bit for the war effort to worry about me. 'ATA - Anything to Anywhere'. Isn't that what they say? Think about all the wonderful aircraft that you'll be flying, and the places you'll be visiting every week. I'll be back before you know it.'

Bernard reached into his canvas kit bag which was packed full and on the verge of bursting and pulled out a small leather wallet with a photo of himself inside, and he gave it to Molly. As she looked at the small photo of Bernard, his smiling face glowing as he leaned against the trunk of a tree, she struggled to hold back her tears and she barely managed to get the words out.

'I love you.'

'I adore you, Molly.'

They kissed tenderly and held on to the moment for as long as they could before Bernard pulled himself away, threw his kit bag over his shoulder and joined the throng of soldiers heading for the ramp.

Molly watched him depart.

Four

A dark green MG Roadster two-seater sports car was speeding along a country lane on its way to Hatfield Aerodrome, with its top rolled back and Arthur Marshall at the wheel. The colours of autumn were just starting to arrive as trees in various shades of amber and red lined the road as far as the eye could see, occasionally forming dramatic canopies overhead through which the little car seemed to temporarily disappear as it blended into these natural surroundings. In an effort to confuse the enemy in the event of an invasion, basic defensive measures were in place including the removal of signposts, railway station signs and milestones, some of which had their carved details obscured with cement. Arthur was thus navigating from memory. However, his sense of distance and direction had never failed him before, and he confidently took great pride in his abilities.

Molly was seated in the passenger seat, her head protected against the wind by a silk scarf which she was beginning to wonder whether she had tied too tightly as her jaw was beginning to ache. That minor discomfort however was paled into insignificance by the dread of her brother's driving, as he continued to hurtle the little car around the bends as though he were at the controls of his Tiger Moth in a series of aerobatic display manoeuvres. His voice was raised to be audible against the oncoming wind and Molly struggled to hear him.

'So, Molly, this is a bit better than your old bicycle and the train, don't you think? I've used up a month's petrol ration, but it's worth it to get the old bus out on the road again; and if I can get you to your ATA interview in style, so much the better. I'm excited for you.'

'Yes Arthur, but you may wish to slow down around these bends as I would very much like to arrive in one piece.'

'You'll need to speak up Molly. I can't hear a blasted thing.'

Molly smiled and raised her voice slightly.

'I'm excited too, but it's only an interview. Arthur dearest, please do slow down. I can't hear myself speak'.

Arthur hit the brakes and the car slowed down as he came out of his racing driver trance and Molly's scarf stopped flapping around her face for the first time in the last hour.

'Sorry about that Molly. It's been a while since I've had her out on the road and it's all rather exciting, plus driving amongst all this stunning scenery is quite what this little car was made for.'

'It's quite alright. I love speed but only when I'm the one in control. As I was saying, it's only an interview but I'm not there yet.'

'Oh, but you will be. And don't take a damned bit of notice of those bloody newspapers and their poppycock; women have as much right to fly as any man; and to hell with anyone who tries to stop you. And anyway, you can fly a damn sight better than most men I know.'

'I know and thank you.' said Molly, 'It's a bit odd that women can't be encouraged to fly, instead of it all being so difficult and negative. I told Mrs Denby in the village about my interview, and she was most upset. She gave me a piece of her mind, saying that women shouldn't be taking men's jobs.'

'For goodness sake! Does she not realise just how many women are working in this war, or the last war for that matter?'

'I suppose not. There will hopefully come a day when men and women can stand side by side and be accepted equally for the same task, and whether or not there is a war going on.'

'Yes, well I'm thrilled that you have got this far, as even being asked for an interview is quite an honour. I wish that father and mother could have been with you today. They would have been so proud.'

'I feel that they are with me Arthur'.

As the car approached the perimeter of Hatfield Aerodrome, the noise of aircraft taxiing and taking off grew louder, drowning further conversation. Although the aerodrome was the base of Ferry Pool No. 5, the first all-female ATA unit, its main activity was aircraft manufacture as a result of the de Havilland Aircraft Company, which originally operated from some local farmland until moving to the aerodrome due to the increased level of production for the war effort. de Havilland was also a repair hub for damaged aircraft, many of which were shipped in by rail or road on a regular basis.

As a result of the large-scale production, the Luftwaffe had recognised the value of the airfield and for this reason it was now partially camouflaged. Only a few years earlier, a single Luftwaffe Junkers Ju 88 dropped multiple bombs, resulting in the death of seventy-seven people and with many injured.

Arthur was clearly excited at any close proximity to an airfield or any aircraft for that matter, and his increase in speed matched his increase in enthusiasm. They drove past the end of the runway, as training aircraft took off over the top of the car, which made Molly slightly nervous as Arthur was more interested in looking at the aircraft above than at the road ahead, and the car swerved just a little too much for Molly's comfort. Despite Molly desperately gripping to anything that came to hand in the hope of averting potential injury due to Arthur's non-concentration, he remained oblivious to the road. His attention was firmly captured by one aircraft in particular - the de Havilland Mosquito, as this was very much of great fascination to Arthur and indeed closest to his heart.

De Havilland used high-performance design methods to produce the Mosquito, or the "Mossie" as it was affectionately known. The twin Rolls-Royce-engine, shoulder-winged multi-role combat aircraft was one of the fastest operational aircraft in the world. Constructed primarily of wood, it introduced woodworking companies and furniture manufacturers into the building of wartime aircraft. Arthur was truly gripped in its magnificence.

Having arrived at the aerodrome gates, Molly was by now quite desperate to get safely out of the vehicle and she quickly climbed out of the passenger seat, picked up her bags from the rear seat and leant over to kiss Arthur goodbye.

'Wish me luck'.

As Molly walked towards the gates of the aerodrome, the Mosquito passed out of sight, disappearing into the clouds, and Arthur re-focussed and called out to her.

'Molly … be prepared. There may possibly be some resistance within the RAF too.'

'Don't worry,' she said, 'I can deal with it'.

Molly stopped at the security gate which was actually two wooden bollards over a dirt track and with one young uniformed man from the junior military ranks whom she assumed to be the guard, and who was quite relaxed and content as he sat on a crate and watched apathetically as she approached with her papers ready. Molly originally thought that she would be nervous at being interviewed by Joan Hughes, one of the famous 'first eight' women pilots of the ATA, however, having experienced the elation of surviving the car journey only moments before, she was now brimming with confidence and feeling as though she was ready to tackle anything.

'My name is Molly Rose and I'm here for an interview. With Joan Hughes of the ATA.'

As Molly looked at the young man, she wondered just how old he could be as he looked fresh out of school. He was quite the serious type and did not smile, perhaps in an effort to impress Molly by showing an element of maturity as he handed her back the papers.

'Head on over to the Ops Room by following the road down about four-hundred yards and then turning right.'

'Lovely,' she said, 'thank you.'

Several officers looked at Molly as she walked quickly by, but even though she could feel the burning stares, she tried not to notice and focussed instead on the various military buildings, one in particular which captivated her attention, and was a lovely example of Art Deco architecture. Molly wondered what its purpose was prior to it being requisitioned for war, and then she thought about some of the larger houses of her friends that had been converted temporarily into army bases and hospitals; and if that fate was soon to befall Whitehill. She also noticed a group of young women in a classroom and, without approaching the window, briefly stopped and craned her neck to peek in, as an instructor had what looked like a piece of an aircraft dashboard propped up on the table as his uniform-clad students made notes. One of the students just happened to look out of the window and saw Molly looking in, and she quickly moved on.

She reached the Ops Room and entered the main door, where she was met by a young woman in uniform with a set of pilot's wings above her breast pocket and three stripes on her shoulder flash. Molly was standing face-to-face with Flight Captain Joan Hughes, and Molly had to remind herself to breathe.

Joan was petite and pretty at just over five-feet tall and with blue eyes and copper-coloured wavy hair, which was held back by a forage cap. Obsessed with flying from an early age, she qualified for her pilot's license at seventeen and was, at the time, the youngest female pilot in Great Britain. Joan was also the youngest of the 'first eight' women to join the ATA in January 1940, as part of an undertaking which was considered by many purely as an experiment. She had since developed into an exceptionally good, level-headed and accomplished pilot, and although she was cleared to ferry nearly all types of aircraft, most of her time was now spent instructing both male and female pilots at the Advanced Flying Training School (AFTS) at White Waltham.

'Hello! Molly is it? Ah, good. I'm Joan Hughes. Pleased to meet you and welcome to Hatfield and the Air Transport Auxiliary. I'll be looking after you today and sitting in on your flight test.'

'Molly Rose. How do you do.'

'I've been looking forward to meeting you,' said Joan, 'we'll be doing your check ride here first before we send you off to see Pops d'Erlanger and Queen Bee for your grilling! How much do you know about the ATA?'

'Only that it's a civilian organisation that ferries military aircraft for the RAF. Other than that, just what I've read in the newspapers.'

'Just so,' said Joan, with an element of cheeriness and tone of voice that showed a complete pride in her job. 'We've been going for over a year now and we have two-hundred-and-forty-four male pilots and twenty-seven women so far. We started off flying the air taxis - ministry bods, senior officers, RAF personnel and so on - from one place to another; we still do all of that of course, but now we also have the ferry work and air ambulance work. When - if - you join us, you will be doing some or all of that.'

'So how much ferry work is there?' said Molly.

'Actually, that's becoming the biggest part of the job. The factories are ramping up production, and the RAF can't spare the pilots to collect the new aircraft. That's where we come in; not only delivering new aircraft but transferring various machines between maintenance units and active service squadrons. So, Molly, how much flying experience do you have?'

For a fleeting moment, Molly felt that the bravado she confidently armed herself with upon entering the base was beginning to diminish. She resisted the temptation to be overwhelmed and resorted instead to her inner strength of second nature, convincing herself that being there with Joan was exactly where she should be.

'I've had my license for about four years,' said Molly, 'and I've been flying mostly Tiger Moths for the past several months. It's part of my job as an aircraft maintenance engineer at my family's company.'

'Wonderful, said Joan, 'you should be right at home then. We'll be going up in a Moth today. You probably passed the classrooms on the way down and we'll have a look at the hangars as we go out to the airfield. First, take a look at this …'

For the first time, Molly's attention turned away from the all-consuming presence of Joan Hughes, and she looked around to see a busy Operations Room in the throes of its daily activity. Every facet of the room was most likely a small but essential part of the overall war effort; and this realisation left Molly in awe. The space was not overly large and there were huge windows on two sides; one of which overlooked the airfield and the other with a clear view of the apron, dispersal and parachute storage room. It was not messy, but it was clearly a room which was well used, as the rigidity and cleanliness of a tidy aircraft administration office had been overshadowed by a somewhat haphazard, albeit thriving, working environment, with files and notebooks strewn all over and more pieces of paper on the floor that one would have imagined.

There were several Ops Officers and admin staff, some of whom talked on the phones whilst simultaneously passing instructions to a man filling in a blackboard covering almost the entire upper part of the rear wall. The backboard was made up as a large grid, the columns of which were headed 'aircraft'; 'from'; 'to'; 'category'; 'priority'; 'pilot'; 'code'; and 'specs'. There was also an extra-large table at the other end of the room, which was completely clear of even the smallest object, and was perhaps the cleanest space in the room.

Of the five Ops Officers and admin staff who were oblivious to Molly, three were female, and Molly noticed that they were dressed in what she considered to be quite smart uniforms. The female tunics were a cross between single and double-breasted design, and of a deep blue, almost black colour, and fastening on the female side. The buttons were black and featured the ATA initials. The female officers wore skirts and light blue RAF shirts with black seamed stockings and flat black shoes.

Another ATA female officer who had walked in with a small package was wearing a forage cap upon which was a gold metal badge of the ATA's insignia; oval in shape and surrounded by a wreath with a spread-winged eagle mounted on top. The insignia was made up of the letters ATA, with the letters A being smaller and the T being in the middle and taller. Molly noticed that all officers wore the same insignia on their tunics.

Joan walked over to the Ops Officer on duty; and acknowledged him, although he did not reciprocate as he had a phone to his ear, held there by his shoulder, and was busy scribbling something down on a notepad. She pointed to a large chart on the wall.

'This is the flying area,' said Joan. 'It's a busy airfield, so you'll need to keep a good look-out as de Havilland have a lot more traffic coming in and out than we do, and they think that we are guests here so we play the game and try to stay out of their way. I'll run through the operational procedures for the aerodrome whilst we wander over, and we can go through the manoeuvres that you'll need to demonstrate. But first we need to get you kitted out. Even though we'll be at low altitude, you'll still be issued a parachute, which hopefully we won't need to use today.'

Molly smiled as Joan took a slip of paper from the bulletin board.

'Weather report,' she said. 'I'm sure I don't need to tell you how vital it is to check conditions continually. The weather can get you into an awful lot of trouble if you're not prepared for it.'

After Molly and Joan had changed into flying kit, they threw parachutes over their shoulders and walked out onto the airfield. Molly noticed that it was not as overcrowded with aircraft as she had envisioned, except for a few Tiger Moths flying high in the air above. Molly began to feel relaxed; she knew that she was far more comfortable in the air than in an interview. She also felt that, despite Joan's legendary status, Molly was in fact quite at ease in her company.

'I've heard that you were one of the first eight women to join the ATA?', said Molly.

'Yes, that's right. It seems an age ago.'

'That must have been an incredible experience.'

'This whole war is an incredible but horrid experience,' said Joan, 'but yes - it was quite an honour to be one of the original eight women asked to join. There were some challenges of course, still are in fact, but I think we are working through them.'

Molly and Joan reached the apron where a number of training de Havilland DH.82 Tiger Moths stood in line; and they were greeted cheerily by an engineer who accompanied them to their aircraft.

Primarily manufactured in Cowley, Oxfordshire, the dual-control Tiger Moth was the favourite of flying schools throughout the Commonwealth and elsewhere. It had been formally adopted by the British Air Ministry as the new basic trainer of the Royal Air Force due to its robust design and ideal handling capabilities for the training of fighter pilots. Although the Tiger Moth was generally responsive and easy to handle during normal flight phases, it required great skill to avoid stalling or spinning during formation flying or aerobatics training, and was hence known as "easy to fly, but difficult to fly well".

Despite its many accolades, there were several disadvantages to the Tiger Moth. Its upper wings were large and inclined; and could be easily de-stabilised by heavy gusts of wind. It also had no electrical system and therefore needed to be started by hand, which could be a hazardous process if not exercised with extreme caution.

Molly was well aware that even though the weather was warm, it would certainly be cold at three-thousand feet, and she was dressed ready with several layers under her leather flying jacket. She climbed up onto the wing and into the cockpit in one smooth and graceful manoeuvre as she had done many times before and Joan smiled to herself as she finished the external checks and climbed into the front seat, giving a thumbs up. Although Molly was slightly nervous, it did not show, and she took deep breaths as the engineer handed her the shoulder straps. She strapped in, and as her hands checked over the familiar controls, she visibly calmed.

Molly switched the fuel valve on, turned on the mags before setting the throttle to zero and the mixture to rich. The ground engineer stood in front of the propeller, initiated the priming process and swung the prop, and then, after a tentative few chugs, it roared into life, drowning any further conversation. The propeller created a whirlwind which tugged at Molly's scarf as it flapped around wildly, and for more seconds that she was comfortable with, she reached up and unsuccessfully tried to catch it, finally grabbing it by the neck end and tucking it away safely under her jacket. "That's a good start", Molly thought as she laughed to herself.

Joan spoke through the Gosport tube telling Molly to taxi out to the end of the runway and Molly gave another hand signal to the engineer and pushed open the throttle. The engine noise and slipstream increased, and the aircraft began to move forward, bouncing across the grass to the take-off point as every part of the aircraft rumbled in that familiar way that Molly had become so used to. She leaned out over each side of the cockpit to see where they were heading, as her ahead view in the "Moth" was obscured, resulting in the lower wing being particularly prone to hitting obstructions.

When they reached the end of the runway, Molly pushed the throttle further forward and as the aircraft gathered speed, she gently pulled back on the stick to lift the aircraft into the air; quickly climbing to one-thousand feet, past the airfield perimeter fence and heading off across the Hertfordshire countryside. This was the time when Molly was most relaxed in her comfort zone, with the familiarity of the moment suddenly and calmly kicking in, lowering her heart rate and slowing everything down in stark contrast to the madness of the world below.

Above the engine and wind noise, Joan shouted through the speaking tube the various manoeuvres.

'OK. Do a three-hundred-and-sixty degree turn and come back to your original heading and track.'

'Continue this heading, take us up to fifteen-hundred feet, hold steady the altitude while making a ninety-degree turn left, then right.'

'Throttle back to stall speed and show me a stall recovery.'

Molly completed each manoeuvre with confidence, before Joan gave a thumbs-up.

'Right - let's see how you get on closer to the ground,' said Joan, 'circuits and bumps next.'

'Roger.'

Molly banked left to see the airfield in the distance; as a few other biplanes followed each other round in a wide circuit. It was a beautiful sight, both calming and captivating, and Molly started to feel that everything was going well, even to the point of her thoughts drifting off about her father; and wondering if she was really closer to him at altitude.

Joan interrupted Molly's thoughts with her next instruction.

'Give them a wide berth, let them clear the circuit, and then in we go.'

Molly lined up the landing strip on the nose of the aircraft and eased into a gentle descent; with the airstrip getting larger as the aircraft approached, its nose high. She made a slightly erratic front wheel landing, keeping the tail up and bouncing a couple of times. She pushed open the throttle and took the aircraft back up for another go-around.

'That was a bit wobbly but it's OK,' said Joan. Keep the nose a bit higher next time round and keep the revs up.'

Molly gritted her teeth, and completed another two 'circuits and bumps', getting better each time.

"OK, that's better. Back to one thousand feet and take us round again. Keep an eye on traffic.'

Molly complied; looking left and right to spot other aircraft which were a long distance away. She was feeling good and that all was going well. After a couple of seconds, Joan slammed the throttle closed.

'Engine's out, you'll need to do an emergency landing.'

Molly calmly dropped the nose, circled back towards the airfield and lined up for approach, gliding towards the grass strip as the wind whistled through the wings of the biplane, and performed a perfect three-point landing.

At the end of the landing strip Molly throttled forward and taxied back to the apron, guided into position by the same engineer. The aircraft came to a stop and Molly shut down the engine. The only sound was her gentle breathing, the pings from the cooling engine and the creaks from the aircraft cables. Molly and Joan climbed out onto the wing and jumped down.

'Well done,' said Joan, 'not bad at all. We'll get sorted out and I'll make an appointment for you to get over to White Waltham to meet Pauline Gower, or Queen Bee as we all call her. She's the Head of the Women's Section of the ATA. But important matters first. Cup of tea?'

'Righty-o. And absolutely, yes please!'

'I think that you'll do splendidly Molly and I'll no doubt see you again soon. Don't look so worried; The Queen Bee is not nearly as scary as she sounds!'

Five

White Waltham Airfield near Maidenhead in Berkshire had a significant history of pre-war flying training as the de Havilland School of Flying, teaching students for the RAF Reserve. It had since been taken over by the government to become the headquarters of the Air Transport Auxiliary and Ferry Pool Number 1. From here the civilian pilots of the ATA had replaced the RAF in facilitating the routine movement of aircraft between factories, maintenance units and front-line squadrons.

Molly had arrived at White Waltham for her interview with Pauline Gower. The weather had turned colder, and Molly was wrapped up in multiple layers, with a scarf pulled up over her mouth and nose and a matching woolly hat, both of which her sister Violet had knitted as a birthday gift. The heating on the train from Cambridge had not been working and the carriages were cold, much to the chagrin of the passengers; and together with the sudden November frost, Molly was desperate to get inside to a warm office where she could thaw out.

Pauline Mary de Peauly Gower was 32 years old and the daughter of Sir Robert Gower, a Conservative Party politician and solicitor who, after giving up on his dream of presenting his daughter to society as a debutante, reluctantly gave her an aeroplane as a 21st birthday present. That gesture was the first of two beneficiary acts by Pauline's father towards her future career in aviation; the second of which was a gift of a Spartan two-seater to alleviate his concerns of Pauline hiring 'unsafe' aircraft to pursue what was clearly becoming an obsession. Aside from those two generous gestures, Pauline worked hard to find the money to fund what had become one of her greatest loves.

In her early twenties, Pauline taught music to enable her to fund a partnership in a touring air circus, followed by the co-ownership of an air-taxi service. With her persistent dedication, she had developed into one of the most accomplished women in British aviation. Pauline was a council member for the aeronautical section of the Women's Engineering Society, and in 1936 was the first woman to be awarded the Air Ministry's Second-Class Navigator's License. In 1938, she was appointed as a Civil Defence Commissioner with the Civil Air Guard and later that year, she published *Women with Wings*, a book about women in aviation.

At the outbreak of the Second World War, Pauline used her high-level connections and determination to implement her vision of a women's section within the newly formed Air Transport Auxiliary. She was now the Commandant of the women's branch of the ATA with overall responsibility for the testing and selection of women pilots.

As Molly entered the office building, she was greeted by an elderly and bespectacled lady in a woollen jacket and skirt which was the same shade of grey as her hair, and who introduced herself as Pauline Gower's secretary. Molly tried to think about the last time she was so nervous. At once, her mind flashed back to her wedding day as she stood beside her father about to walk down the aisle. She half-remembered faces, organ music and the smell of the freesias in her bouquet, but most of all she recalled Bernard's face at the end of the aisle glancing back towards her; his nervousness even more palpable than her own. With war declared, they thought it important to marry before the hostilities started although there was an element of underlying tension shrouded by the colourful activities of an English village wedding. Molly heard herself say the words "I do" and then she flashed to the train station ... "I'll do everything I can to help keep you safe".

Molly followed the secretary along a stark corridor lit with naked lightbulbs and lined with fire extinguishers and neatly arranged notice boards. The sound of their footsteps echoed loudly on the polished wooden floor and was pounding in Molly's head. Her eyes were fixed on the door at the end of the corridor, on which a white-lettered name plate gradually came into focus: 'Pauline Gower - Head of ATA (Women's Section)'.

Molly's hearing de-focussed as she heard phones ringing in the background, shrill against the backdrop of aircraft activity, and a woman's voice finishing a telephone conversation could be heard behind the door. Pauline's secretary stood next to Molly and smiled at her as she knocked on the door. After a couple of seconds, a clear and commanding female voice shouted from behind the door.

'Yes, come in.'

The secretary opened the door and ushered Molly into a small austere office with windows overlooking the airfield. Molly saw a stern looking young woman seated behind a large desk, head down over paperwork. The secretary gave Molly another encouraging smile and a thumbs up, and closed the door, leaving her standing nervously on the carpet in front of the desk. After what seemed an age, and during which time Molly began to count her own heartbeat, Pauline Gower looked up, and studied Molly for a few seconds.

Pauline was petite and feminine with dark brown expressive eyes and dark hair. Although a trifle stern at first sight, Molly sensed some compassion and warmth underneath what seemed to be a layer of formal rigidity.

'Molly - come in, come in. Please take a seat.'

'Thank you.'

'I've just got off the blower with Joan; she spoke very highly of you; your flight test was OK. Well, pretty near perfect actually, but we don't want to get swollen heads now do we. So, no problems with the flying; tell me about your job.'

'Well, I'm an engineer: an aircraft engineer. I service mostly Tiger Moths, working in my late father's business. Actually, I was the first female engineering apprentice. Anyhow, my job is to check the engines to make sure that they're performing properly, you know, to maximum efficiency, ready for air-testing. So, I get involved in all levels of maintenance and repair, especially now, with all the war work.'

'It sounds like jolly hard work,' said Pauline.

'It is, and I suppose because I'm a woman, and the boss's daughter, I feel I have to work twice as hard as anyone else, otherwise the others think I'm getting privileges.'

'Ah yes, we know all about that. Good, good. And the flying?'

'Yes, aside from that, I also fly. I've had my flying license for nearly four years now, so I'm allowed to flight test some of the aircraft. I have fifty-seven and a half hours in Gipsy Moths and Harts, of which almost nineteen hours are solo. To be honest, that's my favourite part of the job.'

'Excellent. Yes, I see that you have a good deal of experience. And do you have any time for recreation?'

'Well, I play tennis. And I try to find time to read about the war when I have the chance. You know, the newspapers I mean. My husband is in the army and has recently been posted, so I very much want to keep up to date with the news from wherever he is. But most of all, I love everything about aviation … engineering … aircraft … flying, and doing anything that makes me feel, even in a small way, that I am helping in this war.'

Pauline at last broke from her somewhat stern attitude and she gave Molly the warmest smile. Molly was clearly relieved and suddenly felt the tension drain from her body as she breathed out.

'You would fit in well here Molly,' said Pauline. 'It seems as though you have already encountered a few of the issues that we face regularly. Although attitudes to women pilots are changing, slowly.'

The office door suddenly flew open and Gerard d'Erlanger entered, full of apologies for being late. Molly did not expect a second interviewer, and her eyes widened as d'Erlanger crossed the room; the nervousness that had ebbed away moments before swiftly returning. Pauline registered Molly's anxiousness and smiled, wondering whether it was the interview or the surprise of meeting the most important man in the entire organisation that provoked such a response in Molly.

Gerard John Regis Leo d'Erlanger was thirty-six years old and affectionately known within the ATA as "Pop". He was a French-born Baron and the only son of the international banker Baron Émile Beaumont d'Erlanger, and his wife, Marie Rose Antoinette Catherine de Robert d'Aqueria; daughter of the Marquis de Rochegude of Bollène in France.

Formerly a director of the British Overseas Airways Corporation (BOAC), d'Erlanger foresaw that the war would create a demand for experienced and capable pilots, who for one reason or another, would not be considered suitable for operational service in the Royal Air Force. He successfully lobbied Harold Balfour, the Parliamentary Under Secretary for Air, and Sir Francis Shelmerdine, the Director General of Civil Aviation, and proposed the creation of the Air Transport Auxiliary as a civilian organisation which could be of great service to the war effort.

D'Erlanger flashed a dazzling smile at Pauline before acknowledging Molly's presence.

'So sorry I'm late; affairs of state, and it all dragged on a bit. It's a pleasure to meet you Miss Rose; and thank you for coming to see us.'

'Molly,' said Pauline, 'this is Gerard d'Erlanger, the founder and Commodore of the ATA.'

Molly stood up and held out her hand.

'Delighted to meet you sir,' she said, 'I've heard a lot about you.'

D'Erlanger stood by the desk at which Gower was seated. He was tall and portrayed an air of the archetypal suave spy; sophisticated on the outside, but ruthless nevertheless; and although slightly intimidating at first sight, his gentle way came across as he started to speak.

'Please, please, sit down,' he said, 'we don't stand on ceremony here. I'm sure that Pauline has filled you in, so you probably know by now what you'll be getting yourself involved with.'

'Very much so, sir.' said Molly.

'Good good,' continued d'Erlanger, 'Well we've come a long way since we first started, so as well as the usual run-of-the-mill stuff, we are now authorised for over a hundred different types of aircraft: from Tiger Moths to Sunderland Flying Boats and everything in between. And I am delighted to say that the women have just received authority for single seater fighters; Hurricanes, Mustangs and Spitfires!'

Pauline acknowledged and smiled, however Molly suspected that she was already well-aware of this news.

'Yes, that is marvellous news,' said Pauline, 'we've been lobbying for long enough.'

Molly sensed that d'Erlanger and Pauline had a close relationship; a familiarity and relaxing spontaneity with each other. D'Erlanger smiled again at Pauline before continuing.

'Indeed, indeed; I have no doubt that our pilots can fly anything on the RAF and Fleet Air Arm's books. Well. Where was I? Oh yes. We now have a number of women pilots, so have set up two 'all-women' Ferry Pools; one at Hamble, the other at RAF Cosford. But Pauline's in charge of all that so I won't steal her thunder. Although we're sometimes called "Ancient & Tattered Airmen", we are anything but!'

D'Erlanger sat on the edge of Pauline's desk.

'Our motto is '*Aetheris Avidi* – Eager for the Air'. Is that you Miss Rose?'

Six

A storm was raging over a flotilla of ships heading south in the Atlantic Ocean as the fore-deck of the huge troop-carrier *HMT Aorangi* plunged into the bottom of the trough of an oncoming wave which crashed over the deck. As the bow rapidly changed its trajectory reaching the crest of the swell, the full force of the gale hit head-on causing the huge iron and steel ship to shudder before disappearing again in a drop which seemed for a brief moment to defy gravity. In the hold, tanks in British desert camouflage markings were strapped down, creaking and straining noisily against their chains as the ship made slow and laborious progress, struggling through the freezing oncoming seas.

The journey to North Africa had been far worse than Bernard had expected, even though it was December, as the weather took its toll on everyone aboard with seasickness affecting several of those below decks. He thought that the sleeping quarters were the tightest he had ever slept in and had commented "Fine, if you are less than four feet tall" to one of his pals. Bernard looked decidedly queasy and was jammed into a corner table in the cramped ward room opposite Edward Egerton-Reed who seemed to hardly notice the turmoil and who had been annoyingly positive since leaving port. Bernard was trying to write by the feeble and flickering bulk-head light, stopping and starting to coincide with the corkscrewing of the ship.

★★★

Back in Cambridgeshire, three weeks had passed since Molly's interview with Pops and the Queen Bee and she had resumed her 'normal' life as an aircraft engineer. She was finding it more and more difficult to concentrate on her work due to the frustration of not hearing from Bernard, together with the anxiousness of waiting to hear from the ATA. Molly made a habit of checking the post first thing every morning and then again in the evening and becoming solemn for a brief period afterwards having been disappointed when still no letters arrived. Her disappointment was contagious and subsequently infected Annie the housekeeper, who adored Molly and was desperate for her to be the recipient of some good news. The only positive distraction was the upcoming Christmas, and Molly tried to focus on preparations for the family's favourite time of the year, planning gifts and a menu for the family's traditional Christmas dinner.

Molly arrived home after a tiring day of pulling apart a Tiger Moth engine to look for leaks in the oil, coolant and petrol systems; and then ground testing another engine to ensure that it performed to maximum efficiency before being air-tested. It was one of those cold factory days with no flying, and a thoroughly downhearted Molly was ready for a hot bath and creeping into bed with a good book.

As Molly walked towards the front entrance of Whitehill Manor, the door sprang open and her sisters Mary and Brenda rushed excitedly towards her. Brenda could hardly contain herself as Mary was holding two letters addressed to Molly. Molly tried to remain calm and to resist joining in the whirl of excitement, as Brenda had begun to jump up and down.

'Is that your ATA letter?' said Brenda, 'Pleeeeease read it to us Molly. Are you going to be an ATA pilot and shoot down the Germans? DakaDakaDaka…'

Mary tried to remain calm and dignified, although being inwardly as excited as Brenda and curious to ask Molly the same question. Instead she mildly reprimanded her young enthusiastic sister.

'You are so immature Brenda; stop it,' said Mary, 'Everyone knows ATA pilots don't have guns … or even radios.'

As the three young ladies demurely entered the house, Molly calmly took the letters from Mary and immediately made a dash for it up the imposing staircase, almost knocking over Annie, the housekeeper, who was coming downstairs with a tray. Her sisters hastily followed and as all three girls were running and laughing, Molly turned and made an out-of-breath apology to Annie, who was smiling and clearly au-fait with the amusement of the situation and hoping that this was the news that Molly had been longing for. Molly just managed to reach her room and lock the door escaping the clutches of her sisters who were by now both in determined pursuit.

Breathing heavily Molly ran to the bed and leapt on the soft blankets, rolling on her back and gazing at the envelopes in her hand.

Outside the door, Brenda poked out her tongue to Mary and ran around in circles with her arms aloft, pretending to be an aeroplane.

Molly adjusted herself into a comfortable position on the bed and tried to calm her breathing as she looked at the leather-bound photo of Bernard which sat on her bedside cabinet. The first letter was from Bernard. She opened it and read aloud.

'Dearest darling Molly … I am missing you terribly and I so wish that we were in each other's arms as opposed to me being thrown around in a cramped and extremely dull ship due to horrid weather. Most of the chaps have been seasick … except of course for Fruity who seems to be enjoying the ride (much to the annoyance of everyone else). I have had some good news and yes, it's the news that I have been waiting for - I am being posted as a 'replacement officer' with the 4th Royal County of London Yeomanry ('the Sharpshooters'). I've also been promoted to Captain and I will be a tank commander; it's going to be a little bit different from composing orchestral music, so I have lots to learn! Can't say too much, it's all a bit hush-hush and none of us really knows, but it looks as if we might be heading for the Med. We're rostered to be there sometime soon, so we will no doubt spend a few weeks on His Majesty's Royal Navy Troop-Ship Cruises on the way to the sunshine … should be a bit of fun, those Navy boys know how to travel in style. Until I see you again my angel, your own Bernard'.

Molly had mixed feelings of concern at Bernard's news, but she was reassured by his jovial tone. With excitement and anticipation, she quickly tore open the second letter which was marked 'from the Air Transport Auxiliary'.

'Please be good news …' she thought.

Molly read aloud.

'… Dear Mrs Rose, thank you for your recent visit to White Waltham … ba ba ba ba ba … and as a result, we would like to invite you to join the ATA as soon as possible.'

Molly was rhapsodic with excitement and could hardly control herself. She leapt off the bed and jumped around the bedroom not knowing whether to laugh or cry. It was a whirlwind of relief; ecstatic happiness punctuated with flashes of trepidation – Would she be good enough? What a responsibility! How proud she would be! She would give her very, very best! She then calmly stopped, settled down and regained her composure; standing straight, as she looked in her mother's Edwardian Mahogany Cheval mirror, tidying her cardigan and capturing the wisps of hair that had broken free from their pins. As Molly opened the door to leave the bedroom, her sisters had been listening outside the door, and they leapt up, almost knocking Molly over. "Horrors" she shouted as she chased them in a flood of laughter, which echoed down the stairs.

Annie was smiling.

Seven

After the Great Fire of London in 1666, Regent Street was one of London's first planned developments and a shining example of Neoclassical and picturesque design. The famous London street had now become overcast by the greyness of war; devoid of all its usual joviality and colour; and scarred by demolition as a result of the Luftwaffe's bombs. Snow had fallen but it had quickly melted into a grey mush that further added to the uninspiring scene.

The street was busy with wartime traffic; as red London buses growled alongside civilian motor cars and military vehicles. Bombed out buildings and ground defences including sandbags, air raid shelters and anti-aircraft guns were clearly evident.

Shoppers and military personnel in heavy winter coats crowded the pavements, some walking purposefully, others enjoying looking in the shop windows. Among them was Molly who dodged the slow-moving traffic, pedestrians and fallen debris, as she made her way to Austin Reed, the tailors, for her ATA uniform fitting. Austin Reed was one of the main designers and manufacturers of uniforms for the armed forces and its flagship premises had adorned Regent Street since the beginning of the century.

As Molly reached the shop, two damaged taxis were standing in water from a burst mains pipe and people were clearing rubble from bomb damage to adjacent offices and shops. She navigated her way around the obstructions and found her way to the door just as three RAF Officers finished paying for their uniforms and prepared to leave. As Molly entered, the doorbell tinkled and, as she was removing her overcoat, one of the exiting officers pretended to almost collide with the young and attractive Molly.

'Oh, I am so sorry, do excuse me,' he said, 'and a VERY good morning to you ma'am.'

Molly smiled but did not answer. At the far side of the expansive display area, another young woman was trying on gloves; and the two made eye contact and rolled their eyes skywards as the officers departed.

Molly walked towards a smartly dressed bespectacled middle-aged male shop assistant, who looked her up and down as she approached.

'Good morning, my name is Molly Rose and I have an appointment for a uniform fitting - for the ATA.'

'Yes, of course. I won't keep you a moment ma'am.'

Molly's beaming face said it all. This was one of the proudest days of her life. As she examined the displays of rank badges, hats, gloves and uniform-clad mannequins, she thought about what she would look like in the uniform. How proud she would be to wear it!

A strong New Zealand accent broke her daydream.

'Hi, I'm Jane, Jane Winstone; looks like we're here for the same reason, eh?'

Jane was a little older than Molly, taller in stature, and although forward in her approach, she portrayed an underlying element of shyness.

'Oh, hallo. I'm Molly, Molly Rose. It's lovely to meet you. I must say, it sounds as though you're rather a long way from home.'

'Yeah, too true. New Zealand; I'm a Kiwi! I've been asked to join the ATA, and I did my air test and interview a few weeks ago.'

'Oh, me too! So you're a flyer as well? How wonderful.'

'Yeah, been flying since I was sixteen actually,' said Jane, 'not sure I'd be any good at anything else.'

'I know what you mean - me too: Have you just arrived in England?'

'About six months ago', said Jane, 'and I'm missing home already. But I really needed to get away.'

A look of sadness came over Jane's face and Molly saw that something was clearly troubling her.

'Nothing too serious I hope? Tell you what, let's get sorted out here and go for a nice cup of tea and a chat shall we?'

Their conversation was interrupted by the tailor's assistant Mr. Grimbly. He was around fifty years of age and very skinny to the point of looking decidedly weak. Both Jane and Molly were somewhat surprised that a man whose clothes did not fit him at all well should be working at Austin Reed. His voice was commensurate with his overall appearance as he mumbled something barely decipherable to Molly.

'We are ready for you ma'am. Please follow me.'

He moved slowly and ineffectually, and as Molly walked away to follow Mr. Grimbly, she looked around at Jane and gave a slight indication of her feeling that she was part of a surreal theatrical performance. Jane was wondering what delights awaited the young and charming Molly.

Mr Grimbly led Molly into a side-room separated from the shop reception by a curtain, which he left open. There was a large Singer sewing machine in the corner, and pieces of fabric and half-made suits and uniforms were strewn all over. Unlike the beautifully arranged main shop, the whole room was very untidy, and Molly stood for a moment visibly surprised.

'Now, Miss, I'll measure for the jacket first. If you could kindly hold this end of the measure.'

He attempted to pull the measure round Molly's chest without touching her, and Molly became even more concerned.

'Might the measurement be more accurate if I were to remove my jacket?' said Molly.

'Quite so miss, quite so. If you insist. Er, yes, if you would be so kind as to, ahem, to remove your jacket.'

Molly complied and stood with her arms outstretched for her measurements to be taken. Mr Grimbly, tape measure in hand, approached Molly again. He was clearly exceedingly embarrassed and unsure about how to measure a woman, desperately trying not to touch her at all. After a few ineffectual attempts to throw the tape measure round her and failing to catch the free end, in a look of complete panic he looked towards the back of the shop.

'Mr Smithers! Mr Smithers! Are you free?', he shouted.

Mr. Smithers, the tailor, an elderly, balding but well-dressed portly gentleman, appeared through the curtain; a tape measure draped around his neck, pince-nez glasses perched on his nose. Given the haughty nature of his response, he seemed to be clearly distraught at having been disturbed from something which he obviously considered to be far more important.

'Yes, I'm free if absolutely necessary,' he growled, 'what's the problem here Mr Grimbly?'

'Well, Mr Smithers; it's a - ahem - a woman ... for a fitting - a uniform fitting. Jacket and skirt.'

Molly was now beginning to find the whole episode rather amusing and she took the opportunity to add to the theatricals.

'And trousers, I think you'll find.' said Molly.

Mr. Grimbly was clearly embarrassed.

'Really? Oh, yes. Jacket, skirt … and trousers,' he said.

Mr. Smithers seemed to have little interest in the proceedings and was quite eager to get back to whatever it was that he was doing.

'Well, Mr Grimbly, carry on!'

'Eh … I think this is a two-man job sir,' said Mr. Grimbly.

Molly was beginning to think that things could not possibly get any more unusual when the shop doorbell tinkled, announcing the arrival of another female customer. Molly looked out from the room to see who it was. Dressed in an elegant winter coat, which she promptly removed to reveal a strikingly smart ATA pilot's uniform, the beautiful Diana Barnato confidently entered.

Diana was thirty years old and the epitome of British sophistication and style. She was the daughter of the wealthy financier Woolf Barnato, chairman of Bentley Motors, and one of the famous Bentley Boys; and three-times winner of the Le Mans 24-hour race in France. Their fortune was as a result of Diana's grandfather Barney Barnato who founded a diamond mine in South Africa.

After coming out as a debutante in the season of 1936, Diana thought that there was more to life than the social expectations of her class and rather than being thrust into the matrimonial fishpond, she decided to become a pilot and learned to fly a Tiger Moth. Soon after the outbreak of war, Diana volunteered to become a Red Cross nurse and in 1940 she was serving as a nurse in France before the evacuation of the British Expeditionary Force from Dunkirk. She thereafter drove ambulances in London during the Blitz before joining the ATA.

Diana saw Molly through the curtain and walked to where she was being fitted.

'ATA is it? God forbid, don't get kitted out here; these two are terrified of being within six feet of you, never mind getting within a foot of your right measurements. Take my word for it, go to Saville Row darling, unless you like the idea of looking like a sack of spuds. I only come here for the buttons, braid and wings. Other than that, I wouldn't trust them to make my hankies. Tell you what, I'm popping down the road for a spot of tea, so why don't you come along? We'll no doubt be working together so perhaps we can get to know each other … and I can give you the details of my tailor.'

Diana opened her jacket to reveal a bright scarlet lining, as she gave a flamboyant twirl, much to the disdain of the tailor and his assistant.

Eight

Despite the war, the Ritz Hotel in London enjoyed a tremendous vogue and was a regular hot spot of social and political life among the elite. The iconic hotel, resembling a French chateau, had a legendary reputation where it felt as though time had stood still since 1906. Incarnations of its name had permeated into popular culture since it opened, denoting something extravagantly stylish and trendy. Its guests included aristocrats, politicians and royals from home and abroad; and even though the hotel had its share of damage and regular shattered windows from bomb blasts, many guests had moved in for 'safety'.

Diana, Molly and Jane entered the Palm Court, the hotel's most widely known facility, which hosts the famous "Afternoon Tea at the Ritz". The cream-coloured Louis XVI setting had been stripped of its chandeliers, panelled mirrors in gilt bronze frames and other finery, and configured with blackout curtains and sandbags for continuing air raids; but still beautiful and quintessentially British. Jane looked over-awed and slightly uncomfortable as she softly questioned Molly:

'What is Saville Row?' she said.

'Somewhere we certainly can't afford to go,' said Molly with a smile.

'So, a bit like here then, eh?'

'Yes, exactly!' replied Molly laughing. 'Guess we better enjoy it while we can - I'm sure that the Crew Room at the ATA will be nothing like this.' They chuckled to themselves.

Diana led the way past the well-dressed clients of the hotel and bustling waiters as everyone made way for her, glancing back at her as she passed. She was supremely confident and quite at home.

'Not a bad old spot really', she said. 'Apart from the Dorch of course, it's probably my favourite watering hole in town.'

Jane caught Molly's eye and they grinned at each other. As Diana made way to her favourite table, she was approached by Margaret Fairweather. Margie, as she was known to her friends, was the eldest daughter of Lord and Lady Runciman of Doxford, both of whom were Members of Parliament.

'Hallo hallo - dearest Diana. Slumming it again I see?'

'Margie - how delightful. You look wonderful as always,' said Diana.

'Oh, thanks awfully. You too darling. And who may I ask are these Bright Young Things?'

Diana took the greatest of pleasure in introducing her two new friends.

'Molly Rose, Jane Winstone - meet my very good friend the Honourable Lady Margaret Fairweather - Margie to her friends - one of the first eight women to join our illustrious organisation.'

Molly immediately recognised Margaret Fairweather as the first woman to fly a Supermarine Spitfire. She also noticed how Margaret's steely green eyes were darting around the room; and although outwardly enthusiastic at their introduction, Margaret maintained a significant air of indifference.

'Golly, how do you do,' said Molly, 'it's an honour.'

'Oh gosh, thank you, but I'm sure there are others in here far more worthy of meeting than me. Anyway, lovely to meet you - and to see you Diana - but I must dash darlings; my impatient husband is already at the table and he'll be a proper old humbug if I keep him waiting any longer for one of his three squares a day. Cheery bye.'

Molly looked around to see a smartly dressed portly gentleman seated at one of the tables, holding a large glass of wine and smoking a cigarette as he looked in Margaret's direction and waved. Margaret hurried off towards him, as Diana, Jane and Molly sat in three comfortable Edwardian armchairs which almost swallowed them whole, and in front of which was a low and beautifully decorated coffee table. Diana summoned a waiter.

'Afternoon tea for three please,' she said.

Diana made herself comfortable as though she was in her own drawing room, settling down for a glass of sherry before dinner.

'So,' said Diana, enthusiastically, 'we'll all be pilots together; what a hoot. Now, Jane, what brings you to this neck of the woods?'

Jane almost jumped to attention, and she felt that the eyes of every guest in the hotel restaurant were directly focussed on her next few words. Diana and Molly waited in anticipation for a response.

'Oh, er, well. My fiancé Angus joined up straight away. The New Zealand Air Force, that is. And he was posted here; to the UK I mean, and he was doing just fine, loving it in fact, but then …'

Jane paused for a moment to get the rest of the words out as Molly and Diana were rigid, preparing themselves for the inevitable. Jane had tears in her eyes.

'… he got himself shot down and killed. About eight months ago. So, I just needed to get away, to come over here … to … well, I don't know what I was thinking really.'

Diana looked uncomfortable, wishing she hadn't asked; but she gathered herself to look very sympathetic. Molly was feeling guilty at having orchestrated a position in which Jane was clearly uncomfortable; and she wondered how she could steer Jane's mood back to that of their first encounter.

'Oh Jane, how awful,' said Molly, 'I'm so sorry. Do you think that being here will give you a fresh start?'

'Getting over here has helped, to be honest,' continued Jane, 'and joining the ATA is a new start for me, yes. I need to be somewhere where I'm not reminded of him everywhere I look.'

Jane paused for a moment and then, much to the relief of Diana and Molly, she smoothly changed the topic of the conversation.

'Do you think we'll be based together at the same place?' she said. 'What do you call it … a Ferry Pool?'

Molly was relieved.

'Well, I hear that there are quite a few of us girls now, and they've set up women-only pools, so I think there's a very good chance. I certainly hope so. What do you think Diana?'

'Yes, quite right,' said Diana, 'the chaps can't cope with us fillies littering up their precious rest rooms, so we've got our own show. It's all a bit like being in an all-girls boarding school; you know, strict military nuns, curfews and such. But I have to do something constructive in this horrid war, and I can't think of anywhere else I would rather be than at the ATA. You'll both love it but it's also hard work. Survival is the key, and you will only survive on your own merits.'

Molly registered the word "survival" which hung in the air like an echo and as a reminder of the risks that she was about to encounter in her new life.

Nine

Spring

It was Molly's first morning of classroom instruction at the ATA training facility at Hatfield Aerodrome in Hertfordshire. She wore her new ATA uniform for the first time and had spent an age in front of the mirror checking that everything looked perfect. As she stared at her reflection that morning, Molly felt a sense of pride in her achievements that had led her to join the ATA but most of all she felt so incredibly honoured to wear the uniform. It was symbolic of her being a part of something bigger, something more profound than anything she had ever experienced; an outwards expression of the responsibility and dedication that Molly felt in her heart.

There was the slight stigma to overcome – that of being a female in a military-style uniform. However, Molly tucked those thoughts away in a corner, and focussed instead on the positive and supportive comments that she had already received from her family.

The uniform was slightly itchy but rewarding, as in addition to its stylish look, the aroma and feel of the fabric was sublime, but the real joy was the ATA badge – a gleaming shining symbol of hope, spirit and freedom; and every glance at it gave Molly a reinvigorated sense of duty and determination. 'I'll never be late for a class', she thought; 'I'll always achieve perfect attendance'; 'I'll be the best pilot that I can possibly be'. Those were only a few of the many promises that Molly made to herself on that morning.

On arriving at the classroom, Molly selected a seat in a spot which she thought would draw the least attention as her classmates shuffled about noisily trying to get comfortable. Looking casually around the small room, she studied for a moment the fifteen male and female civilian pilots who were to be her classmates, and who appeared to be from all walks of life.

The women appeared to be aged from about twenty to thirty-five. Some looked intensely serious, whilst others looked as though they would be tremendous fun, already laughing and joking with each other. The girls had quickly formed into small groups, and as Molly was on her own and with an empty chair next to her, she had a flash thought of isolation which she quickly put aside. Two of the male pilots were quite young and handsome and both kept looking over at Molly, smiling and then whispering to each other.

Molly noticed two men in the front of the class who were maybe too old or perhaps unfit for RAF service, but whom, she thought, may have taken the opportunity to use their skills in the only flying option available to them. Both were well over fifty years old and looked like dashing aviators from a bygone era, as one of them flashed Molly a villainous smile whist twiddling his air force moustache.

Molly reminded herself that everyone in the room held at least an "A" License and had over two-hundred-and-fifty hours of flying experience, and she thought about Gerard d'Erlanger mentioning the epithet "Ancient and Tattered Airmen", and she suddenly became resentful of the term, realising that there was by contrast vast experience in this small room. This was especially relevant to those pilots who had perhaps learned to fly in the 1920s and 1930s or perhaps even served in the First World War, and the body of aviation knowledge they had accumulated which was so valuable to the current war effort. She felt humbled to be seated amongst such people.

Jane Winstone was the last to enter the classroom and she sat next to Molly.

'Hello Molly. I'm a bit late. Would you mind if I sit here?'

'Jane - how lovely. Not at all, please do. So nice to see you again.'

'Good to see you too,' said Jane, 'the uniform turned out OK then.'

'Yes - not quite the sack of spuds, thank heavens.'

They were interrupted by the instructor who was an inconspicuous looking man in his fifties and dressed in the ATA uniform. He was quite small and everything about him was round; from his body to his face, and even his round rimmed spectacles, but his voice was distinctively clear and loud as he started to speak. The room fell silent as all eyes focussed on him.

'Good morning and welcome to the ATA Ground School. You are about to embark on a one-year training programme. However, you are going to do it in three months. You may all be experienced pilots, but we'll be covering a lot of material, which means that you will need total focus. The more you listen and learn, the safer you'll be. The programme comprises of classroom lectures and tests, flying lessons and assessments. You will learn about aircraft instruments, navigation and plotting of flight paths using maps and a compass, technical data, engines, airframes, aerodynamics and more. Your progress will be continually analysed to see if you could be a suitable addition to the ATA.'

Jane leant over to Molly and in the usual quiet and calming tone that was synonymous with her shy demeanour, and whispered;

'We seem to be the youngest ones in the room. Hopefully we can keep up.'

Molly did not answer but she briefly thought about what Jane had said. The idea that she could perhaps fail the training hadn't really crossed her mind until now and she pushed it away immediately. No – she dared not even think it, it would be too much to bear.

The chief instructor continued.

'We'll start with some basics ... ATA pilots are not permitted to fly above the cloud without sight of the ground. You will have limited instruments and even if there is a radio fitted there will be strict non-combat radio silence. So, if you get lost in cloud, you'll have the devil of a job fixing your position once you get clear. You will fly at set cruising speeds, and needless to say there will be no aerobatics. You'll not be fitted with weapons, or navigation equipment for that matter so your dead reckoning manual navigation will have to be exceptional. Aside from all the general airmanship you will learn about the pre-flight checks and cockpit drills for a number of specific aircraft and aircraft practicalities from propeller pitch to petrol carburettors and from hydraulics to emergency procedures. Your life will depend on how much information you retain so please pay attention.'

The instructor held up a small book.

'Now obviously we can't train you on every single type you'll be asked to fly so each aircraft has its own entry in this little blue book: the Ferry Pilot Notes. It's your new best friend and your new bible. Read it, learn it, and if you can, sleep with it by your side; because it will give you the instruction you need when someone asks you to fly a particular type of aircraft for the first time.'

The room was eerily quiet as the sun shone through the window and the muffled sounds of military vehicles and aircraft could be heard outside. All eyes were focussed on the instructor as he held up a second book.

'In addition, this is the ever-valuable ATA Pilot's Reminder Book, as written by various pilots and engineers, and it details the handling and the idiosyncrasies of many types of aircraft. I cannot begin to tell you how important these are. They may very well save your life.'

★★★

During the course of the next three months, Molly attended various lessons and practical tasks, including basic airmanship; navigation; weather; and operational safety, both on the ground and in the air. The instruction covered the principles of flight and a broad range of desirable behaviours and abilities; testing both skill and technique. It particularly focussed on the pilot's awareness of the aircraft and the environment in which it operates. Molly eagerly consumed every word and action with growing confidence, and she spent her evenings reading over the course material; looking forward to the start of each new day.

The parachute fitting and drills were of particular interest and they caused a great deal of excitement; especially to those pilots unused to jumps. Molly and her colleagues were suspended from a gantry in a harness; and taught to jump from boxes while executing parachute rolls. The two eldest pilots that had caught Molly's attention in the classroom completed each manoeuvre with ease, and a good deal of style, Molly thought. They seemed to have as much experience and confidence as the instructor and Molly watched them carefully, hoping to learn something from them.

It was time for their first real parachute drop and Molly and Jane had been paired together. It was a perfectly clear and windless day and ideal conditions for throwing oneself out of a moving plane at altitude, albeit with a parachute. Molly initially thought that Jane looked rather queasy, given her hesitation to jump out of a perfectly operational aircraft, and that her face was turning a delicate shade of pale green as she sat motionless just before the instructor gave them the "Go" signal.

'There's nothing to it. It's just a brolly hop', said Molly as she tried to convince Jane, and herself, that this was as easy as sliding into a Tiger Moth cockpit. The usual 'what ifs' entered Molly's thought process, and she wondered what everyone would think about her if she suddenly changed her mind, but before Molly could even finish the thought, she was dropping like a stone, eagerly looking around to see if Jane was close by. The upcoming rush of air was interrupted by the huge canopy of the parachute opening above in a swift and explosive manoeuvre that instantly turned the howling wind into a calm soothing breeze.

Molly looked around and spotted Jane, and even though she was some distance above and over a hundred feet away, the smile on Jane's face was as clear as day as they both floated towards the ground, exhilarated. As Molly looked below at the beautiful British landscape with its gentle hills, neat fields, railways and cottages, she imagined for a brief moment that there was no war. How could we be at war when the countryside below seems so peaceful, so tranquil, she thought. Molly swayed gently as birds flew below her; their wings catching the light from the sun. For an instant she wondered if this was all real, or was she dreaming. She fantasized about stylishly landing on the lawn at Whitehill and running into Bernard's arms…

***

Towards the end of the intense three months of instruction, Molly was assigned to demonstrate her solo spin recovery and emergency landing drills in a Miles Magister. Two instructors with clipboards stood at the side of the airfield watching Molly push the single engine mono-plane into a steeper and steeper angle of attack, until it was flying almost vertically towards the sun.

Suddenly, the aircraft seemed to lose control, floating precariously as the engine whined loudly, before spinning erratically into a shallow dive. After a few seconds, the engine stuttered and lost power and then cut out completely with the prop stopped rigid. In silence, the aircraft descended steeply towards the ground as the two instructors lowered their clipboards and watched as though frozen in time. Seconds later and only moments before impact, the aircraft broke into a shallow dive, levelled out, and carried out a perfect three-point landing at the edge of the airfield.

Molly was thrilled and beaming with satisfaction as she climbed down from the aircraft. The solo-spin recovery and emergency landing drill was one of the last assignments of the three months of intensive training. Molly tidied herself up, threw her parachute over her shoulder, and walked towards the Chief Instructor and his assistant.

'All done sir,' said Molly, proudly.

'Well done Miss Rose. Let's head over to the office. We have been impressed with your flying and after today's successful solo I am delighted to tell you that you have satisfactorily completed training.'

'Thank you so much Sir.'

As they walked towards the office, Molly began, for the first time, to comprehend the enormity of the task ahead. The past three months had been so busy and hectic, full of late-night study and early morning classes, that she had not had the time to think about actually starting the job of ferrying aircraft.

The instructor entered the office ahead of Molly, and calmly sat down at his desk which was strewn with files and random pieces of paper. As he spoke, he rifled through the paperwork whilst Molly watched, wondering to herself if there was a strategic system to which only the instructor was privy.

'Please sit down Miss Rose,' he said as he pulled a file from the bottom of the pile, toppling others in the process. 'Now let's see, ah here we are. Yes, you have quite a few more hours than a number of our trainees, so you're to report initially to ATA HQ at White Waltham, where you'll get a crash course - well hopefully not, eh? - on Magisters, Harts, Fairchilds and Proctors.'

Molly smiled and thought about how Jane would react to the instructor's bizarre sense of humour. He continued…

'You'll start off on the smaller types, and as you prove yourself the next step will be the single-seater fighters - Tempests and Typhoons, and possibly Spitfires. In any event, your first posting will be to the all-women's ferry pool at Hamble. It's not long been set up, so you'll be starting with a few of the people you have been through training with. Now assuming all goes well and you don't kill yourself, you'll be back in training for the light twin-engine aircraft – Oxfords, Ansons and Wellingtons.'

Molly was by now more than ready to leave; not only to escape the dull witticisms which she was struggling to brush off; but more so, to move on to the next stage of her life.

'Erm … thank you sir,' she said.

'Good luck Miss Rose. You are going to need it.'

Ten

Summer

It was the most memorable of June afternoons for two reasons. One being that the distinctive and exquisitely melodic notes of the little brown skylark could be heard floating across the air against a glorious backdrop of rustling trees in the warm breeze. The meadows were brimming with the soft blues, pinks and yellows of wildflowers in the afternoon light, enhanced by a low creeping mist which had settled onto the fields. Everything looked so utterly beautiful, like an exquisite painting slowly unfolding upon the canvas of a Master.

The second reason was that Molly took the last few steps amidst this magnificent backdrop to the main gate of the ATA's Ferry Pool No. 15 at Hamble in Hampshire, knowing that her life was about to change irrevocably.

Molly had taken the early morning train down from Cambridge and had spent the past few hours contemplating the transformation that lay ahead of her. As she passed through the airfield gates, she saw them as a bridge from her old life to the new and reflected that things could never be the same after this.

Molly had dressed early that morning in her ATA uniform and, as a Third Officer, she had one thin gold bar on her shoulder flash. It took some time for Molly to pull herself away from the mirror as she struggled between fantasy and reality. Her thoughts varied wildly from flying off to the desert as the heroine to rescue Bernard from impending doom, to someone asking her to fly the biggest aircraft that she had ever seen. Arthur and her sisters were so proud, but also sad to see her off, not knowing when they would see each other again, but they managed to hold back the tears as they said goodbye. Annie the housekeeper however had not managed to control her emotions so well as she burst into tears when she saw Molly in her uniform.

Having arrived at Southampton Station, Molly made a quick stop in Hamble-le-Rice village, where the ATA had kindly arranged accommodation at the home of one of the local villagers. Known locally as "Hamble", the village is at the tip of the Hamble peninsula on the south coast, and bounded by Butlocks Heath, Netley, Bursledon, Southampton Water and the River Hamble. The once quiet Hamble still had those quintessential elements of a pretty coastal village but had been transformed as a result of the war, becoming much busier due to the local aircraft-producing factories and the aircraft training centre.

Molly stopped at the home of her new landlady Mrs Collis and carried her small suitcase through the gate towards the house. The path lead through a delightful if somewhat haphazard cottage garden and Molly noticed vegetables growing alongside aquilegias, geraniums and peonies - a sure sign that summer was here. An excited Mrs Collis opened the door in anticipation and came out onto the path to greet her new lodger.

Mrs Collis was seventy years old and had lived in or near Hamble-le-Rice for most of her life. She was a small lady with grey hair and glasses and despite her advancing years she was agile and alert, spending much of her day in the garden surrounding the cottage and always to be found wearing her signature green wellington boots. Molly noticed that Mrs Collis was holding a hen under her arm, and Molly was slightly taken aback at this vision of eccentricity, wondering what her new landlady was about to do with the terrified-looking little hen. Mrs Collis, after a warm and pleasant greeting, noticed the concerned look on Molly's face and explained that it was nothing sinister, thereafter introducing her "favourite hen" as "Lancaster".

It did not take Molly long to realise that living with Mrs Collis was going to be quite fun, and an unusual contrast to life as a pilot. Molly was particularly relieved that she did not need to justify her officer's uniform, nor her role at the ATA, as Mrs Collis seemed to be immensely proud to be hosting a serving officer, albeit female, for the war effort.

After a quick cup of tea and a chat, and being shown to her small but comfortable room which contained more patterned fabrics in different colours than Molly had ever seen, and with chintzy little ornaments in every available space, she felt settled and happy and made her excuses to depart, setting off for the short walk to the ATA air base. The thatched cottage was on the edge of the village and as Molly exited the gate, she could see the air base in the distance and could faintly hear the sounds of aircraft taking off and landing. The walk was short, along one winding country lane which was mostly dirt track, on one side of which was a grassy hill leading up to woodland, whilst the other sloped down to a narrow valley and a brook.

The Hamble Ferry Pool was created in September 1940, as a sub-pool of the ATA's headquarters at White Waltham, but it quickly became the 'all women' Ferry Pool No 15. It was situated between the Hamble river and the Solent, and ideally positioned to quickly clear aircraft from the nearby Eastleigh Factory in Southampton which was producing hundreds of Spitfires and Seafires, and assembling Airacobras. Southampton was constantly under attack and as a result, the Hamble base was in a particularly vulnerable position.

After a slow walk through pristine countryside, Molly reached the air base and after showing her papers and clearing the security, was escorted across the base by one of the corporals. The ferry pool was a hub of activity with engineers, pilots and administration staff moving about amidst a flurry of military vehicles. Aircraft were taking off and landing and the sound of engines and propellers was a comfort to Molly, reminding her of home, work and family, and particularly her father.

The corporal accompanied Molly to one of the office buildings which was not exactly the impressive structure that she had imagined, and more like an elaborate wooden hut, as were several of the other buildings on the base. Three women stood talking outside the entrance, and the corporal stopped, wished Molly the best of luck, and returned to his duties. The senior of the three officers had her back to Molly but she seemed to sense Molly approaching as she quickly finished her conversation and turned around with the most radiant and welcoming smile.

'Ah, Molly is it? I'm Margaret Gore and I'm the CO here at Hamble. Welcome.'

'How do you do,' said Molly, apprehensively.

Margaret Gore was accustomed to the overwhelming feelings of nervousness from new recruits, and her perfectly calm demeanour and kindness quickly brought most of them into the pleasant reality of their new situation.

Margaret Wyndham Gore was twenty-nine years old and was slightly built with piercing brown eyes and a soft smile. Initially seeking a career in medicine, Margaret lacked the academic background and so she worked instead to raise money for subsidised flying lessons with the Civil Air Guard and by 1939 she was a qualified instructor. Margaret was not amongst the famous 'first eight' female pilots of the ATA, however she was recruited shortly thereafter and by 1941 she had risen to the rank of Commanding Officer of the Hamble Ferry Pool.

"Margo", as she was affectionately known, was a perfectionist with a natural leadership quality. She was immensely popular amongst the female pilots of the ATA and knew each and every girl; their strengths, weaknesses and their personalities; all of which was vital when choosing assignments, promotions and new training opportunities, which she continually encouraged.

'Walk with me Molly. I've heard some good things about your flying and your training, so you should fit in very well here.'

'Thank you ma'am.'

'Now, as you probably know, we're a newly established all-women pool, so we don't yet have any women's accommodation on base. We have taken on a number of hirings not far from here; and as I understand, you're billeted with a Mrs Collis in Hamble-le-Rice village?'

'Yes, that's right,' said Molly, 'I met her briefly when I dropped my suitcase off on the way here. She seems very pleasant.'

'Jolly good. It's a lovely village - nice and quiet - and some of the other girls are close by. And by all accounts Mrs Collis is a dear and quite a fun character so you'll be good company for each other in the evenings; a bit like having a home from home. If you have any problems Molly, any at all, you can come and chat to me.'

'Thank you ma'am. Will do. It all sounds splendid.'

As they reached the Crew Room, Margo gave Molly another warm smile.

'Right, here we are - the Crew Room. Brace yourself Molly.'

Margo opened the door and they entered the Crew Room which was full of pilots and buzzing with noise and activity. There were forty or so people in the room; mostly female, however there were also several male RAF and Fleet Air Arm officers who were standing at what looked like a bar. Tables and chairs filled most of the room at which many others were undertaking a variety of activities including a bridge four; backgammon; jigsaws: pattern-cutting for a dress; letter writing, reading and sewing. Several pilots and ground crew were simply sitting and chatting and only a few noticed Margo and Molly as they entered.

'We currently have thirty-one female pilots at Hamble,' said Margo, 'and from every corner of the world, so you will hear many different accents and languages here ...'.

Margo looked at one of the female pilots who was doing a handstand in the corner.

'... and you'll see a lot of different activities,' she continued. 'The girls are friendly, but they do tend to keep in their own groups, so you'll get used to that.

A female pilot walked by and Margo saw Molly glance at her thick fur-lined boots.

'I know,' said Margo, 'regulations state that we girls are supposed to wear skirts outside of flying hours, but most of us stick to the trousers and boots - which is fine.'

'So, can we wear flying kit all of the time?', asked Molly.

'Officially only when on actual flying duties,' said Margo, 'Some of the COs of outlying stations make a point of picking us up on "dress and deportment". Humbug really, you'd think they would have better things to do. But it would be good if you can try to adhere to the rules as best you can.'

Margo and Molly walked to a table where Diana was seated with several other girls.

'And about time too,' said Diana, 'I've been telling the girls all about you and how you barely escaped the clutches of the tailors from hell.'

'Hallo Diana,' said Molly, with a smile, 'lovely to see you again.'

'You too Molly,' said Diana, 'welcome'.

The pilot who had, up to that point, been in a handstand in the corner for fifteen-minutes, flipped herself upright in a very smooth manoeuvre and gracefully walked to the table.

'Ladies,' said Margo, 'please meet Molly Rose, our newest pilot, fresh from training. Molly - Diana Barnato whom you know; and this is Mary Wilkins, Joy Gough, Lettice Curtis and Irene Arckless ... and our fitness guru from South Africa - Jackie Sorour.

The girls all smiled and said hello to Molly, who was by now beginning to feel a lot more comfortable.

'A new blonde hair,' said Lettice, 'how charming.'

'Blonde hair?' said Molly, confused.

Jackie smiled and tapped the tiny gold bar on Molly's shoulder flash.

'She means *this* blonde hair,' said Jackie, 'We were all blonde when we started, so take no notice Molly. Come and join us when you're through with the tour.'

'Oh, right,' said Molly, smiling and seeing the funny side. She liked Jackie instantly.

Jackie had a gift of making people feel good no matter what the circumstances. She was about the same size as Molly and with short dark hair and dark features. Her world was colourful, inspirational and sensual; and spontaneous to a point of unpredictability. Jackie pushed the limits of social convention and, although she would live in the moment, she often relished stepping out of the personality spotlight to be by herself to recharge. Her non-stop charisma made her likeable and popular with the other girls as she was always fun to be around.

'I'm sorry Molly,' said Lettice, 'couldn't resist it. It's lovely to meet you. I heard that you're billeted in the village. We'll be neighbours.'

'Yes,' said Molly, 'with Mrs Collis. She seems very nice.'

'My landlady is Mrs Merrivale' said Jackie, 'and I've been trying to teach her yoga, but she's having none of it. She's a dressmaker, so I've also been helping her to make dresses in the evenings. Such a therapeutic contrast to flying aircraft.'

'So *that's* why you always look so feminine,' said Mary.

'I may have tailored my uniform a bit, yes,' said Jackie confidently as she started stretching, 'But you can't get on in a man's world by pretending to be a man.'

'I have digs at The Bugle pub but it's a bit of a bore,' said Diana, 'I hardly stay there as I travel back and forth to London most evenings as I much prefer the Savoy.'

The girls all looked at each other and laughed.

'Oh, stop being such a luvvie,' said Lettice.

Margo saw that Molly would be comfortable with the group and she started to think about carrying on with essentials.

'Well,' she said, 'it seems as though you have the domestics sorted out, so I'm going to whisk Molly away as I'd better just run through our daily routine. We'll see you girls later.'

Before they left, Margo briefly turned her attention to Irene who was seated in front of Jackie. Molly noticed that Irene seemed to be lost in her thoughts as Jackie's hands rested protectively on her shoulders.

Irene was a humble and reserved young woman, with a tendency to underplay her accomplishments. She could always be relied upon to get the job done on time and her caring and sensitive nature and generosity touched the hearts of her friends, and especially her closest friend Jackie. Irene's current predicament however, immersed her mind in a gloomy fog as she sat motionless and thoughtful, seemingly harassed with many disquieting fears.

'By the way, Irene,' said Margo, 'I heard that your fiancée was shot down. I am sorry.

'Thank you Margo,' replied Irene, 'I heard from the War Office that he survived the crash, but he's now in a POW camp, which may be horrific. I do hope that he's not hurt, and I've been told to contact the Red Cross to find out more. It's all too horrible to think about.'

She lowered her gaze to the floor.

'Do please keep me posted if you hear anything more,' said Margo, as she led Molly away towards the door.

Molly and Margo entered the Ops Room which, unlike the Crew Room, was relatively quiet. New information was coming in by phone, and which was being relayed to one of the Ops Officers who was hastily scribbling on the board with a chalk stick. Margo and Molly approached the efficient and stately blonde Operations Officer, Alison King, who seemed to be the central focus of the room and wielding a Churchillian command of proceedings.

Flight Captain (Operations Division) Alison Elsie King was thirty years old and had known Margo from before the war. She joined the ATA in 1940 as a 'sub-adjutant', with responsibility for administration, and was meticulous to the point of perfectionism. Her keen efficiency and attention to detail resulted in her becoming the first female Operations Officer with responsibility for allocating the daily ferrying movement of aircraft.

'Molly,' said Margo, 'this is Alison King, our Ops Officer. Alison, please meet Molly Rose, our new pilot.'

'How do you do,' said Molly.

'Welcome Molly. I've heard good things about you. So happy that you're here.'

'Do you have a few minutes please Alison,' said Margo, 'just to run Molly through your empire?'

'Of course. So, Molly, it all looks a bit haphazard, but it's actually very organised. Aircraft movements are shown every day on this large blackboard. Pilots are chosen depending upon their familiarity and experience of each aircraft type. You will obviously start on those you are familiar with, and as you gain experience and rank, you'll be given other aircraft to fly. That, of course, is Margo's decision.'

'Indeed,' said Margo, 'It's not all Tiger Moths nowadays. You may have heard that we're expecting some of our women to soon be authorised on Typhoons and Spitfires for instance. With your hours Molly it shouldn't be long before you join them.'

'So,' continued Alison, 'once we have our daily allocations, I or my Ops Assistant update the board and fill out an authorisation chit. Each pilot signs to accept the aircraft allocation. We lay out the chits on the table over there each morning. If there's anything specific related to a task, I'll hand those chits out personally. The "Priority" column there shows the urgency of the delivery.'

Margo added: 'It's important to remember that we are not permitted to fly at night, in bad weather or above a fixed cloud layer, so it can be a devil of a job getting airborne for a high priority delivery if the weather has closed in. In that case you'll be expected to stay with the aircraft until it's possible to get off.'

Alison continued: 'But as far as possible we will try and schedule you to be home every evening. We now have the taxi-flight Ansons, so it's a lot more efficient than it used to be when we had to rely on trains and taxis - we sometimes lost days on end as pilots tried to make their way back. Well, that's about it; all pretty straight-forward really.'

'One of our junior officers will show you around the other parts of the base,' said Margo, 'and the girls will fill you in so you'll soon get the hang of it. Any questions? No? Good. See you tomorrow then, bright and early.'

After the rest of Molly's tour, and with her head still buzzing with excitement, she returned to the Crew Room just as Mary and Joy were about to leave. Mary informed Molly that she was also heading back to Hamble village and she asked if they could walk together, which delighted Molly.

At just over five-feet tall, the twenty-six-year-old First Officer Mary Wilkins was a farmer's daughter with a middle-class upbringing, diminutive in stature and about the same size as Molly and with blonde curly hair and blue eyes. At first impression, Molly thought that Mary was polite although somewhat reserved and quietly spoken but she also sensed that there was a lot more to this petite and pretty girl, hoping that Mary could perhaps be the ideal person to show her the ropes.

Mary and Molly walked along the country lane into Hamble village just as the sun began to go down, signifying the close of the most perfect and eventful day. Mary told Molly that she had been inspired by aviation from an early age when she saw a de Havilland 60 Moth during a childhood visit to a flying circus. She thereafter learnt to fly in 1938 and, having heard a BBC radio broadcast asking for qualified pilots to apply to the ATA, she successfully applied and joined the organisation. Molly listened with intent and Mary asked what Molly thought about her induction.

'It was quite a lot to take in all in one day,' said Molly, 'but I must say that it's all very exciting.'

'Exciting and daunting at the same time,' said Mary. 'The girls are lovely - don't you think? You'll love it here Molly, and from what you told me about your background, it seems to be perfect for you.'

'Perfect, yes it is - in many ways,' said Molly, 'and I feel as though I'm exactly where I should be. But I'm also very aware of all the risks and especially the consequences of any mistakes. Well, this is my digs; See you tomorrow Mary - and thank you.'

'Yes, bright and early for day one. I'll see you in the morning. Goodnight.'

Molly entered the cottage as Mrs Collis was taking a vegetable pie from the oven, the smell of which was detectable from the garden gate, and Molly realised in that moment that she had not had anything to eat all day. Her body had been running on pure excitement, but a sudden hunger overwhelmed her when she saw the most perfect pie emerge from the oven, and with her name written all over it.

'Hallo Mrs Collis, said Molly, 'that looks wonderful.'

'It's a Woolton pie,' said Mrs Collis, smiling, 'I thought that you may be hungry.'

Mrs Collis had been closely following the Ministry of Food's "Dig for Victory" campaign, cultivating flowering plants, herbs, vegetables and a few small fruit trees, from which she tried to be as self-sufficient as possible. She owned a few Maran hens which provided a regular supply of eggs and which, along with home-made jams and chutneys, the entrepreneurial Mrs Collis often sold to her neighbours. She reminded Molly of her mother, who was also full of charisma and ever so slightly eccentric but always full of wonderful surprises, and she hoped that Mrs Collis would perhaps help fill the void created by Molly's separation from her family.

'I am actually very hungry,' said Molly, 'and I must say that it's most kind of you to think of me, thank you.'

'You are so welcome my dear,' said Mrs Collis, 'I grow these vegetables myself so we have a small supply of essentials, thank heavens. Strawberries have just arrived and we have plenty of things from the garden. Hitler is trying to starve us all you know, and I for one am not going to let that happen. My few hens lay eggs daily, and I like to think of them as dropping their own little bombs on Hitler's head'.

'Ah, Lancaster, yes, now I see', said Molly laughing. 'I think that I'm going to love it here Mrs Collis,' she said, as she sat down at the table with her eyes widening at the feast before her.

'I would so love to buy a cow,' added Mrs Collis, 'but I don't quite know where to put it ...',

That evening they laughed and joked and enjoyed each other's company and Mrs Collis asked Molly about her job at the ATA, about her family and about her husband. Mrs Collis told Molly about her life during the First World War and how she had lost her husband and her two sons who died whilst fighting alongside each other at the Battle of the Somme. They had all served at Gallipoli and then on the Western Front. Prior to the First World War, the family had a smallholding outside Hamble-le-Rice village; and spent their days milking, and growing fruit and vegetables which they sold. She told Molly about their adventures growing up in the countryside, and how their biggest thrill was to take their small boat out onto the River Hamble estuary and catch fish.

As Molly sat and listened to Mrs Collis, she thought about how difficult it must have been for her to rebuild her life after the First World War, and how this delightful lady was a stoic example of Britain at its best. Mrs Collis then moved on to the topic of life in Hamble-le-Rice village, not least of which was the local gossip, telling Molly about some of the scandals that had been unfolding whilst the 'menfolk', and a few of the women, were away. Molly thought about how positive Mrs Collis was, despite all that had occurred, and she also wondered how she could contribute to her happiness during the period in which they would be staying together.

The following morning, Mary was waiting outside Molly's digs with two bicycles, one of which she was seated upon as she munched strawberries. Molly was surprised as she came through the door and into the garden; not only at the site before her, but more so because a large strawberry was in mid-air with a trajectory towards Molly's head.

'Catch,' said Mary.

Molly just managed to catch the strawberry before it did any damage; as a strawberry juice-covered uniform would not have been a good start to Molly's first day.

'Oh thanks,' said Molly, 'how wonderful!'

'Early strawberries,' said Mary, 'my landlady grows them in the garden and she amazingly allows me to pick a few here and there. Don't you just love summertime. Even the word conjures up images of freedom.'

'Yes, it does. What's with the two bicycles?'

'Oh yes; that's your other welcome gift,' said Mary proudly, 'my landlady has a spare which she hardly uses.'

'Golly, that's wonderful!' replied a delighted Molly, as she finished the strawberry, threw her bag over her shoulder, and hopped on.

As the two girls cycled towards the base, Molly told Mary of her first evening with Mrs Collis and, although perhaps a little on the eccentric side, how perfectly inviting she had been, and about the wonderful Woolton Pie. Mary laughed at the story of Lancaster, the "Home Guard" hen and its egg-shaped bombs. Mary told Molly about her life growing up on an Oxfordshire farm and how she remembered as a little girl that RAF aircraft would regularly fly overhead due to the farm's proximity to the local airbase.

'I was determined to learn to fly, and nothing was going to stop me,' said Mary. 'Luckily, father was very supportive, and he paid for my first flying lessons'.

As they cycled further and chatted as though they had known each other for years, Molly began to see that, underneath Mary's outwardly kind and gentle nature, there was a core of inner steel and a strong sense of independence, focus and determination. Molly also confirmed what she had hoped for earlier: that here was a person who would be a great source of inspiration and influence.

The bicycles made the short journey to the base even shorter, although the upward slope of the hill made it slightly challenging as there was a good deal of dependency on pedal-power; but the thought crossed Molly's mind that it would be nice to glide home in the evenings after a long day of ferrying aircraft.

The girls left their bikes outside the Ops Room, and as Mary opened the door, the sound of the noisy and hectic room was overwhelming, as about forty pilots were moving about and it seemed that every one of them was talking simultaneously, with the only discernible words being the muffled names of aircraft. There was something unique and exciting about it all and Molly followed Mary inside, who seemed to jump straight in, chatting to Jane Winstone who had emerged from the crowd waving a chit, and thereafter greeting Molly with an enthusiastic hug.

'Jane, you look wonderful,' said Molly.

'I feel good,' whispered Jane, 'this is just what I had hoped for'.

The Ops team was busy listing the day's flights on the huge backboard as phones continually rang, and ferry request messages from Central Ferry Control were handed to various uniformed personnel who were rushing around in what seemed like organised chaos. Most pilots picked up their chits that were laid out on the table, although Alison King was handing out several chits personally and giving more detailed instructions to the pilots. Pilots were looking at their ferry tasks and then chit-chatting about aircraft technicalities, map sourcing, navigation plotting and weather research. Molly waited patiently, watching and listening, and she noticed that the scene playing out before her eyes was a collaboration en-masse; as pilots were simultaneously sharing information with everyone in the room in a 'free for all', imparting their valuable knowledge and experiences in a cohesive and co-dependent effort to help and protect each other. It was quite overwhelming, and she had never experienced anything like it before.

When the pilots started to drift out to the waiting taxi Anson and Fairchild, and the table was clear, Molly walked towards Alison to collect her first ferry assignment as Jane walked by her in the opposite direction waving her chit.

'A Swordfish,' said Jane,' thank God. Something that I've actually flown before. The girls were teasing me all last evening.'

Molly smiled – nervously.

'Hello again Molly,' said Alison, 'a pretty straightforward delivery of a Miles Magister from Yatesbury to Odiham, so not such a long trip to get you started.'

'Oh, thanks,' said Molly.

'The taxi Anson is waiting for you on the apron to get you to Yatesbury.'

Molly collected her kit and left the Ops Room as Mary wished her good luck. Molly was relieved when she heard that her first ferry task would be in a Miles Magister, as she had logged many hours in that aircraft during training and had demonstrated her solo spin recovery and emergency landing drill in the "Maggie", as it was affectionately known.

Molly arrived at the apron to find the waiting taxi which had its engines running. The British twin-engine Avro Anson was the standard taxi aircraft for the ATA and could carry groups of up to eleven ferry pilots to and from aircraft collection points. Four pilots, none of whom Molly knew, embarked before her and she was the last.

The portly pilot Douglas Fairweather was at the controls, a cigarette hanging from the corner of his mouth, and although Molly thought that he looked familiar, she could not recall when she had seen him before. Douglas greeted Molly as she embarked.

'Ah, hello,' he said, 'not seen you before; you must be one of the new girls? Pleased to meet you; I'm Douglas Fairweather, pilot extraordinaire and all-round good egg … and I'll have no comments about my roundness, thank you very much.'

'Hallo, oh, yes, Molly Rose. It's my first day. Nice to meet you. I thought we weren't allowed to smoke?'

'Well if you don't tell, I won't,' said Douglas, taking another puff and blowing smoke all over the cockpit.

Just before the door of the aircraft closed, Margie Fairweather clambered up onto the wing and embarked and Douglas looked her up and down, with a broad smile across his face.

'You look exceptionally gorgeous today if you don't mind me saying so,' he said.

Margie smiled without saying anything and took her seat next to Molly.

'It's lovely to see you again Molly,' she said, 'so good that you're here at last'.

'Thank you,' said Molly, 'good to see you too. By the way, he's a bit fresh, isn't he?'.

'Well I don't mind,' replied Margie, 'he is my husband after all.'

Molly thought back to meeting Margie for the first time at the Ritz Hotel in London, and she suddenly remembered that Douglas was the man waiting for her at the table. She smiled to herself. After meeting Margie on that occasion, Molly had suspected she may be quite difficult to get to know, and she suddenly hoped that she had not just said the wrong thing about Douglas being 'fresh'. But as they sat and chatted throughout the flight, she realised that, in addition to Margie's obvious modesty and devotion to duty, she had a soft core, and those layers of iciness and rigidity which Molly had experienced at their first meeting, were slowly peeling away to reveal a person with a good deal of warmth and humour. Margie told Molly about her flying experiences before the war and how she had been an instructor at the Scottish Flying Club; and how she had over a thousand hours from flying all over Europe. Molly was in awe at having the chance to meet such a legend and one of the "First Eight".

Molly hoped that Margie would mention the famous pioneering aviatrix Amy Johnson, who was also one of the first female pilots at the ATA and a friend of Margie's, and who was tragically killed in a plane crash earlier in the year. She dared not ask though and suspected that when the time was right, Margie may tell her more. Margie did however talk at length about her daughter Ann, a thirteen-year-old child from her first marriage whom she adored, and who was away at boarding school. Molly noticed that Margie's face lit up when she described her daughter, and how it quickly became solemn when she spoke softly of the anguish at being apart. Molly fantasised about her own life and the possibility of having her own children with Bernard, happily living in a world at peace.

The taxi Anson landed at RAF Yatesbury in Wiltshire, which was Molly's pick-up destination and she got up to disembark. As they said goodbye, Molly felt that she had clearly "broken the ice" with Margie and looked forward to their next meeting.

The main purpose of RAF Yatesbury was as a training centre for radar operators, and there were actually very few aircraft to be seen on the wide and flat airfield, which was quieter than Hamble and with only a few people moving about. Molly checked in at the Ops Room and did not quite know what to expect but she sensed that the Ops officer knew that it was her first assignment. She was shown to the apron where three Miles M.14 Magister two-seater low-wing monoplanes sat side-by-side. The Maggie was favoured by the ATA as a trainer unlike the RAF which preferred Tiger Moths.

It was not long before Molly was airborne and flying across the beautiful North Wessex Downs with its pastoral vales and rolling chalk hills, and looking down to see numerous footpaths, trails and bridleways and atmospheric Medieval churches dating back to the 12th century. As the distance between Yatesbury and Odiham was no more than sixty miles by road, Molly's flight time was short, and upon seeing the landing runway on the horizon, she was left feeling that the flight was nowhere near long enough.

After a quick check-in at the RAF Odiham Ops Room, Molly was back in a taxi Anson, and landing at the ATA Ferry Pool No.15 Hamble.

She had successfully completed her first day as an ATA pilot, and the addiction had quickly set in. She wanted more.

Eleven

Winter

The prevailing mood was one of uncertainty, as the world had been plunged further into war. New conscription laws were brought into effect in the United Kingdom to include women and men up to the age of forty-five and the government had introduced rationing of electricity, coal, and gas alongside the numerous other rationed items. The American Air Corps had firmly established bases in the UK and the presence of US officers was increasingly noticeable. Malta had received more fighters for its ongoing defence, as the small island continued to sustain heavy bombing attacks.

Molly had settled into her role at the ATA and she was initially assigned a steady flow of aircraft ferrying tasks commensurate with her training and her Class 1 status; including the Swordfish, Albacore, Tiger Moth and the Miles Magister. Molly quickly adapted to her new life and received each new ferry task with enthusiasm, and all the time looking forward to the next. The thrill of experiencing new aircraft was wonderful and she found it easy to adapt from one to the other, as although the cockpit and instrument panel designs differed, flying a variety of aircraft had much in common.

Following additional training which Margo strongly encouraged and supported, Molly progressed to Class 2 pilot and was thereafter flying the heavier single engine aircraft such as the Hurricane, Defiant and the Fairey Battle. Molly had also flown her fair share of the Fairchild Argus, the ATA's favoured taxi and that was a good opportunity to navigate to and experience additional airfields and ATA Ferry Pools, and also to meet people. Included in the Class 2 rating was the Spitfire, the one aircraft that always seemed to find its way into and thereafter dominate conversations in the Crew Room

70

and bar; but that particular entry had so far not managed to find its way into Molly's log book.

During Molly's night-time cycle trips down the hill and back to Hamble village, it was a regular occurrence to see the distant searchlights throwing rods of white light into the black sky, and to hear the thrum of heavy aircraft in the distance. Flashes of light were usually followed by a series of low "crumps" and the chilling view of fires on the horizon. By contrast, the mornings were glorious and quiet, albeit getting colder as the season had changed all-too-quickly from autumn to winter. One morning as Molly cycled along, and as the sun rose through a thin mist in layers over the airfield, she was transfixed by the figure of a man on a bicycle as he meandered around, stopping occasionally to pick the last of the mushrooms, and placing the haul into a wicker basket.

The extremities of war were complex and were now intertwined with every facet of Molly's life; from the dark horrors of night to the radiance and relative safety of the morning; from the sheer joy of reading Bernard's letters to the cold reality of his vulnerability; and from the camaraderie of Molly's new colleagues to the dangers that each and every one of them faced on a daily basis.

The weeks went on and the weather became colder. Arriving at the base promptly at 07:00 one brisk morning, Molly entered the Crew Room to see who was about. Just as she arrived, Mary, Diana, Lettice, Irene, Jackie and Joy were preparing to leave, and Molly joined the six girls as they walked side-by side towards the Ops Room. They all wore leather flying jackets, underneath which were multiple layers; thick woollen trousers and fur-lined boots, with parachutes slung haphazardly over their shoulders. Golden wings were stitched above their top left pockets and they all carried small overnight bags. It was a vision that only a few years before, no-one could have possibly anticipated, other than perhaps Gerard d'Erlanger and Pauline Gower.

Seven pilots, seven diverse characters, each unique in their own special way. All of them on the mission of their lives and sharing a common goal: to make a difference in the pursuit of peace, each prepared to risk their life to make that dream a reality.

'Did you see the fireworks last night over Southampton?' said Irene, 'it's not as though we're completely safe here with the Spitfire factory being so close. It's certainly going to be one of Jerry's main targets.'

'They were miles away last night,' said Joy, 'and I heard that Portsmouth got it too. But I wouldn't worry about it too much. I mean it's not as if we're actually *in* the factory.'

'One seems to spend more time climbing in and out of the cockpit than actually flying,' said Lettice, trying to change the subject. 'I much prefer the long hauls than several short hops in a day. It keeps one fit I suppose.'

'I mean surely Jerry knows that those Spits are being manufactured there,' continued Irene, and ignoring Lettice. 'But then again, who's to say that *we* are not the targets anyway.'

'I try not to think about it,' said Molly, as she thought about the searchlights, flashes of light and fires on the horizon that she had seen the night before. 'I flew a Harvard from Birmingham to Southampton through storm clouds yesterday and that was certainly no fun; There's enough to think about whilst being up in the air, without worrying what might happen when we're on the ground.'

'I flew from Southampton to Birmingham yesterday,' said Irene, 'and if I'd been in that cloud, I might have met you coming the other way.'

'Well there's a pleasant thought,' said Lettice.

'Golly, you are all being so dreary,' said Mary, 'I like the long-hauls too. Yesterday, I followed the roads and railway lines all the way from start to finish. Pretty straightforward really.'

'You really are the Fog Flyer and definitely the queen of navigation,' said Joy to Mary, 'Where did you get that sixth sense?'

'I was born with it I suppose,' Mary replied.

'Five minutes of standing on my head every morning clears my brain,' said Jackie, 'I'm sure it helps me get from A to B.' Jackie threw down her parachute a few feet in front of her and she performed a perfect cartwheel over it, picking it up as she span over.

'Hmm, quite!' said Diana, 'But I can think of much more civilised pastimes to be enjoying first thing in the morning.'

Lettice could not resist the urge to quip Diana about her newly painted life-vest.

'Diana,' she said, 'you've painted your life-vest yellow! Oh, how very chic darling.'

'Well a *dark green* life vest is hardly any use when one is bobbing about in the English Channel,' retorted Diana, but Lettice was not prepared to let Diana off her hook so easily.

'Quite, and all very haute couture,' she said, 'but it doesn't exactly go with your outfit.'

As the girls walked and talked, Irene seemed to be getting more irritable until at last, she could no longer manage to restrain herself.

'Oh stop it,' she said, in a tone which was angry but also sad.' How can you be so jolly when this bloody war carries on – and with my poor Tommy still rotting in some POW camp while these bloody Jerrys fly over dropping their awful bombs.'

The girls were silent.

'He'll be back Irene', said Joy after a pause, and as she slid her arm though Irene's. 'Our boys will eventually get him back'.

Irene quickly calmed down after the volcanic interlude which usually ended most conversations about her fiancée's predicament. 'I'm going to borrow a Spit,' she said, 'it'll only be a day or two's hop over the Channel to Germany to rescue him. Thirty-six hours max I'd say.'

'Oh, don't talk rot,' said Joy, 'that kind of madness will get you dismissed, or worse - killed. And anyhow, we are not allowed to fly across the Channel, let alone borrow an aircraft for such hair-brained exploits.'

'If I don't do it, who will?' retorted Irene angrily before walking on ahead.

The other girls were quiet for a few moments until Joy broke the silence.

'Do you think that she's serious?'

Just after everyone entered the Ops Room, Margo Gore followed and instantly rapped the table for quiet.

'Good morning all,' she said, 'Now listen closely. Before you sign for your chits we have a huge backlog to clear in the next couple of weeks, so it's all hands to the pump. The weather coming in looks a bit beastly to say the least, so as far as we can, we'll be allocating you to fly in groups; that way the less experienced can tag on behind the, shall we say, veterans. It'll also help the ack-ack gunners to identify you as friendlies.'

'The air-taxis are going to be absolutely maxed-out,' said Alison, 'so I'm afraid if we can't fly you home one way or another it's going to be trains and cars, and those of you going to North Wales and Scotland may have to stay over until transport's sorted.

Everyone quietly groaned.

'I know, I know,' continued Margo, 'it's not ideal, but that's what it was like for us on every trip when we started; we didn't have the luxury of the

Ansons then you know. Isn't that right Margie? So, think yourselves lucky. Now, back to accommodation – it's still almost impossible to get you in to any of the Officers' Messes; the usual rot about not having facilities for women and such. We're working on it, but until this situation is resolved it'll be local hotels; the senior pilot will hold the imprest and take responsibility for the junior ranks. That is all, carry on.'

The noise increased as the girls started to pick up their chits to see their daily allocation and within seconds, the entire room was buzzing again. As none of the pilots knew what was on the daily agenda, there was an air of excitement and anticipation.

'Hey, has anyone flown the Barracuda?' said Mary.

'It's the air ambulance again for me,' said Joy, 'it's so awfully sad to see even one of our boys in distress.'

'Oh, how simply charming,' said Diana, 'Yet another long-distance flight to the frozen north in a Tiger Moth. Do you know how beastly cold it is in that part of the world at this time of year; I'd better get an extra layer on!'

'I've got a Tiger Moth to Scotland too,' said Margie, 'so I guess I'll be flying with you Diana.'

'Me too,' said Jane.

'Yeah, and me,' said Jackie, 'Sod it. I was hoping for an easy one this time. Something with heating would be nice. Or even just a decent canopy.'

'Good,' said Diana to Margie, 'that makes *you* the veteran of our little gaggle. Hell's teeth, I can't imagine *me* being considered as the grown-up - thank goodness.'

'I'll head off to the Met Office to check the forecast for the North Pole and then pick up some dosh,' said Margie, 'Oh, and a map of course, if we actually have any. I had to use the page out of a school atlas last week.'

Lettice quietly scanned her chit and then walked over to Alison.

'Morning dear heart,' she said, 'I have a new Mossie delivery today, first time for me on the new version; could you be a darling and dig out the updated deets for me? Oh, and do you have a more detailed map I can take with me?'

Molly stood quietly amongst the hub-bub and was the last to be allocated her chit by Alison, who smiled as she handed it over. Molly hesitated for a few moments after reading it, and then she walked over to Mary, with a huge smile on her face.

'My first Spitfire,' she said.

Twelve

The taxi Anson stopped at the apron at RAF Cosford, engines still running; and with Douglas Fairweather at the controls, the stub of a cigarette hanging from the corner of his mouth. Several people disembarked, including two men from the Air Ministry, and Molly.

'Go get'em Molly!' said Douglas, as Molly smiled and walked with the other personnel towards the Ops Room.

Molly entered the large Ops Room and, aside from two engineers who were standing and chatting in the corner, the room was fairly quiet and sparse. Two Ops Officers were seated at desks and with their heads down, quiet and fully focussed. Molly approached the Ops Officer seated closest to her and handed him her chit, which he took without looking up and then carefully checked his clipboard. The two engineers in the corner stopped talking and all eyes were focussed on Molly.

'Spitfire V8 No BL634 just out of the factory and going to RAF Cranfield in Bedfordshire,' said the Ops Officer.

'Okey-Dokey,' said Molly, at which point the Ops Officer, surprised at hearing a female voice, looked up.

'Oh. Hello. Well she's all ready for you; the weather report's on the board, and, er, the locker room's over there if you need it. Good luck. I'm afraid we'll need to post a guard if you need to use the loo - we've only got a men's room.'

'Thank you,' said Molly as she smiled and headed for the door, as the two engineers in the corner, clearly smitten at the pretty young female pilot, both smiled.

'Ma'am,' said one of the officers as Molly walked out.

The weather was gloomy and quite cold. Molly wrapped her scarf twice around her neck and pulled the collar of her flying jacket up to protect her from the cold wind which was blowing across the airfield. She walked quickly towards the apron past a small group of male ground crew and engineers who were gathered at the entrance of one of the close-by hangars. Molly lifted her chin, trying to ignore them, but at the same time wondering if their attention was due to her being a woman, or a woman in a pilot's uniform.

Molly had never flown a Spitfire, despite her longing to experience this iconic aircraft. She had undergone training in many similar types of aircraft; particularly the Master, the British trainer most similar to a Spitfire in characteristics. Even though it was quite 'normal' for ATA pilots to be given the task of ferrying an aircraft that they had not previously flown, assignment of a Spitfire without training was not unique, but it was rare. Molly heard Mary's voice in the back of her head … 'Don't worry, you'll be surprised at how easy they are to handle.'

Molly reached the apron where a number of aircraft were being prepared for flight. She checked the tail numbers of the Spitfires, conscious of the eyes of the predominantly male factory workers staring in her direction.

Spitfire No BL634 was at the end of the line and Molly stood for a few moments and looked at it. Underneath the dull colours of the camouflage, there was something quite beautiful and graceful about this aircraft. Its lines were perfect, and the airframe was elegantly shaped, making it unique amongst the other aircraft that Molly had previously flown.

A young military engineer from the group walked over to Molly, interrupting her thoughts on the Spitfire. Molly acknowledged him without saying anything and moved on to get the essential ground checks completed, referring to the Blue Book for each step. She took her time, diligently working through each step as the engineer jumped from one foot to the other trying to keep warm as he watched her closely.

'Have you ever flown a Spitfire before ma'am?'

'No, actually this is my first,' said Molly with a smile, 'but I've been told that the Spitfire was built for female pilots, so I'm sure that I'll be absolutely fine.'

'I'm not too sure about that ma'am,' said the engineer, returning the smile.

'Well, I've been looking forward to this day for as long as I can remember, so it jolly well will be fine!'

'In that case ma'am, I'm sure it will be.'

Molly tucked her maps into her boot, and then hopped up onto the wing and dropped her parachute on the seat. The engineer raised his eyebrows to his watching pals as Molly climbed into the cockpit; and he then climbed up behind her to help as she strapped in.

Molly made herself comfortable and took a quick look at the Ferry Pilot Notes, touching the various dials, controls, knobs and switches to make sure that the instrument panel was the same. She took a sigh of relief before noticing the red metal emergency crowbar attached to the door.

'Hopefully I won't need that,' she said.

The young engineer returned Molly's smile and then hopped down and backed away from the aircraft without taking his eyes off Molly.

'Good luck ma'am.'

Molly gently placed the palm of her hand on the instrument panel of the Spitfire. It rested there for a few seconds as she smiled and took a deep breath. 'Right,' she said, 'let's see if I can remember this. Oh golly. Fuel; brakes; idle cut-off in the off position; pre-oiler switched on; fuel pump primed; prop set to fine pitch; throttle set; booster coil uncovered; and starter button.'

The engineer moved the trolley battery away and stood by to remove the chocks as Molly took a look around the aircraft.

'Clear – prop', she shouted, as she pressed the booster coil and start button. Instantly the propeller began to turn; the engine caught and the prop span to a blur as the crescendo of noise from the twelve-cylinder Merlin engine made the whole aircraft, and Molly herself, vibrate. It felt as though she was sitting on top of an erupting volcano. She pulled the overhead canopy to the partially locked position so that she could stick her head out while taxiing.

Molly felt an overwhelming sensation of elation that took her breath away; a pure and utter joy to be sitting in the Spitfire, knowing she was about to take her up. This was surely one of the most spectacular moments of her life, she thought, a huge smile spreading across her face.

'OK, let's do this Molly,' she said to herself as she waved the 'chocks away' signal, released the brakes and very slowly taxied out to the take-off point on the runway, weaving from left to right to see where she was going, as the Spitfire's elevated nose was blocking her vision. She then turned the aircraft on to the take-off strip to see the hangars in the distance, and the wind had dropped as the wind-sock showed a light breeze on to the aircraft nose. At the take-off point Molly made the final checks and increased the revs. Hers was the only aircraft to be seen, standing majestically alone, prepped and ready to be unleashed into the sky.

'Right, here we go. Open throttle ... slowly ...'

The power of the Merlin engine sped her down the runway and into the air.

'Oh ... my ... God.'

The Spitfire soared higher into the air quickly reaching one-hundred-and-fifty miles per hour and Molly was in complete control as she banked the aircraft hard right to fly directly across the hangars. It was exhilarating. As she looked down at the airbase, for a brief second, she thought that she could see the young ground crew mechanic who had stood to attention and was saluting her as he watched the Spitfire disappear into the distance.

Molly flew the Spitfire gracefully between the sun-lit cloud formations over beautiful countryside; some of which was covered in a blanket of frost. The aircraft weaved gently between the clouds, and the sound of its engine sent a small herd of cows running as a group of farmers looked up and waved as she flew overhead. Molly was having a perfect flight and was amazed at how responsive the Spitfire was to even the slightest touch of the controls and she realised why it was jokingly called a female's aircraft. She checked her position several times against the map on her lap, whilst looking down at bomb-damaged towns and railway stations and eventually saw the RAF Cranfield airfield fast approaching.

'Golly, I'm here already. That's a bit quicker than the Moth. And not a bad bit of navigating; even if I do say so myself.'

Molly's Spitfire touched down smoothly on the grass at RAF Cranfield which, unlike some of the other airfields she had flown into, was perfectly flat. The ground crew engineer marshalled her to an allotted space near the control tower where the aircraft rolled to a secure halt, and Molly's humbleness waivered for a moment as she wondered how many people from the tower were watching her. The Merlin engine stopped and the sharp pings from the cooling cylinders mingled with a gentle breeze were all that could be heard. Molly sat quite still, gaining her breath and listening to the pinging of the engine.

'Thank you,' said Molly, as she put her hand on the instrument panel again.

Molly composed herself, opened the canopy and hopped out onto the wing and down. Several RAF officers had emerged from the building, curious to take a look at the ATA 'female' pilot and then they turned away, continuing to chat amongst themselves without acknowledging her. As Molly gathered her kit and headed over to Ops to check the aircraft in, an Anson taxied in with Douglas Fairweather at the controls.

Molly walked through the Ops Room door and saw instantly that the room was busy, with several officers standing around and chatting. As she entered, she heard the voice of Flt Lt McAlpine; one of the senior officers.

'Who the devil gave these upstart women permission to fly our ... '

He stopped abruptly when he saw Molly and the whole room was suddenly quiet. Molly walked towards him; her face showing not a trace of emotion, although conscious of everyone staring at her.

'Sign here,' he said, abruptly.

Molly signed with a smile, turned around and slowly walked away. It had been a perfect day so far; the fulfilment of one of her greatest dreams. She was damned if anyone was going to spoil it, she thought to herself. Before leaving the Ops Room, she briefly noticed that one of the other officers was smiling at her.

'A VERY good morning to you again after all this time,' he said, 'I see that Austin Reed did you proud with your uniform.'

'Oh, yes, yes, indeed.' said Molly, recognising him from their brief encounter at the entrance to the tailors. 'And I even got my trousers. Nice to see you again, but I must dash as my transport's here. Toodle pip.'

Molly looked fixedly in the direction of Flt Lt McAlpine. 'I *so* look forward to seeing you all again,' and then she left.

The ATA taxi Anson had turned around to face the airfield, its engines running and with Douglas seated at the controls, his ubiquitous cigarette in his lips. Molly jogged out onto the apron and hopped in.

'Well if it isn't Miss Molly Rose. How was your day Molly?'

'Extraordinary, absolutely extraordinary,' she said as she sat down, strapped in, and the Anson taxied out.

Thirteen

The light was grey and flat and there were flurries of snow swirling in the air, although not cold enough for it to settle for too long. The penetrating wet could turn to ice at any moment which made flying conditions precarious and the short winter days narrowed the window to get from A to B.

Diana, Margie, Jackie and Jane were dressed in multiple layers as they disembarked the taxi Anson and hurried out to the apron at Finningley Airfield. Waiting for them was a line of Tiger Moths. Margie had carefully checked the weather report before leaving the Ferry Pool at Hamble and she had set a timetable for the ferry flight before identifying and marking on her map the emergency landing points in the event that conditions changed.

A thin layer of frost sat atop the camouflage of each aircraft, and Margie's thoughts drifted for a moment to cosy fires and being at home with her daughter. The biting cold consigned such luxuries to a distant blur, and she turned her attention to the immediate task at hand.

'So, ladies,' said Margie, 'as briefed, stay in a loose formation; keep an eye on your wing-man and I'll do the navigating, and if there are any changes in the weather, just follow my lead. And for God's sake please don't hit each other.'

Assisted by ground crew, the girls threw their small overnight bags and parachutes into their cockpits and awkwardly clambered in, their bulky attire making it difficult to wriggle in. Once strapped in place, they started their checks as the ground crew, dressed in woolly hats and thick jackets, blew on their hands and jumped from one foot to the other to keep warm. The four young men were looking at each other and smiling, knowing that they were all looking forward to telling their pals about the 'four girl gaggle' later that evening.

Within a few moments, and despite the cold, the propellers were turning, and the aircraft taxied out to the end of the runway where they sat in a two-by-two formation, ready for the long journey to Scotland. Margie and Diana were the first to take off, and Jackie and Jane quickly followed, taking a few moments to adjust their speed and altitude before the four Tiger Months were as coordinated as a small flock of undulating seagulls. Jane was in the rear-most aircraft in a staggered line, and each aircraft was separated by about one-hundred feet.

Margie quickly assumed the lead through wisps of cloud which occasionally obscured the aircraft behind her as she oscillated in altitude. She concentrated hard, trying to keep her place leading the formation and not to lose sight of the three pilots behind her, occasionally becoming tense as they temporarily disappeared into the cloud.

Here they were, not simply pilots, but three friends whom Margie cherished, and who were for the short term, her full responsibility. She felt every pang of guardianship, duty and obligation, but also an overwhelming apprehension of potential loss. Such is the burden of leadership she thought.

Meanwhile, Jane was at the rear of the gaggle; her sole aim not to lose the aircraft in front as she stared ahead, continually sniffing and wiping drips from the end of her nose. She felt as if the flight was going on forever, the cloud becoming thicker and the snow swirling around her, sometimes completely obliterating her field of vision. Then Jane lost sight of the first two aircraft in front of her. She maintained composure and focussed on the faint silhouette of the third, following carefully and hoping that the flight would soon be over. Jane began to feel an odd sensation, as if her mind was becoming numb and her thoughts slowing down. They flew further north and as they progressed, Jane found it increasingly difficult to focus. Suddenly, a gap in the cloud revealed the lead aircraft and much to Jane's relief, she saw Margie signal that they were landing. A thin film of frost coated both the windscreen and Jane's flying helmet and she noticed that her fuel gauge showed almost empty. She tapped it several times as she shivered uncontrollably, trying hard to concentrate on landing.

After a long and laborious flight, the gaggle crossed the mouth of the River Esk and circuited the airfield at RAF Annan in Scotland, as the runway emerged from the snowy landscape, becoming clearly discernible as they peeled off one by one to touch down.

They taxied in and parked line abreast; the props cutting out one after another as the ground crew scurried out from the warmth of their hut to chock the aircraft. Margie, Diana and Jackie struggled slowly out of their cockpits, and clambered to the ground, stamping their feet and blowing on their hands. Jane however remained strapped in and motionless. Diana, her face ashen white, with grey-blue lips, was beating her arms around herself in an effort to warm up as she walked over to Jane's aircraft. She looked at Jane and immediately saw that her lips were blue, her breathing was fast, and she was shivering uncontrollably.

'Are you all-right in there old thing?' said Diana.

'I, I think so,' said Jane, 'I think I m..m..might have frostbite on my nose and I c..c..can't feel my feet or hands, but a..a..apart from that I'm f..f..fine. I don't suppose some-one c..c.could undo my straps; I'm afraid my h..h..hands don't seem to work and I'm s..s..stuck.'

'Oh dear, a bit the same here I'm afraid,' said Diana, quickly realising the seriousness of the situation but remaining calm, 'but hang on, we'll have you out of there in a jiffy.'

Diana turned quickly to Margie and Jackie, and the look on her face told them instantly that something was very wrong.

'Quick - help me get her out,' said Diana, as she carefully climbed up to release Jane and helped her out of the cockpit, 'I think she may be on the verge of hypothermia.'

Jane followed Diana stiffly out of the aircraft and as she stepped down, the other girls thought that she looked frozen to the bone. Diana and Margie glanced at each other, saying nothing but both clearly concerned. They each put an arm around Jane to support her and walked her towards the line hut.

'Right, let's get her into that line hut fast,' whispered Diana to Margie, 'and find some warm blankets and something hot and sweet to drink. I don't like this at all.'

'W..w..what are we doing here?, mumbled Jane drearily, moments before her legs buckled and she collapsed. Jackie sprang forward to help Diana and Margie carry the weight of their unconscious friend.

Fourteen

London's Savoy Hotel in The Strand is adjacent to the River Thames. It was the first luxury hotel in Britain to introduce electric lights throughout its building, together with electric lifts, and bathrooms with constant hot and cold running water in its lavishly furnished rooms. The hotel had become a meeting place for war leaders, including Churchill and Mountbatten.

On a cold night in October, a number of high-ranking RAF officers, government ministers and Air Ministry civil servants departed the hotel after a formal dinner; some of whom chatted in the lobby while their cars were summoned. Sandbags were stacked around the famous entrance, and black-out wardens shouted warnings as the doors were opened allowing the bright lights from the foyer to cast elongated and distorted human shadows across the courtyard.

Gerard d'Erlanger and Pauline Gower stood amongst those in the lobby.

'Please tell me that you haven't spent yet another entire evening lobbying for equal pay for our female pilots,' said d'Erlanger, 'I want it as much as you do, but there are other things going on Pauline.'

'Well as a matter of fact I have,' said Pauline, 'It worked getting us to fly anything other than Moths didn't it? And I'll keep lobbying until we get it. It's about ability, not whether one is a man or a woman; it's the most competent person for the job. And by the way', she added tersely, 'I want something done about the Commanding Officer at Whitchurch who still refuses to allow my girls onto his base.'

'That's the least of our worries at the moment,' said d'Erlanger.

'Look Gerard, you know as well as I do that most of our girls have more hours and experience than those poor boys with less than forty hours who are sent to Spit squadrons. I'm not saying that we should be operational, but our girls are more than capable of flying anything the RAF can.'

'I quite agree. Talking of which, what do you know about Operation Calendar?'

'Officially, not a huge amount,' said Pauline, 'but a couple of father's cronies in the cabinet were over for dinner the other night; and I did rather interrogate them – poor things. It seems that Churchill has been on the blower to President Roosevelt to discuss the reinforcement of Malta. Apparently, he's asked for loan of the Aircraft Carrier - *USS Wasp*, I think - to ferry Spitfires down there. Extraordinary.'

'Quite,' said d'Erlanger, 'Malta is getting the most horrendous hammering, so Operation Calendar is quite urgent. The Hurricanes haven't got the range or power to keep the Luftwaffe at bay; so Spitfires are being sent out. But getting them to Malta will be the fun bit. It's obviously too far to fly, so they're going by sea. The RAF are going to fly them off the carrier.'

'Really?' said Pauline, 'they're planning to fly them off? But Spitfires don't operate off carriers, surely?'

'Well, not so far they haven't,' said d'Erlanger, 'but how things change when needs must, eh? So, when, *if*, this all comes off, we'll be asked to get the Spitfires to the embarkation port for loading; that means that we'll need as many pilots as possible to be Spit qualified.'

'Righty-o. Well, that's great news; I know for a fact that the girls will be up for this task as well as the chaps.'

Gower and d'Erlanger put on their heavy winter coats, picked up their belongings and moved through the doors to the steps of the hotel. Snow was in the air and Gower and d'Erlanger said goodbye to each other as their taxis waited with open doors. As d'Erlanger was about to hop into the taxi, he turned to Pauline.

'By the way Pauline,' he said, 'if Jerry gets wind of this, I'm sure that you can imagine the consequences.'

'Well let's make sure that doesn't happen.'

The taxi driver was a young man in his early forties, and he was wrapped up for winter, with a scarf doubled around his neck and breathing condensation.

'Bloody hell it's cold,' said d'Erlanger, 'Whitehall please. Would you mind driving along the river?'

'Yes sir,' replied the taxi driver, 'it's probably much safer.'

'I don't think anywhere is safe at the moment,' said d'Erlanger.

'You're right about that Sir. I hope that you had a nice evening at The Savoy Sir. I've not been in of course, but it's certainly my favourite hotel entrance in London. Well, before the sandbags that is.'

'Hmm, quite. My evening was interesting, to say the least.'

'I saw you with a number of RAF chaps on the steps; Are you in the Air Force Sir?'

'No, the ATA actually,' said d'Erlanger, 'The Air Transport Auxiliary.'

'Ah, I have a pilot's license myself Sir; and forty-nine hours in Hawks and Falcons. Before the war I learnt to fly at the Civil Air Guard, and was then an instructor for Marshalls in Cambridgeshire. I was up in the air at every opportunity.'

'Good heavens man! Then why aren't you flying now?' exclaimed d'Erlanger.

'After I was sent to South Cerney for advanced flying training, I, well, I had a medical problem; kidney stones. So I was refused a position as a pilot in the RAF. But it turned out to be nothing serious, sir, and I'm fine now.'

'That's rather bad luck. And taxi driving was your only option?'

'I was actually planning to join the ATA Sir.'

'Marvellous,' said d'Erlanger as the taxi pulled up at Horse Guards Avenue, 'What's your name?'

'Lead, Sir. Dennis Lead.'

As d'Erlanger hopped out of the taxi, he smiled and handed the taxi driver his card.

'Well, Mr. Lead - consider yourself joined.'

D'Erlanger walked over to the entrance of a terraced Edwardian building, outside which two guards were standing, and after showing his security papers, quickly walked inside. Although d'Erlanger and Pauline Gower were as close as two colleagues could be, she was unaware of the message that d'Erlanger had received by hand at the end of dinner, asking him to attend a late-night "Highly Confidential" meeting with one of Churchill's senior war strategy advisors.

D'Erlanger had no idea what the meeting was all about and of the task which was about to be set before him.

Fifteen

During the Second World War, black paint was applied to the seven-acre roof glazing of the vast Carlisle Citadel Railway Station as a precautionary measure against enemy air raids. It was not unknown for the occasional piece of glass to come crashing down onto a platform as a result of a nearby bomb blast or from the general rot due to neglect of the age-old building.

At 21:00 on a cold night in October, one such incident occurred and as a result, one of the two last trains to London was cancelled, culminating in a severely overcrowded night train to Southampton. The grubby train was cramped with military personnel, many in Scottish regimental attire, and tired-looking, harassed civilians as it chuffed out from the bleak Cumbria station, steam billowing against the snow-covered tracks.

The train consisted of six carriages, all of which were full, and with a corridor down one side, with each individual small compartment having its own glass-panelled sliding door. Diana, Margie, Jackie and Jane were tired as they struggled down the narrow corridor, still in their flying jackets, trousers and boots, and carrying their parachutes. They stepped over baggage, most of which was in piles of military canvas bags, as soldiers, sailors and airmen stood aside to let them pass.

'Just our luck that there are no sleeper berths left,' said Margie angrily.

'A railway system in wartime is the epitome of inefficiency and discomfort, *and* with no First Class,' said Diana, 'how dreary.'

'First class!' exclaimed Jackie, 'There's no bloody seats, let alone sleeper berths or first class. There's certainly no room for meditating in here.'

'The luggage racks look quite comfy though,' said Margie, 'certainly more room up there than in the Moth cockpit; positively luxurious!'

'As long as we can find a carriage with a bit of heating, I'll be very happy,' said Jane, who was still looking quite unwell after the exploits of the previous twenty-four hours. 'I thought I'd never feel my feet and hands again.'

'We were worried about you old thing,' said Diana, 'you were rather blue.'

A uniformed guard pressed himself against the side of the corridor to let them pass.

'I'm afraid we're a bit packed tonight ladies,' said the guard, 'what with falling glass and cancelled trains n'all, we've also lost a couple of carriages. It'll be a longer journey than usual too I'm afraid, as we have to get around Crewe which took a bit of a battering last week. There's a bit of space two carriages up.'

The girls smiled their thanks and continued through the carriages until they found one with a couple of spare seats amongst civilian-clad men and two uniformed RAF pilots. Two stern-looking matronly ladies, dressed in hats, high collars and long skirts, approached down the corridor from the opposite direction. On seeing the girls, they sped up and pushed quickly into the carriage, grabbing the two empty seats and smiling demurely at the male RAF officers, one of whom spotted the girls looking exasperated at having missed the two seats. The civilian men remained stoically behind their newspapers or looked fixedly out of the frost covered window.

As the two matrons, like two large pigeons in a small nest, wedged themselves between the newspaper-reading men, one of the men took a cigarette from a silver case, and was about to light it. The elder of the two matrons glared at him angrily, fixing him with a steady gaze like that of a predator, about to despatch its prey ruthlessly and efficiently. The man froze immediately, registered the potential danger of the situation and then quickly replaced the cigarette in its case before lowering his head behind his newspaper. The elderly matron pursed her lips and huffed in satisfaction, and then turned conspiratorially to her friend.

'Did you see those girls in the corridor?' she asked in a feigned whisper which was actually loud enough for everyone in the carriage to hear. 'If only they knew what an absolute sight they look in trousers, I'm sure they wouldn't wear them. And their hair ... well! Why on earth do girls today want to look like men?'

'Oh, leave them be Hilda,' said the other matron, 'I think they look nice.'

Hilda was struck dumb by this unexpected reaction from her friend, her mouth dropping open slightly before recovering her composure, raising her eyebrows and suddenly busying herself by looking for something in her handbag.

One of the two RAF officers grinned at Diana, who rolled her eyes. Diana and Margie stood apart, theatrically looking each other up and down, and they burst out laughing.

'Oh, how *frightful!*', said Margie, theatrically.

Jane was oblivious to the goings-on as she leaned against the door staring vacantly at the floor, the tiredness and exhaustion of the last twenty-four hours having finally caught up with her. Her complexion was pale and she had dark circles under her eyes. This was noticed by the elder of the two RAF officers and he stood up, nudging his colleague to do likewise, before offering their seats.

Flt Lt Rory McTavish was twenty-eight years old and from St. Andrews on the east coast of Fife in Scotland. Two years earlier, he had decided to serve his country as a fighter pilot and rather than waiting to be called up as a conscript, he took control of his own destiny, volunteered and enrolled.

'Only two seats I'm afraid,' said McTavish in a broad Scottish accent.

Jane and Jackie dumped their parachutes in the corridor and gratefully squeezed past McTavish and his colleague in an awkward dance, squashing newspapers to a chorus of "tuts", and "watch out" until they had changed places, and the two officers stood in the corridor with Diana and Margie. Jane and Jackie settled into their seats. Margie eyed the empty luggage rack, working out how she could clamber up there. Diana had a "surely not" look upon her face but knowing her friend well, she knew exactly what was coming next. Margie struggled to move two large and heavy bags from one luggage rack to the other, leaving the first one empty as people in the carriage watched, wondering what she was doing.

'Righty-ho,' said Margie, 'Sorry, I'm not standing in the corridor all night after the day I've had, especially when there's a perfectly good luggage rack with my name on it.'

Margie looked at Jackie who was thrilled that the evening's entertainment was about to begin and trying hard not to laugh out loud.

'Be a sport darling and give me a leg up will you,' said Margie, as she held up her booted right foot.

The matrons looked on aghast; as the men peered over their newspapers and harrumphed as Jackie got up from her seat and grabbed Margie's boot, laughing as she hoisted her unceremoniously into the luggage rack, where she lay out full stretch, hands behind her head, and looking very contented.

The expressions on the faces of the people in the carriage ranged from mild shock and bewilderment to polite smiles, and the elder of the two matrons sat with her mouth open, unable to say anything.

In the corridor, which had since quietened down as the majority of those on the train had found seats or quiet corners, Flt Lt McTavish, his young colleague and Diana arranged the parachutes on the floor as make-shift seats, and settled themselves down as best they could in the limited space. Two soldiers stepped over them, apologising, until the trio were eventually alone in the corridor.

'Hullo; Flight Lieutenant Rory McTavish at your service. And this reprobate is Flying Officer Callum MacDonald. Take no notice of him staring at you, I don't think he's ever been this close to a woman!'

'How wonderfully thoughtful,' said Diana, 'thank you so much, I think you've saved the girls' lives. We've had a hell of a day; we came up from Yorkshire in Tiger Moths and the weather was bloody awful. We - well particularly Jane over there - nearly froze to death. We would have stayed over, but we've got another tasking tomorrow so we're on the way back to Hampshire.'

The young lad Callum MacDonald reached into the inside pocket of his uniform jacket and pulled out a silver hip flask. 'Here,' he said, 'have a wee tot o' this; purely medicinal. Single malt. That'll sort you out. Hey, if you think this weather's awful, you should try it in the winter!! Sorry, that was ma wee joke!'

'I don't envy you flying Tiger Moths all that way,' said McTavish, 'I found it bad enough doing wee trips during training. I've never been that fond o' the Moth, and for the reasons that your friend over there experienced yesterday.'

'Where are you chaps off to?' said Diana.

'We've just been posted on ti 601 Squadron near Glasgow,' said Mactavish, 'they're re-equipping wi Spitfires so we're off doon South for a spot o' training before the Squadron gets its new tasking, wherever that might be.'

Callum MacDonald took another 'tot', before joining in the conversation,

'Aye, we're doin some drills wi the Navy for some obscure reason, something that's never been done before is what I heard, and then we're goin where the weather's a hell of a lot hotter than here, I can tell ye! Eh Rory?'

McTavish nudged his colleague and scowled. 'Aye well,' he said, 'I don't know aboot that'.

Diana grinned distractedly as she analysed the words that she had heard from the young officer, wondering what it was that was such a secret. As the train gathered momentum, reaching a steady speed as it passed into open countryside, the sporadic rattling gradually transitioned into a soothing rhythmic beat and Diana closed her eyes and fell asleep.

Sixteen

Christmas

When the war broke out in September 1939, it was not uncommon in Britain to hear the remark, "It will all be over by Christmas!" However, the months passed, and another Christmas came and went with peace still a distant prospect. Earlier in the month, Japan had attacked Pearl Harbour and declared war on the United Kingdom and the United States. Due to the necessities of enhanced national productivity, many traditional holidays were cancelled but Christmas celebrations, albeit limited, had so-far survived.

The Ferry Pool at Hamble had arranged for a Christmas Dinner to be served in the canteen throughout the day, but it was business as usual, with aircraft to be delivered to every corner of the country. The wheels of the ATA did not slow down for anything. A few of the girls had made arrangements to leave the base, visiting their families and friends, and the Christmas spirit had firmly taken hold in the week prior with a few later than usual evenings in the crew bar.

Molly managed to secure a few days of leave to visit the family during the Christmas period, which she was naturally thrilled about, even though there were many changes to the family festive rituals. As with most families, absence marked the traditional family gathering, and it was difficult for Molly to spend Christmas away from Bernard who was still in North Africa and unable to take leave.

Many foods and drinks were in short supply and Arthur had to use much of his influence, sourcing some of the essentials, including a turkey, chocolates, cigarettes, cigars, gin and sherry. Even fruit was an extravagance. It was difficult for the entire family to gather at Whitehill as had been the tradition for many years.

The gifts between Molly and her sisters were mostly home-made, as luxuries were quite hard to come by. Even using paper to wrap presents was forbidden, which naturally made secrecy difficult. Molly did however manage to buy a few bars of soap for her sisters, as that had recently been added to the list of rationed items.

Christmas trees were rare. Apart from a lack of manpower to fell the trees, there was also a shortage of space to ship them by rail. As a solution to this, for the past few years Arthur had arranged for some Norwegian Spruce trees to be planted in the arboretum near the house and he took great pride in cultivating them himself. The tree became the centrepoint of the festivities and the family made a huge effort with the decorations, dressing the tree together as had been family tradition for many years, using decorations that the girls had rescued from the dusty attic. A small photo of Molly's late father, framed as a Christmas tree decoration, was added to the glittering framed images of Molly's late mother and Molly's older brother who had also died, and who had both adorned the tree for the past several years.

Despite the hardships of the current situation it was the simple things that had a huge impact on Molly's Christmas: the scent of pine from the tree, the aroma of mince pies baking, the sight of her sisters carefully making paper chains while they sat in front of the fire. It was these small but cherished pleasures that reinforced what she already knew; that it was all about freedom, and all about family.

Aside from the family's usual evening festivities, the most anticipated and definitely the most enjoyed, especially by Arthur, was when Molly picked up her log book and proceeded to tell the stories surrounding each new ferry task; describing the various aircraft she had flown, commensurate with the upgrades to her pilot class. To her captivated audience, Molly described trips from one end of the country to the other in light twin engine aircraft such as Ansons and Airspeed Oxfords. She conveyed the thrill of flying heavy twin engine aircraft such as the Blenheim and Beaufighter for the first time. And of course, Molly spoke about flying the Spitfire; her elation evident as she described just why it was so special. Molly's skills had grown immensely and her confidence had blossomed.

Arthur would absorb all the information like a sponge and it particularly helped his business. The company's pilot training school had devised a revolutionary procedure for the rapid training of pilots and their flying instructors, all of which Arthur took great pleasure in overseeing. Molly's experiences and feedback could assist them to refine their training and Arthur was thrilled that his sister was doing something that she so clearly loved.

Molly was unable to stay until New Year's Eve and she returned to Hamble on Boxing Day. The first few months of the New Year were hardly a time for celebration as people waited desperately for a glimmer of hope. The war was not going well for the Allies and Britain was in a vulnerable position. The Ministry of Information, usually distributing positive propaganda, was now waging its own battle. Even though the Government decided not to suppress editorial freedom but chose instead to control the information available to the media, they could not prevent endless grim news from filtering through via newspapers and Pathé newsreels. Stories and photographs of the "glamorous" girls of the ATA became even more sought after.

Transatlantic shipping was being successfully raided by German U-Boats, sinking millions of tons of merchant shipping and threatening Britain's supply of food and arms, resulting in a critical situation which also took its toll on morale. Mrs Collis was as always doing her part in the village and was busy making jams and chutneys which she sold, whilst encouraging her neighbours to embrace the "Dig for Victory" campaign.

Malta continued to sustain heavy bombing attacks after Hitler ordered it to be 'neutralised' in preparation for a German invasion. It was estimated that the small island was hit with twice as many bombs as London. In North Africa, the desert campaign was at a stalemate and Rommel's Africa Corps were pushing hard against the Allies. This was an ever-increasing burden on Molly, and the situation troubled her more and more when she considered the consequences of Britain losing control of the strategically situated island.

Churchill demanded and secured a formal vote of confidence in the House of Commons as he was faced with mounting criticism due to Britain's increasingly dire situation and military defeats. The nation was in desperate need of hope, and as a result, production everywhere was increased, ultimately resulting in even more ferrying work.

The ATA had grown considerably and there were now fourteen Ferry Pools, with plans being considered for even more. Since the outset, and due to Gerard d'Erlanger's connections, the financial control of the organisation had been the responsibility of BOAC. However, as a result of expansion this had now become a challenge and in addition to this, the ferrying responsibilities had become too complex for the Air Ministry. In an effort to streamline the administration, it was gradually turned over to the Ministry of Aircraft Production; a civilian organisation created in 1940 by Winston Churchill to maximise production and distribution of aircraft needed for the war effort.

It was a difficult time for Molly as this multitude of forces tested her resilience and her will to stay positive: leaving the family at Christmas, missing and worrying about Bernard, Britain's worsening position in what seemed to be a never-ending war, and the ongoing dire winter weather which surrounded each ferry flight with gloom, uncertainty and danger.

Molly found solace with her friends during the daytime, and also in the escapism of walking into the cottage of Mrs Collis each evening. She had no idea that the challenges she would face in the near future would test her resilience to its very limit.

Seventeen

Spring

On the first clear and warm day of spring, Molly wasted no time in dressing in her tennis whites and as she headed for the tennis courts, Mary ran up behind her.

'Hallo old thing,' said Molly, turning around 'where have you been?'

'I went to the Signals Office,' said Mary, 'as I need to know where the barrage balloons are. They keep popping up all over the place, and especially if there's an air-raid warning. I narrowly missed so many yesterday and they're damned dangerous. You need to keep a check on them Molly.'

'That's the point though isn't it dear heart? For Jerry I mean, not us. Sorry, joking. Yes, it's quite the obstacle course up there.' Molly noticed that Mary was looking quite concerned. 'Are you OK?', she said.

'Not quite,' said Mary, 'still in mild shock from yesterday, I think. I was delivering a damaged Mustang to the MU for repair; and I got caught in cloud and inadvertently flew across the coastline and was bloody-well fired at by our own anti-aircraft guns.'

'Oh, that's awful and it sounds like a close call. I knew there was something wrong, but I'm so glad that you're OK.'

'Thank you Molly. I saw puffs of smoke and I realised that they were firing at *me*! They must have thought that I was the enemy. It was quite the most frightening thing. Those home-guard types really ought to get up to speed with their aircraft recognition or it'll all end in tears.'

'That's one reason we're flying in gaggles so often,' said Molly, 'it makes us more recognizable to the gunners as friendlies. Not always possible of course. One more hazard on the already long list.'

They reached the tennis court, threw down their bags and took their racquets onto the court. They limbered up as they laughed at each other's warming-up techniques, and then practiced a few shots before starting a game. Molly served an ace.

'Oh, great,' said Mary, 'is this going to be another thrashing?'

'Fifteen love,' said Molly as she served again, 'I saw some of the new American pilots earlier.'

'Me too,' said Mary, who was amazed at her half-decent return of the serve. 'Their boss is Jackie Cochran; and apparently, she's an American millionairess with her own cosmetics business. Her husband is a big Hollywood hot-shot producer and rich beyond belief.'

'Good shot,' said Molly, 'why on earth is she here?'

'I think that she's looking to see how we do things over here as they are starting the same service in America. But why she gave up Hollywood to be a pilot in this god-forsaken war is beyond me.'

'What does she look like?' said Molly, 'sorry that was out; my point. Thirty-all.'

'You'll spot her easily. She'll be in a fur coat and dripping in diamonds. Joking aside, she is the best female pilot in the USA, and she has recruited twenty-five American girls for the ATA. Some of those girls have over a thousand hours.'

'Really,' said Molly, '... and it's forty-thirty.'

'Yes, the delightful Miss Cochran is quite the American 'Queen Bee' with connections to Churchill and Eleanor Roosevelt. Apparently, she is supremely confident and VERY demanding.'

'Quite. But can she fly?' said Molly, 'by the way, I think that's game to me.'

The tannoy at the side of the tennis court squawked into life, and Molly and Mary stood rigid on the court:

"2nd Officer Rose report to Ops immediately... I say again, 2nd Officer Rose report to Ops immediately".

'Oh dammit,' said Molly, 'I know I'm duty bod, but I was hoping it would be quiet today. No rest for the wicked I suppose. I'd better hot-foot it over there.'

Molly quickly dropped her racquet, grabbed her track-suit top and bag, and ran.

'Please look after my racquet,' shouted Molly as she ran. 'It cost me a quid.'

After a good three minutes at a fast pace, Molly ran into the Ops Room, out of breath.

'Glad you could make it Molly,' said Alison, 'hopefully we're not keeping you from anything?'

Three other pilots were in the ops room, two of whom were visiting males, and Molly was clearly embarrassed as all eyes were on her.

'This is a P1-W – Urgent delivery of a Spitfire from Brize Norton in the Cotswolds to Lossiemouth in Scotland,' said Alison, who was enjoying the moment, 'there's a Fairchild taxi aircraft waiting for you on the apron. Oh, and by the way, I love the outfit.'

'I'll need to go and get changed,' said Molly, 'I can't fly like this.'

Alison was wondering if this could possibly get any better. 'No time,' she said, 'your transport's on the apron, engine running. You'll have to go as you are. There's a Parachute in the equipment room.'

Molly looked exasperated and embarrassed as she turned and made a dash for the door and then towards the Fairchild taxi which was sitting on the apron. Douglas Fairweather was at the controls and he gave a look of surprise as he saw Molly running towards the aircraft, clad in her tennis clothes.

'Surely you can't be serious,' he said as he took a cigarette from a silver case, lit it, and shook his head.

'Well, thank you for your kind comments Douglas, but at least I have my priorities right,' said Molly. 'Of course, if you want to wait for half an hour, I'll gladly go and get changed.'

Douglas said nothing, but he was clearly relishing the moment.

'No, I thought not. Now if you could kindly concentrate on flying the aircraft while I put something warmer on.'

'I am *so* looking forward to being in the crew room this evening,' said Douglas as the Fairchild taxi took off; and he smiled all the way though the short flight which landed at RAF Brize Norton.

Although Molly had donned a track suit top, the few missing buttons left her tennis kit still visible as she clambered into the cockpit of a Spitfire, whereupon four ground-crew tried to get near to help Molly to strap in. To enthusiastic shouts of "thirty-love" and "where's your racquet" she gratefully squirmed down into her seat, fired up the engine, and rather more hastily than usual, taxied the aircraft to the runway and took off.

As soon as Molly was airborne, she quickly forgot her awkwardness of flying in tennis clothes, and she calmly looked at her map, banking sharply to the left to head north. The cloud base was low; but visibility on the ground was perfect.

'Right,' said Molly, 'railway line ... where are you', as she struggled with the map for a few moments trying to recognise landmarks, dipping the wings to peer over each side of the aircraft whilst cross-checking the route. Just as she settled in, an aircraft fleetingly appeared behind her from out of the clouds. Molly became aware of it immediately but could not get a clear enough view to make identification. She calmly maintained her route, glancing at the map but suddenly began to feel uneasy. Her heart began to race and she could feel her stomach turning over. 'What *is* it?' she asked herself as the wings momentarily appeared again through the clouds. This time the aircraft flew even closer and was now in full view. Molly's heart missed a beat as she recognised it as a German Messerschmitt.

Molly gazed ahead, her face expressionless and frozen in shock. 'Oh my God, please no, please no...' she whispered.

Hemmed in by cloud and with no weapons; she was powerless to do anything but pray. She glanced in her rear-view mirror and saw the German aircraft gaining on her as flashes of light appeared on its wing stubs as he opened fire. 'Please no...' A split second later, several rounds pierced the outer wing of Molly's Spitfire. She involuntarily screamed as her aircraft recoiled from the impact, but in the next split-second she rolled rapidly and dived into the clouds, craning her neck left and right to see as far behind her as possible.

As Molly looked in her rear-view mirror, the German aircraft kept appearing, staying on her tail as light flashes appeared again, with red tracer bullets streaming past Molly's Spitfire as she hurled it into avoiding manoeuvres. Terrified, she performed a high banking barrel-roll, and then a sharp turn to the left, but still the German was behind her. Molly was struggling to get him away from her rear as she prayed that he would run out of ammo, when suddenly the firing stopped. He was out.

'Please be out,' said Molly, 'OK - I'm taking no chances.'

Molly turned the Spitfire into another barrel roll, but this time deploying the flaps as she entered the cloud, slowing the Spitfire down. As she pulled back into another deep turn, the German overshot her, coming along-side as he attempted to slow down and get back on her tail. For a few seconds the two aircraft were flying side by side.

'Oh my god. Oh my god,' said Molly.

She looked over and was so close that she could clearly see the German pilot's face. He brought his Messerschmitt even closer for a better look and was shocked to see that the pilot with no helmet was female. He stared in disbelief looking at Molly's auburn hair spilling around her face.

Still terrified - Molly mustered every last ounce of willpower and energy and waved to him. The German stared for a moment looking confused, and then his aircraft abruptly disappeared into the clouds.

Molly checked her mirror at intervals, expecting him to reappear at any moment. Her breath was shallow and her heart was still racing. After what seemed like an eternity, with no sign of the Messerschmitt, Molly relaxed a little. 'Thank you. Thank you,' said Molly as she opened the throttle to full power, turned in the opposite direction and descended. She took a deep breath and steadied herself before looking for the nearest airfield.

As she put one of her hands to her face, it was shaking.

Eighteen

For the first two years of the war, although maintaining formal neutrality, the United States of America supplied Britain with war materials and their organisation "Wings for Britain" ferried American built aircraft across the Atlantic to be used by the RAF. The surprise military strike by the Imperial Japanese Navy Air Service against the naval base at Pearl Harbour in Hawaii plunged the United States into the war and thereafter they had maintained two priorities; to defeat Japan in the Pacific, and to help defeat Hitler in Europe.

Proposals were also being circulated outlining the start of a women's flying division in the USA Army Air Forces, which would help to release into combat those pilots who would otherwise be responsible for domestic, non-combat aviation jobs. One woman was given the task of gathering further information, to include sourcing data from the Civil Aeronautics Administration and to assess how many women pilots there were in the USA; their background details, flying hours, skills and their potential interest in joining a new organisation to assist their country in a time of war. She was also asked to join the ATA in an effort to gain experience of such an organisation.

That woman was the record-setting American aviatrix Jacqueline "Jackie" Cochran.

Jackie's task had begun before the US entered the war, and upon joining the ATA, she had recently recruited twenty-five American female pilots, most of whom had travelled to Britain by ship, despite the prevalent dangers from marauding German U-Boats. Her ambition was ultimately to create a female pool within the newly formed American ferrying programme and although she had been asked to supply two-hundred women for the British ATA, she convinced her superiors to settle for only twenty-five.

On a bright and clear morning at the ATA Ferry Pool No. 15 at Hamble,

Molly, Mary and Joy were walking towards the Crew Room as Diana and Lettice slowly pulled alongside them in an open top Bentley. Diana was driving; Lettice and Margie were in the rear seat; and another female in a pilot's uniform was in the front passenger seat and wearing sunglasses.

'Girls,' said Diana, 'meet Jackie Cochran. Jackie has joined us with several other pilots from the USA.'

Mary, Joy and Molly stopped, taking some moments to comprehend the sight that greeted their eyes and which was decidedly out of place in the middle of an operational air base during wartime.

Diana continued: 'Jackie - This is Mary, Joy and Molly.'

'How do you do,' said Molly, as she reached in to shake Jackie Cochran's hand, noticing the glittering diamond on her finger. 'I heard that you had joined us. Welcome to England'.

Before Jackie Cochran had a chance to answer, Joy, who was stroking the Bentley, interrupted: 'Is this the new standard issue for ATA pilots, Diana?'

'If my father had his way, it certainly would be,' said Diana.

'Molly Rose is it?' said Jackie Cochran in a broad American accent. 'I heard about your close encounter with the Luftwaffe. That must have been terrifying. I can just imagine what he told his Luftwaffe cronies back in Berlin … *oh, those Brits must be in serious trouble if they're recruiting female pilots*. It's a shame that you couldn't just blow him right out of the sky.'

'Yes, quite,' said Molly, temporarily lost for words.

'Must dash darlings,' said Diana, sensing Molly's uncomfortableness as she prepared to drive away. 'Late for lunch. Toodle pip.'

'Anyway, fab to meet you girls, so-long,' said Jackie Cochran.

Molly, Mary and Joy stood for a few moments watching them as they drove off and then they continued towards the Crew Room.

'You weren't joking,' said Molly to Joy, 'Miss Cochran is quite the character.'

'I would certainly not want to be in her bad books,' said Mary, 'she seems quite formidable.'

'Oh, she is!' said Joy, 'I heard that she already had a run-in with Pauline Gower and I gather they're on non-speakers. The delightful Miss Cochran was most upset about her American girls having to strip naked for their medicals. She complained to Pauline and soon put a stop to that!'

'Well I quite agree with her,' said Molly, 'damned liberty'

'What did Diana mean about her father wanting Bentleys to be standard issue?' asked Mary.

'Diana's father is Woolf Barnato,' said Joy, 'the Chairman of Bentley Motors, and her mother Dorothy is actually American. I heard that her grandfather is big in the diamond business. They are truly positively rich.'

'Perhaps you should invite the delightful Miss Cochran to your gathering in Cambridge this weekend, said Mary.'

'Oh golly. I don't think so,' said Molly, 'Pauline Gower will be there. Two Queen Bees in the hive - that will never do.'

Nineteen

The golden age of the weekend house party in the country was at its peak before the start of the war, but the tradition had for obvious reasons, taken a severe downturn. Despite this, it was Arthur's intention to have a "gathering", as he called it, with the aim of entertaining those most valuable to his business; and several of his company's most important contacts, along with a few friends, were invited for cocktails.

Under normal circumstances, the extensive patio of the house would have been perfect for the evening's entertaining due to the warmer weather, however the blackout restrictions made that impossible. It was therefore decided to host the entire evening inside and Arthur set about working with the housekeeper to make arrangements, specifying that the event should be decidedly low-key and avoiding any over-indulgence which would be highly inappropriate in a time of war.

The housekeeper Annie had been with the family for twenty-five years, and although the war made it necessary to let the other members of the household staff go, Annie stayed on. She had grown very close to the children throughout her years of service and was now regarded as one of the family.

Arthur also delighted in the opportunity to invite Molly along with several of her colleagues from the ATA. Aside from the pleasure of seeing his sister, which was becoming far too infrequent, Arthur loved to hear about the ATA and the various aircraft that Molly had flown. On the rare occasion that Molly did have time to chat with him about her work, he would ask questions about the most detailed aspects of various aircraft; including their performance and capabilities, often baffling Molly, but reflecting Arthur's amazing level of knowledge about his industry. The cocktail party would be a rare opportunity to extend his information gathering, and from Molly's colleagues too, and Arthur was in eager anticipation for the evening.

Molly was, as always, delighted to be home. Whitehill had remained her sanctuary and refuge in a time of uncertainty and she cherished her visits there.

Several Bentleys and Rolls-Royces, together with a number of military vehicles, arrived into the forecourt of Whitehill Manor and Arthur had arranged for two of his factory employees to help park the cars. The vehicle headlights shone weakly through the brownout and blackout restrictive covers fitted to hinder detection by aerial reconnaissance and bombers. Driving at night along dark country roads was therefore a very slow and arduous process as all external lights, including streetlights, were either dimmed and shielded to deflect light downward or switched off entirely. This, in effect, more than doubled the travel times for those who were willing to take the risk.

The Air Ministry had forecast that Britain would endure more air bombing attacks at night than during the day, causing mass destruction and many civilian casualties. The countryside was not immune to this; being vulnerable to attack from marauding bombers looking for military airfields. Thus, the windows and doors of Whitehill Manor were covered with heavy blackout curtains to prevent the escape of even a glimmer of light that might aid enemy aircraft.

A number of guests alighted the vehicles and approached the grand entrance of the eighteenth-century manor. As they walked through the main door into the hallway, the full opulence of the house revealed itself. Yet despite its grandeur, Whitehill was warm and inviting; a comfortable family home in which guests felt relaxed.

Despite Arthur's original intention not to overdo things, the whole place was abuzz with excitement; music was playing and Annie and one of her friends moved about with trays of drinks and hors d'oeuvres. Arthur had succumbed to slight extravagance at the last minute, deciding that his guests deserved an escape, albeit temporarily, from the dull anguish and sorrows of war.

It was a small gathering of about twenty-five guests, several of whom were in uniform, and all stood chatting in couples and groups. Molly was the epitome of courtesy and hospitality, moving about the room, introducing those who did not know each other and generally making everyone feel comfortable.

Douglas was close by entertaining a group of officers as puffs of smoke defined his presence. He looked like the perfect gentleman in a beautifully cut pin-striped suit; and with a crisp white shirt and his favourite university tie, and highly polished hand-made Oxford shoes from Church's. Vividly present, surprisingly energetic for a man of his size, and a master of the anecdote, Douglas was as always, the centre of attention.

Molly moved over to join Diana, Lettice, Margie and Mary, who were all drinking Champagne; despite Diana having previously declared that she avoided Champagne unless she was thirsty. Molly looked stunning in a beautiful black dress which she had borrowed from the wardrobe of her late mother, and as she made even the slightest movement, the sequins caught the light from the overhead chandeliers and the flickering candles, enhancing her slim and petite figure and her pretty face.

Molly's auburn hair was swept back with a small hair pin made of tiny sapphires to match her earrings. She did not often wear make-up, but on the rare occasion that she did, it was difficult not to notice her perfect features. Diana was wearing a long emerald green gown that was sparkling, and her hair was held back by a beautiful but simple diamond tiara, which was a gift from her grandfather.

The five girls stood together and drew stares from the other guests in the room. Their graceful presence and demeanour was devoid of all conceit and projected an aura to those around them. An astute observer would perhaps conclude that they each possessed a gift; a very special gift, and should they ask them it would at once become clear…They were pilots…ATA pilots.

Arthur approached the group, holding a glass of Champagne.

'Please don't forget our little arrangement,' he said to Lettice.'

'Looking forward to it,' Lettice replied, as Arthur wandered off.

Molly was perplexed: 'What was all that about?' … it all sounds very clandestine'.

Lettice smiled: 'I promised your brother at least an hour tomorrow. He wants to talk about the Mossie'.

'Oh golly, you'll need more than an hour for that,' said Molly.

'I don't mind at all,' said Lettice, 'I learnt quite a lot the last time we chatted.'

'I suppose I've learned quite a lot from him too,' said Molly, 'his mind is like a sponge and he can retain the most detailed information … aircraft and motor cars … he is like an encyclopaedia. Speaking of motor cars, I do like your new Bentley,' said Molly to Diana.

'Thank you. Me too,' said Diana, 'it's a birthday present. Father is far too generous, however he has no need for a collection of Bentleys whilst being a Wing Commander with the RAF. Positively superfluous.'

'My father said that the ATA is still receiving considerable criticism in the House of Lords,' said Lettice.

'Unfortunately, there are not enough women in the House of Lords,' said Diana, 'I had no criticism from any man when I was a nurse, nor when I drove ambulances in London during the Blitz, so why should being a pilot be any different?'

'Father does defend us of course,' said Lettice, 'and I know that your father does too Margie, but if there's any word of an accident, then we are all accused of being inexperienced at best, incompetent at worst.'

'Oh, how little they know,' said Mary.

'In any case, accidents are caused by carelessness, not inexperience,' said Margie.

Joy, Jackie and Jane entered the room, still dressed in their ATA uniforms. Molly saw them and quickly broke away from the group to greet them.

'Hallo - welcome,' said Molly, 'I so hope that the journey wasn't too horrid.'

'So sorry for being late,' said Jackie, 'the trains were delayed as North London was hit quite badly so we had a bit of a long way round. We've left our things out in the hallway. If you tell me where our rooms are, I'll take them up.'

'Oh, don't worry about that,' said Molly, 'Annie will make sure that everything is taken to your rooms and unpacked, ready for you later. Now come and have a drink and let me introduce you to a few people.'

A server walked over to where the girls were standing and Joy and Jane each took a glass of Champagne. Jackie took a glass of water from the tray, and all three followed Molly who escorted the girls towards three male guests who were in the midst of a conversation.

'Excuse me for interrupting gentlemen,' said Molly, 'however may I introduce Jackie Sorour, Joy Gough and Jane Winstone. Ladies, this is The Right Honourable Charles Appleton, Father Hanbury, our local vicar, and Group Captain Martyn Paxton.'

The men stopped their conversation to say hello. The three of them had been thrown randomly and temporarily together for one evening, and were slowly realising that they were as incompatible as fire, oil and water.

Charles Appleton was a Conservative Member of Parliament and his family owned several factories in the north of England, which had made a fortune supplying a multitude of aircraft engine parts since the outbreak of war. He was a large man with a waxed moustache and expensive clothes which seemed to be well past their expiry date. Appleton was thrifty to say the least, believing wholeheartedly that if one counted the pennies, the pounds would look after themselves. Highly intelligent and confident yet opinionated to the point of stubbornness in an effort to reinforce what many would consider his archaic values. Charles was also a product of the 'Old School'; preferring that women should listen rather than express an opinion.

RAF Group Captain Martyn Paxton was a long-time friend of Arthur's from a local farming family, and who had decided at an early age that he wanted to fly. Paxton excelled at school and university and was recognised by his teachers and peers as an extremely talented and cultivated individual, who was certain to achieve great success in his chosen career. That career was the RAF; and one which further developed Paxton into a man of commitment and honour; considered by those who made his acquaintance as a fine example of style and good form.

Father Hanbury was the local vicar. He had been a friend of the Marshall family for many years and had presided over Molly and Bernard's wedding ceremony. He was an odd-looking man. Extremely thin and squinty eyed and dressed quite oddly. He was in his mid-50s and had a child-like stare and a bony face with sunken cheeks, light brown eyes and flaming ginger hair which stood up in swirls around his head.

'It's a pleasure to meet you all,' said Group Captain Paxton, 'and I do hope that your journey was not too tiring.'

'It was horrible on the trains,' said Jackie, who was immediately taken with the affable and charming Paxton. 'Thank goodness that we are staying here for the whole weekend,' she continued, perhaps hoping that the dashing Paxton would not be hastily returning to his duties.

'I haven't been on a train since I was a boy,' said Father Hanbury as he chuckled and genially nodded his head. 'In fact,' he continued, 'I can't remember the last time that I left Cambridgeshire. I suppose that I'm not quite the intrepid traveller'.

Charles Appleton was at a loss as to whom he would talk to, given that Paxton's attention had now turned to the lovely Jackie Sorour. Having no intention to engage in what he considered would be meaningless conversation with the three new arrivals, Appleton therefore had no alternative than to turn his attention to Father Hanbury.

'It's a bloody disaster that the Japanese have invaded Singapore you know,' said Appleton', 'I do hope that they're not planning a takeover of my club.'

Father Hanbury was visibly perplexed, as the goings on in the Far East were considerably outside of his field of expertise.

'Perhaps it's been converted into someone's residence or a headquarters by now' said Joy, jokingly. She continued, 'I read that Churchill referred to the invasion as "the worst disaster and largest capitulation in British history". Apparently, under the terms of the surrender, one-thousand British troops will be left in Singapore city to maintain order until the Japanese Army completes its occupation.'

Charles Appleton stared at Joy as though she had entered the party via the chimney flue, and was bewildered at how a woman - and worse, a woman in uniform - could express such a contribution. There was a slight pause, and then Appleton turned decidedly to Father Hanbury, who seemed to be oblivious of the unfolding drama.

'Actually,' said Father Hanbury, 'I may have inadvertently wandered into a village in Norfolk once.'

'Yes - well - ahem, as I was saying,' said Appleton, 'the last time that I was in Singapore …'.

Joy was somewhat taken aback and two frown lines appeared on her forehead as her mouth opened slightly to form the words of her response. In a split-second Group Captain Paxton had noticed her annoyance and before Joy had a chance to register her displeasure at Appleton's conduct, he quickly rescued the potentially inflammable situation.

'So ladies, how are you finding the ferry work?' he said, 'it must be jolly tiring doing the number of flights you do per day; day in and day out. I have the greatest respect for what you and your colleagues do. Without you, my chaps would spend so much less time available for combat missions'.

'That is very kind, thank you,' said Joy, 'although I'm not sure if that opinion is generic across the RAF', and then she looked at Charles Appleton, 'or in Parliament for that matter.'

'That may be so,' said Group Captain Paxton, 'but they will all come around - eventually. Another glass of Champagne?

Twenty

Upon Italy's entry into the war in June 1940, the Western Desert Campaign, otherwise known as the Desert War, began to unfold in the Libyan and Egyptian deserts. The German Africa Corps commanded by Erwin Rommel, otherwise known as "The Desert Fox", was sent to bolster Italian forces and a fluctuating series of battles against the British Commonwealth forces, commanded by Lieutenant-General Bernard Montgomery, was ongoing. Molly had tried to keep up with news and visited the cinema at every opportunity to look at the Pathé newsreels, but she was concerned that they painted a different picture to the actual events unfolding in North Africa. She was desperate to hear from Bernard.

★★★

In a dry wadi-bed in the North African desert, a number of dusty tanks with British markings were scattered under camouflage netting as a group of officers sat in the meagre shade, their weapons close at hand. The searing sun baked the arid landscape and the heat was stifling; almost overwhelming. Bernard and his colleagues were waiting to be rushed up, however orders had not been forthcoming.

Propped against the tracks of one of the vehicles, Bernard was writing a letter to Molly:

> *"… so I haven't managed to pick up any letters from home, but I'm hoping you are all keeping well. We are all in great spirits, the chaps are a wonderful bunch and all enjoy a good old sing-song - not quite Ad Majorem Dei Gloriam, but still quite tuneful! The weather here is absolutely lovely, very warm and sunny, I've got quite the sun-tan …"*

He put aside his letter as Edward Egerton-Reed appeared from behind the tank and walked past Bernard towards the group of officers.

'Writing home old chap?' said Edward, 'Please send Molly my love.'

'Will do Fruity.'

Edward stopped in front of one of the tanks as the Commander was spreading a map on the sand, holding it in place with a rock on each corner. All eyes focussed on him.

'So, chaps,' said the Tank Commander, 'we've had reports that the Africa Corps are coming on as strongly as ever in the last two weeks – they continue to advance at a hell of a rate here and here. Unbelievably, Rommel has been pushing forward up to sixty miles in a single day. Our orders are to outflank these units here and fight through heading North to meet up with A Division. The next push will be Tobruk.'

The small group gathered closely around the map as he continued:

'If Rommel's moving at that pace, I can't see how his logistics chaps can keep up with the forward units. At some stage he'll have to pause and re-group, re-fuel and so on. But we can't bank on that, so we need as much intel as possible on their movements before we set out. If those units there are still in the game, we'll have the devil of a job breaking through.'

Bernard moved in even closer to take a better look at the map.

'When's the next update due?' said the Tank Commander to Edward.

'We're getting snippets in all the time Sir,' replied Edward.

'Well we can't sit and wait for too long; We'll billet here tonight and set off tomorrow at the crack of dawn. Tell the men to get as much rest as they can, as it'll be one hell of a day tomorrow. Especially if Jerry is managing to get his supplies through.'

Bernard picked up his letter and continued writing:

"... and so my sweet girl, I do hope that you're not having to do anything too dangerous with those kites of yours. Please keep safe. I couldn't bear it if anything happened to you. Until we can be reunited. I adore you."

★★★

111

Molly walked into her room, quickly dropped her bag and jumped onto the bed, where she opened a letter from Bernard. This was always the time that Molly both loved and hated, as it was wonderful to hear his news, but there was always an element of worry.

She read aloud:

"My darling, just a short billet-doux to let you know all is well. We're on the move quite a bit ..."

Molly read the letter twice and then a third time to analyse specific sentences and words, anxious to discover if Bernard was hiding anything; his feelings, details of his health, and the prospective dangers that lay ahead. Molly knew that Bernard was not allowed to give away too many details, and that letters were censored by military personnel and post office workers to protect sensitive information being leaked to the "enemy aliens." She tried over and over again to imagine exactly where he was and what he was doing, wishing that things could be different and longing for the day when she would see him again.

As Molly's eyes started to close, and her thoughts wandered, she lay back on the bed with the letter clutched to her chest and fell asleep.

Twenty-One

On a quiet evening in March, three members of the ground crew of No. 218 Squadron at RAF Marham in East Anglia were waiting, throwing a cricket ball between them as they sat on the blue-grey ground equipment. One of the engineers was a young boy of nineteen who caught the ball and immediately froze, his head tilted slightly and his eyes focussed towards the sky. His two colleagues were rigid and silent in anticipation as the only thing that they could hear were birds chirping in the airfield grass.

The other two engineers knew exactly what was happening, for here was a young lad with hearing abilities way beyond normal and, much to the regular entertainment of his colleagues, the boy's senses once again proved right as the thrum of heavy engines and props could suddenly be heard in the distance. The three young lads jumped up and walked to where they could see the shape of an incoming Vickers Wellington twin-engine, long-range bomber, as it appeared on the skyline, lining up for landing.

In the cockpit of the huge aircraft, Mary looked tiny in the pilot's seat, concentrating hard and fighting with the controls as it wallowed and sideslipped. Behind her sat the male flight engineer. Mary had the blue Ferry Pilot Notes book open on her lap and was going through landing procedures.

'Undercarriage down,' said Mary to the engineer, 'Half Flap.'

'Undercarriage down,' repeated the engineer, as he pulled the flap lever. 'Half Flap. Roger'.

The aircraft slowed and the nose dropped as Mary heaved on the controls to steady the huge aircraft, and to give extra throttle. The entire aircraft was shaking as Mary tried with difficulty to read her notes, which were jumping about on her lap, when suddenly the aircraft dropped. Mary reacted quickly, again fighting the controls.

'Bleedin' 'eck,' said the engineer, 'have you flown many of these before ma'am?'

'Nope… first one…,' said Mary, distractedly.

'Full flap then ma'am?' said the engineer, as he tightened his straps.

'NO!' said Mary, 'too early, we'll undershoot.'

The engineer was turning white as he waited for Mary's instruction, and beginning to wonder if he would be back at the base for supper.

'OK, NOW,' said Mary, 'Full flap.'

It was a magnificent sight as the brand-new Wellington approached the runway with its flaps and wheels down, as it was backlit against the amber sky. The wheels kissed the runway and the aircraft settled heavily but perfectly as it taxied towards the hangar, gleaming in the light as the colours and details gradually revealed themselves. As the aircraft and its propellers slowed to a dignified halt, the ground crew moved forward to marshal the fuel bowser into place and threw the chocks under the massive tyres.

It took a few minutes for the door of the aircraft to open, and a small figure hopped down - the petite Mary, carrying her parachute. She approached the engineer.

'Hello,' she said, 'no snags, so just a sign in.'

'Hello Miss,' said the engineer, 'I'm afraid passengers can't sign, it needs to be the pilot. Where *is* the pilot?'

'I am the pilot,' said Mary.

The other two engineers stopped what they were doing and stared.

'Ha-ha, very funny,' said the engineer, 'of course you are. Here, let me up and I'll give him a hand.'

The engineer put his paperwork on top of the huge tyre and climbed up into the aircraft. Mary shook her head and reached up to remove the paperwork from the top of the tyre. The other engineers looked on, bewildered. Mary took out a pen, signed in the aircraft before reaching up to replace the paperwork on the tyre. She then walked away, smiling.

'Good luck with that,' she said to herself.

***

Later that evening, Mary arrived back at the Hamble Ferry Pool in the last taxi Anson of the day and, having no time to change out of uniform, she quickly made her way to Southampton, catching her friends just as they were about to enter the cinema.

Cinemas were becoming a sanctuary for escaping the realities of war, even if only for a few hours. Molly and her friends paid a shilling each to visit the cinema at every opportunity; not only to lose themselves in movies with Hollywood stars such as Bing Crosby, Carole Lombard and Clark Gable, but also to see the Pathé newsreels. The newsreels were producing some incredibly dramatic footage and were as popular as the feature films themselves, keeping the public informed, or possibly misinformed, on developments in the war.

A few years earlier, the government had re-created the Ministry of Information, which had also been active during the First World War, to influence popular opinion. The Ministry was the central government department responsible for propaganda and publicity, with a function to present the national case to the public at home and abroad. Another of its aims was to convince the public of German brutality; emphasising wherever possible the evil and wickedness perpetrated in the occupied countries.

Molly, Mary, Joy and Lettice were in uniform as they stood in the foyer where posters were advertising the newly released film 'The Ghost of Frankenstein', starring Lon Chaney as the monster.

'They didn't believe that I was the pilot and so they searched the plane,' said Mary, 'can you believe it? They probably thought that the flight engineer was the pilot.'

'Oh, I so wish it had been a Lancaster,' said Molly.

'Ha-ha; yes,' said Mary, 'That would have kept them busy for a while longer. Come to think of it, it shouldn't be too long now before our more experienced girls are trained up on Lancs.'

'Talking of which, where are the other girls?' said Lettice.

'Irene and Jackie went to the local hospital to cheer up the wounded servicemen,' replied Joy'

'Those two are inseparable' said Lettice.

The girls reached their seats and the lights dimmed. Smoke filled the air and latecomers were silhouetted against the screen as they stepped gingerly to their seats. The Pathé newsreel started, showing a map of Europe and the Mediterranean; and zooming in to the tiny island of Malta in the Eastern Mediterranean.

"The siege of Malta – the brave people of Malta stoically endure daily Italian and German bombardment of their tiny but strategically important island in the middle of the Mediterranean. British forces continue to defend the island while the RAF and Royal Navy launch attacks against vital Axis Forces' shipping lines re-supplying Rommel in North Africa.

The British Prime Minister is determined that we defend Malta - "It is imperative that Allied Forces help the people of Malta and hold on to this strategic island," he continues, "'our unsinkable aircraft carrier' will make sure that Allied Forces keep control of the Eastern Mediterranean supply lines and defeat the enemy in North Africa. Until reinforcements arrive, the relentless enemy air attacks continue…"

The girls sat quietly through the remainder of the newsreel, and then waited excitedly for the start of the film. Molly, however, found it hard to concentrate on the horror unfolding on screen as Doctor Ludwig Frankenstein unveiled his gruesome creation, which was, for the short term, restrained in chains. Molly's thoughts were drifting in and out of the newsreel, as she gradually began to piece together the connection between potential victory, Malta and its impact on the battles in the North African desert, and the most vital piece of the puzzle … Bernard.

As the film came to its conclusion, with the monster trapped in the burning chateau and the film's hero and heroine walking away into the sunrise, Molly came out of her thoughts and stood up to leave, alongside Mary, Joy and Lettice. As they exited the cinema and walked along the street, Molly's thoughts were in a far-off place.

'Well, that film was a bit unbelievable,' said Lettice, 'why are the women always pathetic and drippy, and terrified at the drop of a hat?'

'I don't know what was the more terrifying,' said Mary, 'the film or the Pathé Newsreel.'

'Yes, those poor people in Malta,' said Molly, 'it must be terrifying being bombed like that night and day. I didn't realise how jolly vital Malta is for defeating Jerry in North Africa.'

'I feel for them too,' said Joy, 'It's because Malta is at the very centre of North Africa's supply lines so whoever controls Malta also controls the Mediterranean *and* those supply lines. No wonder Jerry wants it flattened.

If we hold Malta, we control the sea lanes and Rommel doesn't get his supplies.'

'But that newsreel said that Malta is being pounded to bits,' said Molly anxiously, 'How can they possibly hold on much longer?'

'We need to hold on to Malta,' said Lettice, 'or Rommel will have everything he needs to give our chaps in the desert what for. The Desert Rats can only hold out for so long if Rommel keeps getting his supplies.'

Mary immediately noticed Molly's worried look, and she nudged Lettice in an effort to change the subject.

'I wish that I could do more to keep it all from going terribly wrong,' said Molly.

'You already are Molly!' said Mary, frowning at Lettice, 'We all are. If we weren't doing exactly what we do, it would be up to the fighter pilots to get all these aircraft from A to B. But they need to be in action. Every time you jump into a cockpit, you are helping the war effort.'

'I really do hope so,' said Molly, lost in thought.

Twenty-Two

The following morning, Molly entered the Ops Room as three other pilots were leaving. She was approached immediately by Alison King, which was unusual as Alison generally stood in the same spot and pilots went to her. Alison gave Molly her chit.

'Good morning Molly,' said Alison, 'this is a double-hop P1 high-priority delivery of a Swordfish from Abingdon to RAF Coastal Command in Northwood. You'll make a slight detour to High Ercall in Shropshire as the aircraft is being looked at by two engineers and then on to Northwood. It has classified equipment onboard Molly so read these procedures whilst you're in the Fairchild. When you get to High Ercall, you're to call Commander Hamilton at Coastal Command who is the HQ contact and let him have your ETA'.

'Thank you. Will do.' said Molly.

As Molly walked away she thought about the last time that she had flown the Swordfish and particularly how her overalls and goggles were covered in oil from the consistent spluttering of its noisy engine, but that thought quickly passed when she saw Mary and Jackie who were waiting for her outside the Ops Room. Both girls had late-afternoon tasks and so had decided to spend the morning together, planning the coming evening's entertainment. As Molly left the Ops Room, she was surprised to see them loitering around.

'Golly, it's all right for some.' said Molly, 'Why don't you both put on bathing suits and get a sun-tan?'

'Now that's a good idea', said Jackie, 'but first we're planning a little soirée this evening at The Bugle Pub in Hamble. Will you join us Molly?'

'Of course,' said Molly, 'delighted'.

'Where are you off to?' said Mary.

'I have a P1 to Northwood,' Molly replied, 'in a Swordfish'.

'Oh dear,' said Mary, 'a string-bag ... oil and noise in abundance'.

'Ooh, lots of lovely American pilots at High Ercall,' said Jackie, 'It's the HQ for the US Air Force 309 Fighter Squadron. Do you know that they fly British Spitfires with US Air Force markings?'

'I'll be sure to bring one back for you.' said Molly as she walked away, 'Cheerio'.

'Do you mean a Spitfire or a pilot?' called Jackie as Molly headed off towards the apron.

Molly took off in the Swordfish, heading for East Shropshire. The flight was clear and uneventful, and Molly felt relaxed at the controls. She decided to climb slightly to avoid the high ground of The Wrekin, a large hill and prominent landmark near Telford which rises to a height of thirteen-hundred feet above the Shropshire Plain. As Molly approached the hill, a family with two children waved excitedly at the aircraft as their dog ran around in circles. Molly thought about how blessed they were to be together... Suddenly, and without warning, the engine stuttered and cut out.

'No no no no ...' said Molly, as she became rigid, looking into the cockpit to identify the problem. She reacted swiftly to push the aircraft into a gentle dive and began the process of running through emergency procedures.

'Focus Molly!' she said, 'Procedures ... check altitude; check throttle, check switches, check fuel cock; check airspeed; check slip meter; check externals; attempt re-start.'

Molly tried to re-start ... but there was nothing except the noise of the wind.

'Damn, damn, damn ...'

She scrambled to open the emergency procedures checklist.

'Check externals, check altitude, turn in to wind, wings level, reset switches, reset throttle, recycle fuel pumps, check prop, attempt engine re-start.'

Again, Molly tried to re-start ... but nothing.

'Damn it!' she cried, 'Right Molly; land the damned aircraft.'

The aircraft had descended, and Molly looked desperately for a landing site as she tightened her straps. The fields in the area seemed extraordinarily small and, having no power, she was gliding into the wind in a rough approach as it whistled across the fuselage. Molly spotted a likely looking field that seemed bigger than the rest, and drifted erratically lower and lower, lining up to avoid the boundary hedges and a wall. But as she descended, she had a nasty shock.

'Oh my god, it's a downhill slope. Molly, what *are* you doing?'

Molly adjusted her angle of approach to compensate ... but then she saw a farmer walking slowly behind his horse and plough on the other side of a hedge at the bottom of the field; directly in line with her landing path.

'Please – no!' she cried, 'Get out of the bloody way!'

A young farming lad was plodding behind a horse-drawn plough, encouraging the shire-horse on by flicking its reins. In the background, the noise of the aircraft flying overhead had suddenly stopped. The farmer was unaware of the events unfolding in the sky above him until the horse started to fidget, ears back, and snorting. The farmer grabbed the reins, and then stared in disbelief at the aircraft which had appeared out of the blue and was heading directly for him.

'Jesus Christ,' he said, as he dropped the reins and ran as fast as he could, which was difficult through the uneven ground, all the while looking back over his shoulder, but he suddenly tripped and fell face-down into the mud behind the hedge.

The aircraft continued to bear down on him, committed to its emergency landing, and the wheels thudded down onto the grass, rolling for a few yards before Molly hauled the aircraft violently to the left to avoid the horse and plough. The farmer was transfixed as he looked through the hedge at the oncoming aircraft. His horse turned and bolted, with the plough careering wildly behind it, bouncing over the muddy troughs as though it was about to disengage and turn over at any second.

The aircraft continued to veer left, its wheels digging into the soft ground, and then the right wheel ripped off and bounced towards the farmer. As if in slow-motion, the right wing hit the ground, spinning the aircraft and slowing it down, as the propeller dug into the soft earth with a dull thud, and the aircraft gently turned over and, almost gracefully, came to an abrupt stop with its tail high in the air.

Molly was hanging upside-down by her straps.

The wheel bounced towards the farmer and stopped entangled in the hedge only a few feet in front of him. He was lying prostrate in the muddy ditch, his arms covering his head. He tentatively lifted his head as the noise stopped to see the wheel in front of his face.

Uninjured but slightly bruised and very angry, Molly struggled to unhook herself from her harness and fell unceremoniously out of the aircraft in a heap on the ground. She looked around to see if the farmer was OK, and then looked at the damage to the undercarriage, wing and prop.

The farmer stood up gingerly, looking at the wheel in front of him, and then over his shoulder at the distant horse, which was contentedly munching grass as if nothing had happened.

Molly was aching all over as she limped slowly over to the farmer.

'Are you OK?' she said.

'Yes Miss,' he replied, 'I think so. Are *you* OK Miss?'

'I'm fine – I think - but I need you to do something for me. It's very important. Firstly, tell me where the nearest phone is.'

'It's in the village Miss, about half-a-mile that way.'

'OK, thank you. Now, ... what's your name?'

'Tomlinson Miss. Jack Tomlinson.'

'OK Jack.' I need you to stand guard over this plane. No-one must come anywhere near it. Don't stand too close. Over there is good. I'll be back in half an hour. Can you do that for me?'

'Yes miss,' he said, still in a state of confusion.

Molly limped towards the village. So many thoughts were going through her head; she would be disgraced and fired, ostracised by all who knew her, she would be the source of endless 'female pilot' jokes, as told by RAF officers as they laughed at the bar in the Officer's Mess ... Then Molly thought about all the other ATA pilots who had crashed, and particularly those who had lost their lives and the thought rallied her. Her worries suddenly seemed so trivial and at that point, she realised that she was incredibly lucky to be alive.

Molly reached the small village and a few elderly ladies chatting outside a cottage said hello; wondering who this rather suspicious-looking person was. Molly timidly said hello before entering the safety of the village phone box and pulling out the procedure document that Alison had given her. She asked the operator to put her through to Navy Commander Hamilton at Coastal Command (Northwood) and waited for the connection.

'Commander Hamilton's office', said a voice on the phone.

Molly paused … 'Hallo Sir, this is Second Officer Molly Rose from the ATA. I was delivering the P1 high-priority Swordfish from RAF Abingdon via High Ercall, but I'm afraid there's been a bit of an accident.'

***

In the sick bay at Hamble Ferry Pool No.15, several patients were being tended to by the resident sisters as Molly passed them, wincing at the sight of some of the patients' wounds. She had a small dressing on her forehead and a bruise on her right cheek but other than that, she felt fine if a little shaken. She hurried outside into the fresh air and stood at the entrance, taking deep breaths; the incident playing over and over in her mind. She thought again about how lucky she was and about the young farmer. What a relief that he was not hurt…

Margo was walking past heading towards the Control Room and she stopped when she saw Molly.

'Been in the wars I see,' said Margo, 'are you OK?'

'I had a bit of a prang - the engine cut out completely. But yes, I'm fine. I feel a bit of a fraud compared to the poor lot in there.'

'I know, I've heard about the accident,' said Margo, 'and you're quite the talking point … but don't worry about it Molly.'

'Thank you ma'am,' said Molly nervously, 'but I suppose this will affect my promotion?'

'Can't see why it should,' said Margo, 'it happens to the best of us. It wasn't your fault and let's face it, that emergency landing could have gone very wrong, and then what? There was some vital equipment on that plane that's still intact. You're still here Molly, and that's the most important thing.'

'Yes it is,' said Molly, rather reservedly.

Margo looked at Molly for a few seconds and smiled. 'I am so proud of you Molly,' she said, 'and of the pilot that you've become. Do you know, when we initially proposed to recruit female pilots into the ATA, you were exactly the type of person that I hoped we would find. Despite all the resentment we received from certain members of parliament, the newspapers, the radio, and a few in the RAF and general population, we always knew that we could find the right women for the job and we have. Courage under pressure, and a beacon of hope for all females, not just pilots, but women and girls everywhere who are being told that they're not good enough, that they can't do it because they're weak or intellectually inferior. Now all those women are looking to you and your colleagues Molly. You're changing things for them; redefining their habits of freedom for many years to come.'

Thank you ma'am,' said Molly, who was quite taken aback at such an accolade, and trying hard to keep her emotions in check. Margo touched Molly's shoulder, smiled at her and walked away.

Twenty-Three

Factories continued to ramp up production, which led to an ever-increasing demand for ferrying services. As a response to this, the ATA continued to expand. Additional pilots, ground and flight engineers, and administrative staff were recruited, including meteorological officers, secretaries, drivers, police, emergency crews and canteen staff. Hamble Ferry Pool underwent expansion as additional buildings were constructed to cater for the increase in operations, with several of the older huts and sheds being replaced by more modern brick buildings.

During a visit by a group of dignitaries, Gerard d'Erlanger had, in honour of the enormous amount of ferrying work being carried out, remarked: "Every machine you see in the sky has been, or will be, flown at some period of its life, by a pilot of the ATA".

To maximise the efficiency of pilots, more taxi aircraft were sourced to transport ferry pilots to the factories or maintenance units to pick up their taskings, and then to collect them at their destinations. In addition, a relay system was created for longer ferrying journeys, whereby a pilot would fly the aircraft to the next ferry pool along the way to hand over to another ATA pilot, and so on until the aircraft reached its destination.

The young Princess Elizabeth registered for war service just four days after her sixteenth birthday, joining the Auxiliary Territorial Service (ATS) as a mechanic and driver and was granted a commission as an honorary Second Subaltern for the Windsor Unit. The young princess was keen to help the war effort and the new role was an inspiration to young women around the country. This was of particular interest to the female pilots of the ATA as the young princess was seen as a flag-bearer to women in war services everywhere.

More women were accepted into the ATA, as the flawless and efficient record of the female pilots made a good impression on those in power. New recruits came from all corners of society, including wealthy socialites and the working classes, and new arrivals included a stunt-pilot, a ballet dancer, an athlete, a skiing instructor, an actor, a typist, an architect and a teacher. One of the new recruits was a grandmother.

As many new pilots had little or no flying experience, the necessity to re-structure the training programme became apparent, as new recruits did not have the same level of experience as their predecessors. It was unlike the early days when all new female pilots were versatile and highly experienced, hence unfamiliar aircraft types were assigned knowing that a pilot would soon be familiar with its characteristics.

Pauline was still using all her skills, determination and connections to ensure that women were accepted on the same basis as the men, including continually lobbying for equal pay. Her "iron fist in a velvet glove" approach gained even more respect and admiration, particularly from the female pilots, as she was always friendly, tactful and gently persuasive.

Meanwhile, Margo was encouraging pilots to undergo "conversion" courses at the ATA Flying School in order to fly the single-engine fighters, such as Hurricanes and Spitfires, as well as the multi-engine types. Molly was by now comfortable in most aircraft, with no reservations about flying a new type for the first time.

In those aircraft with which she had become familiar, Molly had also learned to detect the signs that indicated a potential problem. Any sound or movement that constituted an abnormality was reported; which usually meant a visit for the aircraft to one of the Maintenance Units. She also had her fair share of aircraft that had been designated 'NEA' or 'Not Essentially Airworthy', which suggested that the aircraft may be a risk to fly. Molly took each NEA task with her usual courage, however not before she completely understood the fault and had made a "what if" plan should things go awry.

The press became more and more interested in the female pilots of the ATA, and requests were coming in on a regular basis for stories and photos. The newspapers were determined to glamorise the life of the female ATA pilots; not only due to the work but also because the girls looked so chic in their smart ATA uniforms with golden wings above their breast pockets. The editors knew that the varying characteristics and diverse backgrounds of these women would appeal to a broad section of the population at a time when any glamour story of women in service could improve morale.

As Margo entered the Ops Room on a bright and clear Monday morning, five press photographers hurried past her excitedly in the opposite direction, carrying various cameras, flash units and photo bags. Gerald d'Erlanger was standing at the window looking out at the airfield and particularly at the photographers rushing towards a Mk II Fairey Barracuda Torpedo bomber that was taxying in.

'What's going on?' said Margo.

'I thought that a bit of press coverage might be good for morale,' said d'Erlanger with a slight grin.

'Really; and who's flying the aircraft?'

'Maureen Dunlop,' he said.

'Well that will give them a nice surprise,' said Margo as she joined d'Erlanger by the window.

At the side of the apron, the five photographers waited, hurriedly preparing their cameras and flashes as the definitive Barracuda came to a halt and cut its single engine. As the cameras raised, the pretty and elegant half-English half-Argentinian, twenty-three-year-old Maureen Adela Chase Dunlop drew back the sliding canopy and slowly climbed down.

As she gracefully walked across the apron towards the sound of clicking photographers and the popping of flashes, she threw her parachute over her shoulder and ran her fingers through her long auburn curly hair.

'Hello boys!' she said.

Twenty-Four

As the lower circle of the sun touched the horizon, reflecting that elusive moment between dream and reality, the entire sky burned in an amber-red glow. The colossal orb threw out only one shade of orange, pure and crisp but with one tiny blemish - a small grey dot which seemed to be getting progressively larger. As the lower half of the sun merged into the horizon the dot remained, but now splitting into two; each shape becoming larger still until gradually the silhouette of two aircraft appeared in formation. Suddenly, they both barrel-rolled away from each other, spinning and turning and then re-forming; a graceful and balletic display of breath-taking aerobatics.

Jackie and Irene were at the controls of two Supermarine Mk 5s Spitfires as they crossed the green and unending hills of the South Downs on the way towards RAF Northolt. The aircraft dived, spun and swooped sideways, as the girls breathed pure exhilaration, replicating each other's manoeuvres, like a baby dolphin following its mother in a clear blue ocean. As they reached the top of a loop in a "Vertical Eight" figure-of-eight manoeuvre, upside-down and with engines at full throttle, Irene tilted her head to see the setting sun behind her.

The aircraft levelled out and continued the remainder of the journey, with Irene and Jackie both calm, mellow and relaxed. 'Better than any meditation', thought Jackie, as the familiar site of the runway at RAF Northolt came into view. The aircraft touched down, one after the other, and were marshalled by the ground crew to an allocated space near the apron. Irene and Jackie sat quiet and still for a few moments, smiling, before pulling open the hatches and hopping down from the aircraft.

The taxi Anson was nowhere to be seen, and as it was the most perfect evening, the girls decided to sit and wait under a huge oak tree at the edge of the airfield. Both were still in the moment, still in the air, still euphoric; and inwardly reluctant to let those feelings pass. As they sat quietly, the airfield around them seemed to drift into a calm reminiscent of another era. The music of the birds and the gentle thrumming of a cricket in the nearby grass was all that could be heard. The moon became visible in the sky and the low evening sun cast its amber glow as they lay relaxed on the grass. The occasional shaft of light pierced the thick green of the oak overhead and the village church spire lit up in the distance like a jewel.

'There is magic in the most unexpected places', said Jackie, as she imprinted the vista into that tiny corner of her memory together with those unforgettable scenes from her earlier experience in the cockpit.

'That was quite possibly the most exciting five minutes of my life,' she continued, as she laid back and closed her eyes, the imprint of the sun's rays still in her vision.

'Me too, said Irene, 'and it may be best if we didn't mention it to anyone'.

'Well I certainly wasn't planning on telling Margo,' said Jackie, laughing.

The girls were laying completely still until Irene broke the silence.

'It's escapism,' she said.

'From what in particular?' asked Jackie.

'Do you know, those few moments in the Spit was the only time, since I heard about Tommy being captured, that I have been truly happy,' said Irene. 'Only a few minutes in almost a year. I miss him.'

'He *will* be back Irene, before you know it, and this damned war will be in the past, and you'll both be happy … married, babies, life … real life. Not this. This is not life.'

'I wish that I could believe that,' said Irene,' but I know that I'll never see him again. I feel it.'

Jackie sat up on one elbow and turned to look at her friend. 'Don't say that Irene. You don't know that, and you can't think like that.'

'But I do.' She paused again, continuing to stare above her before turning to Jackie and smiling: 'You've been a good friend Jackie. Thank you'.

'I hope that I always will be' said Jackie. She felt a sharp pang of sorrow.

The silence was punctuated by the unmistakable splutter of a taxi Anson approaching, and both girls quickly stood up, grabbed their bags and ran towards the apron.

Jackie was worried about her friend.

Twenty-Five

There were some thirty pilots in the busy Crew Room and a variety of languages were being spoken at different tables. Laughing could be heard from the bar and several Polish pilots were singing to Vera Lynn's 'White Cliffs of Dover' which was playing in the background. Most people in the Crew Room had a copy of the Picture Post magazine with Maureen Dunlop on the cover. Someone had hung the page above the bar.

Molly, Mary, Joy, Lettice and Jackie were seated at a corner table and celebrating. Diana, Margie and Irene were noticeably absent.

I can't believe that Pauline Gower actually pulled it off,' said Joy, 'equal pay for female pilots. That's got to be a first!'

'It is indeed,' said Jackie, 'I was reading it in today's papers. The first time in England that women will achieve equal pay to men; and before the Americans too. A fantastic breakthrough. Well done to Pauline! Nice to get some recognition. We'll be flying across the Channel next' she added.

'And congratulations darling Molly on your promotion to First Officer,' said Lettice, 'Well done!'

'Yes, and jolly well done for surviving that crash last week,' said Mary.

'Hear, hear,' chorused all the girls together as they raised their glasses.

'Yes, the Wrekin should be re-named the Wrecking,' said Molly, 'that damned hill destroyed my Swordfish.'

'You are so very droll,' said Mary laughing, 'where the blazes is Irene?' She promised to be here.'

'I was surprised that Margo took it so well,' said Molly, 'thank heavens. I thought that she would be really upset that I had given the RAF something to complain about. And those two RAF chaps who arrived to guard the Swordfish weren't too happy. They had to miss their Saturday evening dance! No doubt I was positively unpopular in their Mess. Fortunately, I

129

called my brother-in-law Monty who is a Flight Lieutenant at Cosford, and he brought two bicycles and so we cycled out for dinner. That was a good way of spending what would otherwise have been a rotten evening.'

'My landlady - and in fact, pretty much most of the village ladies - think that ATA female pilots would be safer at home and in the kitchen,' said Jackie, 'I so hope that she reads the Picture Post. Maybe I'll casually leave my copy laying around.'

'My landlady still thinks I work in the typing pool,' said Joy laughing, 'so I manage to avoid those discussions. I have no idea why she would think a typist would wear gold wings though!'

At that moment, Maureen Dunlop serenely but hesitantly entered the bar and the entire place erupted in deafening cheers and applause. Copies of the Picture Post were waved around like flags and as people stood up from their tables, shouts of 'Well done Maureen!' 'Hurrah for Maureen!' could be heard. Maureen's cheeks flushed a deep pink as she shyly put her hands over her face in embarrassment, before moving swiftly over to the bar where she was warmly greeted by several officers from the RAF. One of them put his arm around her.

Lettice was slightly irritated: 'Now your landlady will probably think we are *all* just glamour-girls like the ATA's new pin-up. We're not damned celebrities. We are bloody-well hard-working pilots.'

'Well I for one am pleased about it,' said Jackie, 'if it gets us a bit more publicity and recognition and encourages other young women to do what we do then it's OK by me. And anyway, I quite fancy being a glamour girl – just for a few days!'

Lettice frowned but the other girls laughed and carried on drinking.

'Well speaking of glamour girls Mary,' continued Jackie, '*someone* is being persistently asked out on a date by that dashing Fleet Air Arm officer at the bar. Why are you just sitting here?'

Mary theatrically put her hand to her forehead: 'Who needs all the torture and consequences of being in love when one can have the ultimate thrill of speeding through the sky piloting the best fighter aircraft in the world.'

'Quite darling, men are mere mortals compared to the Spitfire gods,' said Joy.

Diana entered the room with Margie and, as they approached the table where the girls were seated, it was evident that Diana was in a foul and angry mood, whilst Margie was trying hard not to laugh.

130

'I heard that you are being promoted,' said Diana to Molly, 'well congratu-bloody-lations. I, however, have just been *de*-moted - to Third Officer no less - just because I made a tiny diversion to a friend's house for a spot of lunch during one of last week's ferry trips. Positively ridiculous.' She scowled.

'How unfair that you're not allowed the personal use of your very own Spitfire for your social life,' said Lettice, 'I'd complain vociferously if I were you.'

The girls all laughed and raised their glasses as Diana and Margie sat down with them at the table.

'On the news front,' continued Lettice, 'I had a taxi flight to Scotland yesterday with two Army and Navy commanders and a couple of American senior bods; and I got some very interesting snippets. They were talking about North Africa. It seems that Rommel's Africa Corps is wreaking havoc. It was all a bit hush hush, but from what I could gather, there's going to be a big push to reinforce Malta as the only way to smash Jerry's supply convoys.'

Molly sat rigid in her chair, focussing on every word from Lettice, and was just about to question her more on the subject when Margo entered the Crew Room and approached the table, looking solemn and clearly disturbed. Everyone at the table sensed that something was wrong.

'I am sorry to ruin your promotion celebrations Molly,' said Margo quietly, 'but I wanted you all to hear this from me; I'm so sorry to inform you that Irene Arckless has had a prang in an Airspeed. She survived the crash and was taken to hospital, but she was very badly injured. I'm afraid she didn't make it.'

'Oh my God,' said Jackie after taking a loud deep breath.

The girls were stunned, rigid in silence and all struggling to hold back their emotions. Lettice reached out for Jackie's hand under the table and squeezed hard.

Molly broke the silence: 'What on earth happened?' she asked.

'Engine Failure,' said Margo, 'she was in an Airspeed Oxford AS-10; and crashed shortly after take-off from Cambridge Airport. Looks like a technical fault; by all accounts she tried to make an emergency landing, but the aircraft hit a tree and crashed head-on into a house. Luckily no-one in the house was hurt. Irene's gone I'm afraid. I am so sorry.'

'Please no, not sweet Irene,' said Molly, 'that's all too horrible.'

'She was such a good pilot,' said Joy. 'It's her 28th birthday tomorrow.'

'Poor Irene,' said Lettice, 'who's going to fly to Germany to rescue her fiancée from the POW camp now?'

A solitary tear made its way down Jackie's cheek as she bit hard on her lip. She had not only lost a friend, but a part of herself, and she could hardly get the words out: 'This is a horrible, horrible war,' she said quietly.

'It's all terribly sad,' said Diana to Jackie as she squeezed her hand, 'but it could be any of us at any time … so get a grip old thing. Feelings are for peacetime.'

The girls sat in silence, contemplating the news, as Margo pulled up a chair and sat down next to Jackie. The pilots on the adjacent tables began to notice the all-too-familiar scenario unfolding in the corner and gradually the sounds of the room diminished into near silence, in an eerie contrast to the noisy celebrations of a few minutes earlier.

Mary broke the silence: 'To Irene,' she said, raising her glass.

'To Irene,' repeated all the girls as they stood up; and then, like a thunderous echo which filled the room, every person stood and raised their glass. 'To Irene,' they all said in unison.

Jackie could not hold it in any longer and burst into tears.

Twenty-Six

Mary had stayed with Molly at her digs in Hamble village as neither of them wished to be alone. They had spent much of the night chatting about Irene and sleeping for only a few hours as all pilots had been alerted to an 06:00 call. By the time they arrived at the Ops Room, both girls were feeling the effects of lack of sleep and a deep and lingering sadness that overshadowed every thought. Both wore sunglasses to hide their bloodshot and tired eyes.

They could hardly get through the door of the Ops Room as it was busier and noisier than either of them had ever seen it, with phones ringing continuously and more Ops staff than usual. Even the calm and organised Alison King looked stressed as pilots tried to make their way to the large table at the end of the room to receive their chits. Molly and Mary decided to stand closer to the admin area at the other end of the room until things quietened down and they found a spot in the corner close to Alison's desk.

Molly noticed that Irene's name was being rubbed off the chalkboard. As she saw the letters disappear, the intense sadness from the night before welled up and flooded through her, leaving her almost breathless. She would never see her friend again: never talk with her, laugh with her, fly with her…Mary tapped Molly on the arm and she snapped out of her thoughts. Without saying anything, Mary looked at Molly and then swiftly darted her eyes to Alison's desk in an effort to draw Molly's attention to a map which was half-exposed under some papers.

Mary smiled at Molly, and then calmly looked around the room to make sure that no-one was looking in their direction, as Molly moved slightly in front of Mary, sensing what she was about to do. Mary slowly and cautiously moved the papers to reveal a map which showed all RAF air bases in the UK. Multiple arrowed lines converged on Shieldhall on the River Clyde, and someone had written in bold red letters … "USS Wasp".

'Whatever this is, it's huge,' whispered Mary, as she quickly covered the map back up, and tried to look inconspicuous, as Joy was walking in their direction.

'Are you both OK?' said Joy, 'You don't look OK. Such a horrid evening. There's a bit of a flap on today,' she continued, changing the subject, 'Urgent tasking apparently and all very hush hush. My chit is pretty much the same as everyone else's this morning. it's a 'P1 W' - "Priority 1 - Wait" - Ferry Spitfire to Scotland.'

The crowd began to disperse, and Molly and Mary moved towards the table, as Margie, Jackie and Diana shuffled past them in the other direction. Alison saw Molly and Mary approaching and reached on to the table to pick up their chits and handed each to the girls.

'I'm so sorry to hear about Irene,' said Alison.

'Thank you,' said Molly and Mary together.

'Is this hubbub because of Malta?' Molly asked Alison.

'Can't say I'm afraid.' said Alison. 'All I know is we're tasked to collect a number of Spits – about fifty it appears - from around the country and to fly them up to Scotland. We've been tasked to drop them into Renfrew.'

Molly and Mary walked over to join Margie, Jackie and Diana, as Molly looked at her chit. 'This is a bit odd,' she said, 'I'm taking an operational Spit from a squadron in Kent – I'll not be popular – they need as many as they can get.'

'I have a "P1 - Wait" Spit to Scotland,' said Margie, 'same as everyone else it seems. This must be serious; but with this forecast we're going to have a devil of a job finding a weather window. We might have to stay on the bases for days to make sure that we can deliver them all on time.'

'At least the P1 status means that we'll not be bound by weather limitations and can proceed at our own discretion,' said Mary, 'I hate waiting around just because of a drop of rain.'

'Alison said that about fifty Spits are being flown into Renfrew,' said Molly.

'Fifty? Really?' said Jackie, who looked in the same condition as Molly and Mary. 'That's nearly four squadrons. It must be important.'

'God Almighty. Renfrew?' said Diana, 'it has the tiniest little landing run ... the approaches are hell, even when the wind is on your side. Why on earth aren't we going into somewhere sensible – like Turnhouse?'

'Renfrew is very close to the docks in Glasgow,' said Margie, 'maybe they're off on their travels by ship?'

'Who knows?' said Diana, 'in any case, ours is not to reason why - needs must dear thing, needs must.'

Molly and Mary looked at each other without saying anything. Having seen the map on Alison's desk, Molly sensed that what she was about to do was exactly what she had been praying for.

The girls wished each other good luck and said their farewells, and after a few moments, the Ops Room was again peaceful and quiet as the girls ran in different directions towards the parachute room and the apron, where several taxi Ansons and Fairchilds were waiting. The taxi aircraft took off one after the other in rapid succession and were all in the air within minutes, heading in different directions.

***

Molly climbed into the cockpit of a Spitfire Vb at RAF Manston, which is located at the most easterly point of Kent on the Isle of Thanet. As she settled in, her thoughts raced at an incredible speed; wild horses tearing through her mind leaving her heart pounding. 'This is it.' she thought. The opportunity that she had waited for since saying goodbye to Bernard; the opportunity to fulfil her promise…

A number of scenarios about the current taskings had been playing out in Molly's head for the past few hours, many of which she did not fully realise, but she was slowly piecing together the various snippets of information from conversations, Pathé newsreels, the newspapers and those few letters that leapt off the map like a thunderbolt … USS Wasp. The last was the final piece of the jigsaw puzzle that connected Molly and her Spitfire to Bernard. She felt like a guardian; with a mission of great importance and with enormous consequences.

RAF Manston was situated on rising ground and usually free of the occasional fog that sometimes caused difficulty at other airbases. It also had minimal approach obstructions. Despite this, Molly did not like the airbase and was always uncomfortable flying in, and relieved to be flying out.

Being situated on the Kent coast and close to the front line, the airfield had become the closest and easiest point for badly damaged aircraft to land after returning from across the Channel. It was the final stop for many aircraft that had suffered from air attack, ground fire or collisions, and given that the salvageable parts were stripped for other Allied aircraft in need of repair, the airbase had become a graveyard for heavy bombers and the like. Molly preferred looking across the Channel, where on a clear day, the coast of France could be seen, rather than looking down at what she considered to be a cold and frightening reminder of how a mission can go terribly wrong.

As her Spitfire soared into the air, Molly had not felt quite so much enthusiasm for several months. The views over the English Channel were eerily peaceful, albeit through a scattering of low grey cloud which cloaked the airfield as she circled overhead. Molly pulled a map out of her boot and spread it on her knees, looking for the railway lines below.

'Righty-o - step one - let's find some landmarks.'

No sooner than Molly had levelled out at her desired altitude, she noticed in her rear-view mirror a speck approaching fast from across the Channel, and it seemed to be getting bigger. Molly flashed back to her narrow escape from the rogue Luftwaffe Messerschmitt only a few months before, and how narrowly she came close to being shot down.

'Oh, please no. Not again,' she said, 'I have nothing to fight you off with.'

As the object approached, Molly nervously banked left, slightly lowered her altitude, and looked back and up to see what it was. 'God, you're fast,' she said.

'Bloody hell. It's a buzz-bomb!'

The dark black silhouette of the V-1 Flying Bomb, or "Doodlebug" as they were commonly known, sped towards her on its murderous journey.

'Where are you going? … It's either the docks or central London,' she said … 'Well, wherever it is, we shall see about that.'

Molly knew that she had only a few seconds to react, as the speed of the V-1 Flying Bomb was much faster than her Spitfire, and she quickly made a decision to try to wing-tip it off course. Molly increased her speed and came up at approximately the same altitude as the V-1, which was rapidly approaching from behind, so that it would pass on her right side. The V-1's engine started pop-popping and it miraculously and fortunately slowed, indicating that it would soon fall to the ground. Molly quickly realised that it was heading for the London docks.

Using all her skill, Molly positioned herself so that the V-1 would come slightly above and close to her right wing and, as the terrifying black mass flew alongside, she manoeuvred her wing tip to within inches of the buzz bomb's left wing. In what seemed like a split-second opportunity, Molly prayed that she was not making the biggest mistake of her life. The dire consequences of her failing in her mission flashed like a bolt from the skies.

Molly tipped her wing so that the two aircraft connected. The noise and shudder were a lot more than Molly expected, and she stopped breathing for a few moments, uneasy in the thought that she was perhaps doing more harm than good. But it seemed to work as the V-1 suddenly veered off course and into a rapid descent towards the cold grey-blue water of the River Medway estuary. A trail of black smoke emerged from the descending V-1 and Molly banked around to see it crash in the water.

Molly was elated, and feeling even more committed, as she flew further across the Surrey Hills and then over the North Wessex Downs towards Colerne. The further west she flew, the foggier the weather became, and Molly was glad to see the familiar sight of the airfield at RAF Colerne, whereupon she lined up for her landing run.

As Molly touched down, the weather seemed to be closing in even more, as three ground engineers rushed to the aircraft in what she thought was more haste than usual. The signs confirmed that this mission was indeed special. She was assisted from the cockpit by one of the engineers as his colleagues carefully looked over the aircraft. He was a young lad of about twenty-two, and full of cheerfulness and enthusiasm.

'Thank you ma'am,' he said, 'We have a quick turnaround on this as she is about to be fitted out with a full complement of instruments and weapons before continuing to Renfrew, hopefully that is, if the weather clears.'

'How many Spits have arrived so far?' said Molly.

'You are only the third ma'am – probably due to fog. We do know that at least two others have been reported as missing, but very little info is available. Perhaps they are just late ma'am.'

'Better late than never,' said Molly. 'They've probably diverted somewhere as the weather was not great on the way in - in fact, I may well be here until it clears. Please let me know if you hear anything. I'm popping to the Mess for a spot of lunch.'

'Will do, ma'am,' he said.

Molly was visibly anxious as she headed towards the Mess. The fog had thickened, and it began to rain. Ever since she could remember, Molly had always hated it when elements out of her control hindered a task. It went totally against her grain and her strong willpower to get the job done no matter what the obstacles. To say that she was now frustrated would be a gross understatement; she was not only furious at the weather, but also deeply concerned for her friends who should have landed before her.

Suddenly she heard the distinctive sound of a Merlin engine and looked up to see another Spitfire coming through the fog to land.

'Thank heavens,' she said breathing a sigh of relief, 'whoever you are'.

Molly entered the Officer's Mess, which was full of male officers in uniform. About twenty people were seated at the tables and a hush fell over the room, with officers staring at the young female in a pilot's uniform. Molly looked around for a place to sit, spotting a table with one other person on the far side which necessitated walking down the middle aisle of the Mess. She was almost at the table as the surrounding officers spoke quietly amongst themselves as they glanced towards her, when the Mess Manager tapped her on the shoulder. Molly turned around to see a middle-aged man dressed in uniform, who spoke quietly to Molly; practically whispering in her ear.

'Good day Miss,' he said, 'I think you'll be much more comfortable in the Ladies Room. I'll have one of the stewards come and take your order. This way please.'

The Mess was almost silent as he ushered Molly through a side door and into a small and chintzy room with one table and four chairs. It was empty. The walls were covered in a dull lime green wallpaper and the only window had no view, looking out onto the wall of the adjacent wooden hut. There was also a slight smell of damp and Molly thought that the room had perhaps not been used for some time.

'We won't keep you a moment, Miss,' he said as he promptly disappeared back through the door, as the hubbub of the Mess dining room gradually became louder in the background.

***

Pauline Gower was in the Ops Room at the ATA Ferry Pool No.15 at Hamble, standing between two harassed-looking Ops Officers, who were seated at their desks, and each with a phone in their hand. The boards on the walls were being updated by a busy clerk and showed a number of Spitfires grounded due to the weather. Pauline was one of the few people who knew the full extent and importance of the current operation and being that Stage One fell squarely on the shoulders of the ATA, she was naturally concerned.

'… Look, you need to get on to them for an update,' she said, '… when is it likely they'll get airborne? … so far less than half have arrived, you say? … and we've lost two? … any news on their whereabouts?

The tone of Pauline's voice was making the Ops Officers slightly nervous as they spoke tersely on the phones, scribbling notes for the clerk to update the movements board.

'And what's the forecast?' continued Pauline, 'can anybody re-route to avoid that front? … The Ministry wants a firm update on when we're going to have them all in, as there's a whole flotilla bobbing about in the Clyde waiting for us.'

'That's another two arrived ma'am,' said Alison, 'and four are reported airborne and in transit, ETA 1300 hours. Nothing on the 2 strays yet.'

***

At RAF Colerne, the rain was hammering down onto four Spitfires parked on the grass adjacent to a wooden hut at the side of the airstrip. A bright orange and rain-soaked wind-sock was flapping wildly in the strongly gusting wind. Inside the sparsely decorated hut, two Ops Officers sat at one end, their desks covered with papers, both frantically dialling phone numbers, answering calls and scribbling; then repeating the process over and over again. Screwed-up pieces of papers littered the floor around them and the smell of pipe smoke and coffee filled the air.

At the other end of the room, Molly and Joy sat in two leather easy chairs which looked as though they had seen better days, distractedly turning the pages of well-thumbed magazines and neither reading nor looking at the pictures. Coffee cups and newspapers were scattered on the low wooden tables which really were on their last legs, and an old iron stove was burning in the corner.

Even though the room was small, the sound of the wind and rain as it pounded on the roof and windows rendered the conversations of the Ops Officers inaudible.

Two male ATA pilots were pacing up and down and smoking pipes, one of whom Molly recognised as Stewart Keith-Jopp; the legendary First World War ace. Stewart had lost an arm and his left eye, yet he was one of the most revered pilots of the ATA. As Molly glanced at him, she wondered if the stories about him were true. It was often said that upon being refused a position in the RAF due to his disability, Stewart stormed into the RAF Central Flying School at Upavon and refused to leave until they gave him a flight test. His subsequent demonstration of skill and expertise in a Harvard was so perfect that the instructor had no option but to pass him with flying colours.

Molly watched as he stopped pacing to peer out of the rain-spattered window. She could feel that he was just as desperate to get into the air as she was. The rain and wind calmed for a few seconds, and Molly focussed on the conversations at the other end of the room.

'No, sorry, we are still on weather hold,' said one of the Ops Officers. 'Forecast shows the situation easing though as this front moves over … Yes, they know the urgency. We'll hopefully have a break in the next couple of hours … Yes, we'll look at a re-route but then they'll have to refuel. We'll keep you posted.'

'I can't believe they dumped you on your own for lunch,' said Joy, interrupting Molly's eavesdropping, 'no wonder you didn't stay in there for long.'

'I would have had the food been any good,' said Molly, 'but it was on about the same level as the hospitality'.

The sound of the rain picked up again and both Molly and Joy looked towards the window.

'If Mary were here, even weather like this couldn't stop her,' said Joy.

'Mary is out there somewhere, and I'm worried about her,' said Molly, 'but I'm also worried about the consequences of not delivering these Spits; I'm sure they are bound for Malta, and I have a promise to keep. One more hour of this, and then I'm going.'

'Me too,' said Joy.

Twenty-Seven

Against a leaden grey sky, a heavy mist had settled over the Shieldhall dockyard on the River Clyde in Scotland. The gloom of the morning rendered the scene devoid of colour as hundreds of dock workers went about their usual routines. Many of these resilient and patriotic men had already sustained incredible loss due to the heavy ongoing aerial bombardment of their towns and homes. Yet each day, they travelled to work in a place that was one of the Luftwaffe's most sought-after targets. Stoically fulfilling their duties and fully aware of their importance to the overall war machine, the men were nevertheless oblivious to the reasons for, and the outgoing destinations of, the cargo which they handled. Day after day their routine continued; bland and non-descriptive boxes, crates and containers hoisted and lowered by cranes, loading and unloading to huge, hulking ships, waiting like iron monoliths on the dock.

It was therefore no surprise at the elation and excitement of this indispensable group of individuals when out of the mist appeared a fleet of massive lorries moving in convoy along the dockside past waiting ships; each truck carrying a Spitfire. The reactions from the men ranged from cheers and applause to salutes and the removal of hats. Some stood still in amazement at the scene, some stood silent in a moment of reflection, and some stood with tears in their eyes; all of them sensed that they were about to contribute even more to the nation's quest to maintain its freedom.

The lorries moved carefully to park beneath three huge cranes, as the dock workers moved urgently, shouting orders and instructions as they attached lifting slings under the fuselage and wings of the aircraft. One by one the Spitfires were winched gently into the air, steadied by men at the end of long ropes. Each aircraft swung ever so slowly over the side of the bulky waiting ship; and each was carefully lowered onto the deck.

The mist lifted quicker than usual as four more Spitfires flew low over the dockyard with their wheels lowered on a landing run to a nearby unseen airfield. The dull grey of the morning was gradually replaced by brightness and colour which elevated the pulse of the dockyard, and which reflected in the joyful and energetic mood of the men. As the mist parted, the full enormity and splendour of the ship slowly revealed itself to the onlooking workers. Across the American aircraft carrier was emblazoned *USS Wasp*.

A few hours later, the magnificent ship with multiple Spitfires lined up wing-tip to wing-tip on her deck was escorted by a flotilla of war-ships as it cut through the cold water of the Clyde on its way to the Atlantic, and thereafter to Malta.

Twenty-Eight

The day after returning from Scotland, Molly had been assigned a Gloster Gladiator biplane fighter from Cambridge to RAF Little Rissington in the Cotswolds. Molly adored the Gladiator and thought it like a Tiger Moth but with much more comfort and power. It featured an enclosed cockpit and possessed a top speed of over 250 miles per hour.

Just before Molly left the Ops Room, she was handed a telegram. With no time to stop, she clutched the envelope and ran out to the waiting taxi Fairchild on the apron. Molly was naturally concerned and could feel the tension rising in her chest as she reached the aircraft. For those with loved ones on active duty, receiving a telegram provoked apprehension and dread, their first thought "What if...?" . Molly embarked the Fairchild, said a quick 'Hallo' to Douglas, and then quickly and nervously strapped herself in before tearing open the envelope and reading the words. It was from her brother Arthur; asking her to call home as soon as possible.

Molly gave a gasp of frustration. There would be no opportunity to use a telephone until later in the evening and that depended on what time she would get back from the last ferry task of the day. Molly resigned herself to a long and anxious wait. But more importantly, why was Arthur asking her to call? She had spoken to him only a few days prior, and all was fine. As the flight got underway and she mulled over a host of possible scenarios in her head, Molly's mood became one of increasing concern.

As the day went on, it seemed to Molly that it would never end. She was mentally exhausted from overthinking Arthur's message, yet trying to simultaneously focus on the Gladiator and thereafter the two additional taskings which she was assigned. When she finally pulled open the door of the phone box in Hamble-le-Rice village later that evening, and breathing heavily from having cycled as fast as she could from the ferry pool, Molly watched her fingers shake as she made three attempts to dial the number to Whitehill.

Arthur picked up the phone immediately.

'Arthur, it's me,' said Molly, 'I received your telegram. Is everything OK?'

'I don't want you to panic Molly,' said Arthur in a tone which Molly instantly recognised as out of character. He was clearly shaken. 'Everyone is OK, but we've had quite the incident here.'

Molly was trembling, and could not bring herself to say anything more, and so she waited for Arthur to continue.

'Unfortunately, an aircraft took off from Cambridge Airport and crashed into the house,' he said.

Molly took a long and loud deep breath, and she had to steady herself by placing her hand on the wall of the phone box.

'It was an Oxford,' continued Arthur, 'apparently the pilot attempted to make an emergency landing, but the aircraft first hit one of the trees in the arboretum and finished up with its nose in the window of the back bedroom which was occupied at the time by your sister Margery and baby Susan, and the nanny was there too.'

'Oh my God,' cried Molly, as she crouched down until she was sitting on the floor of the phone box, shaking.

'They're all fine Molly,' continued Arthur, 'Thank God they're safe. I had to batter down the bedroom door to get them all out, and it's a miracle that there was no fire or explosion and no-one in the family was injured. The tail of the aircraft landed within a few feet of Mary's baby, who was asleep in his pram under the small laburnum tree which was uprooted by one of the wings of the aircraft. Nicholas is fine, don't worry. He slept right through it.'

'This is like something from a nightmare,' said Molly, as she struggled to get the words out.

'The back part of the house is a bit of a mess, but the damage is not anywhere near as bad as it could have been. Someone up there must be looking over us Molly.'

'What happened to the pilot?' asked Molly.

'The pilot was taken to Addenbrooke's Hospital in Cambridge,' said Arthur, 'but was unfortunately pronounced dead on arrival. Actually, she was one of your girls from the ATA.'

Molly went cold; the thought had already started to cross her mind.

'Apparently, her name was Irene ... Irene Arckless'

144

Molly slowly dropped the hand that held the telephone receiver and with her other hand, she covered her mouth to stifle the uncontrollable sobs rising up from her core. As the tears streamed down her face, Molly could only repeat Irene's name over and over, the shock rendering her oblivious to Arthur at the other end of the line. It was several minutes before she comprehended the full extent of the conversation and even then she was on the verge of complete disbelief.

Twenty-Nine

Molly, Diana, Lettice, Mary, Joy and Jackie were all seated at a table in the Crew Room at the ATA Ferry Pool No.15 at Hamble. The room seemed to be even more crowded than usual due to additional pilots and administrative staff, some of whom had been recruited from overseas. The general mood was solemn; most pilots were tired after the long day's deliveries and from the multiple ferry flights of the previous week.

After returning from Scotland, the girls had been thrust into further long days, sometimes with four or five ferry tasks. Journeys were to all parts of the United Kingdom; the initial dawn delivery followed by a second and third, interspersed with taxi Anson flights and sometimes culminating in a return to Hamble only to be given yet another task to the north. Day after day, aircraft were either collected from factories and ferried to Maintenance Units where alterations were made or armaments added, or picked up from the "MUs" and flown to front line units where they would be put into action.

The late-night return journeys were often on crowded trains without sleeper berths and if they were lucky enough to get a seat, the exhausted girls were able to take a nap sitting upright. The work was hard, relentless, and without the glamour that the public had been led to believe.

Despite the tiredness, the six girls were happy in each other's company as they watched two Polish pilots adding their names in white paint to the blackout curtain in the Crew Room, which already contained the names of most of the ATA pilots.

'How are your family?' said Mary to Molly.

'Still in shock I think, as am I,' said Molly, 'I'm still struggling to understand it all.'

'Such an awful and bizarre coincidence,' said Joy.

'My sisters are still shaken up.' said Molly, 'Three of them have moved out of the house, and my fourth sister Mary is talking about returning to her old home. My brother Arthur is making plans to repair the damage but that will take a while, no doubt. I haven't seen it of course, and actually I don't want to. I think that I'll never be able to go into that room again.'

'It's a miracle that everyone in your family survived,' said Jackie, 'I've heard about some unusual things since joining the ATA but that just about tops everything'.

'I don't want to think about it,' said Molly, 'can we talk about something else … have you heard anything more about our trip to Scotland?'

'I don't know why the Renfrew operation was called a "Club Run"', said Diana, 'I would rather be running to another type of club at this very moment - the Embassy, the Astor or the 400 Club to be exact.'

The girls raised their eyes and grinned at one another.

'I would rather be flying one of those Spits off the *Wasp* and into Malta,' said Mary.

'Did you know that they had to fit them all with external fuel tanks to extend their range?' said Jackie.

'I don't know what we were thinking - flying through that weather,' said Joy. 'I heard that there was a mid-air collision, and that miraculously the pilots survived.'

'All our hopes for Malta and North Africa were sitting on that one aircraft carrier,' said Molly. 'I made a promise to Bernard - and those Spits are part of that promise.'

'Oh, I doubt if the *Wasp* was alone,' said Lettice, 'surely she was surrounded by escorts – don't you think?'

Margo entered with a small satchel and slowly made her way through the room from table to table, chatting with various individuals, all of whom were happy for the chance to engage with her. Molly noticed that Margo's eyes kept darting over to their table, and she sensed that something was not quite right. Margo headed over towards them.

'Evening everyone,' said Margo, as she stood beside Molly and handed her two letters. 'Sorry it's a bit tardy, we had a late mail run today. Thought you'd appreciate your letters. Molly, both of yours are marked urgent.'

Molly was deeply concerned, as Margo handed out letters to the other girls.

'Please no more bad news,' said Molly to herself as she tore open the first letter, 'It's from Bernard's pal, Fruity,' and then she read aloud.

'My dearest Molly, I'm in the Queen Alexandra Military Hospital in Millbank. My nurse is writing this letter because I'm in a bit of a bad way; can't actually hold a pen. You may have already heard, but if not, I'm so sorry to be the first to tell you that Bernard's tank was hit, and I think he was one of those that didn't make it.'

Molly dropped the letter into her lap and stared blankly ahead; the colour drained slowly from her face as she tried with all her might not to burst into tears. Margo put her arms on Molly's shoulders and Diana pulled her chair closer. No-one said a word, as they were all looking at the second letter which Molly had placed on the table, and which was clearly marked "The War Office". Molly gathered her composure and quickly tore open the second letter.

'I don't believe it…it can't be true…surely not…' she whispered gently, her voice breaking. Molly was shaking as she unfolded the letter.

'It's from The War Office … Dear Mrs Rose … I am directed to inform you with much regret that notification has been received from the 4th Royal County of London Yeomanry that Captain B W G Rose has been reported missing, believed killed. I am to express sympathy of the Department for the anxiety this communication must necessarily cause you.'

Molly stared down at the letters in her lap, unable to speak and, for a moment, forgetting to breathe. The other girls thought she might pass out as they moved even closer to support her. Molly's face registered the devastation so clearly and so utterly; like a mirror to her heart which seemed to her to be breaking in two; a literal, physical sensation that she felt in her chest. The shock resounded around the table, and then very quickly, as if by osmosis, around the room. Someone turned off the music.

'I am so very sorry Molly,' said Margo. 'I wish that I could do something more than ask you to take a few days off.'

Molly's face was blank, barely registering Margo's words as she continued to stare at the letters. Her hands were shaking. Mary gently put her hand over them to steady them.

Margo continued: 'Mary, would you kindly stay with Molly until … '

Margo was interrupted by Alison King who had hurriedly walked over to the group, unaware of the unfolding tragedy that had consumed all around the table. Alison looked at Molly and sensed what had happened.

'Ma'am,' said Alison, 'we've just heard that all forty-eight delivered Spitfires were destroyed by the Luftwaffe at Malta's Ta'Quali Airfield pretty much as soon as they arrived off the *Wasp*. There's talk of another run.'

'After all that effort?' said Margo, as she squeezed Molly's shoulders again, 'Someone will be paying bloody hell for this.'

'Hell's teeth,' said Diana.

Molly stood up abruptly, much to the surprise of the other girls. She straightened her uniform and surreptitiously wiped a tear from her eye.

'With respect ma'am,' she said, 'surely we'll need to replace those Spits, and if there's going to be another mission, I would like to …' she paused, '*I need* to - be a part of it …' her voice was breaking, 'Please Margo?'

'We'll see Molly,' said Margo, 'I think you might need some time before we can make that decision.'

'I understand Margo,' said Molly, lifting her chin, 'but I'll be fine. Honestly, I will. But until you decide, would you mind if I take a trip to London early tomorrow to visit Bernard's friend – it seems as though he's in a bad way in hospital? I'll be back by this time tomorrow evening.'

Thirty

Molly entered the reception area of the Queen Alexandra Military Hospital at Millbank in London. Her eyes were red and she was still in a daze, not yet fully comprehending her new reality; a shift in the tectonic plates of her world. She had spent the previous night at Mary's digs in Hamble and had called her family, who had gathered together when they heard the news. Molly spoke with Arthur and then with her sister Mary, who had always provided great comfort when most needed. It was her sister's strength that had consoled Molly, and Arthur too, as he took the news of Bernard's death badly.

Mary quickly travelled down from Cambridgeshire to see Molly before the visit to the hospital. They had chatted for a few hours in a small coffee shop near Millbank, where Mary decided to wait whilst Molly saw Edward. Molly summoned every ounce of courage to walk into the entrance of the hospital, knowing what she was about to encounter. She held Edward's letter as she approached the reception desk.

'Hallo,' she said, as she showed the letter to the nurse behind reception, 'I'm here to see Captain Egerton-Reed - he was admitted a couple of weeks ago'

'Ah yes,' said the nurse, 'he'll still be on the ward. Ward 10 - along the corridor to your right, follow the signs.'

Molly hesitantly entered the ward. The rows of beds were full, and there were patients in wheelchairs and on crutches, some at the side of the beds and others chatting in a small group at the end of the ward. Some looked at Molly as she entered and she felt a stab of sadness, not knowing if she should smile. Nurses moved around carrying trays and various medical supplies, some attending to the men who seemed to be most injured, many with missing limbs. One of the nurses looked up at Molly as she wiped the head

150

of a patient; his chest covered with a blood-stained bandage. The sounds of groaning came from every direction and Molly tried to block them out as she walked further into the ward. It was the most distressing and uncomfortable scene, and Molly promised herself never to complain about flying the air-ambulance again.

She was approached by the Ward Sister, and Molly quickly focussed on looking her directly in the eyes, rather than at the collection of small blood stains on her uniform. With unsteady hands, Molly pulled the letter out of the envelope as the nurse gave her a warm smile and gently touched her on the elbow. The Ward Sister looked at the letter and pointed to a bed at the end of the ward.

Edward Egerton-Reed was lying in bed, slightly propped up. He was unrecognisable. His upper body was swathed in bandages and a large, tented cover was spread over his legs. Only half of his face was showing and as Molly walked towards the bed, she could see that he had been severely burned.

For a brief moment, Molly wondered if she had the strength to do this. She hesitated before reaching the bed and stood around twenty feet away; her mind whirling with emotions, a part of her wanting to turn around and leave the hospital. She could feel herself slowly beginning to back away, as if she were not in control of her movement, an instinctual fear rising inside her. Then she heard Edward's rasping voice.

'Molly. Molly,' said Edward, struggling to speak, 'It's me, Fruity. Over here.'

Molly's heart was beating fast as she walked towards Edward's bed. The closer she came, the more disfiguration she could see on his face.

'Hallo Fruity,' she said, nervously.

'You came.' said Edward, struggling to get the words out and as he tried to lift his head, 'I am so sorry Molly. So very, very sorry.'

'Oh Fruity, please try not to move,' said Molly, as she sat on a stool by the side of the bed, 'I spoke with the nurses. They said that you'll be OK. It might take a while, but you'll be OK.'

'I'll never be OK Molly.'

'But thank God you made it Fruity. It must have been hell.'

'It was hell, and such a mess - and then all a blank - until I woke up here.'

'Is there anything that I can get you,' asked Molly.

'A taxi would be nice, Molly, to get me out of here'.

Molly smiled weakly and noticed that Edward's voice was filled with sadness; so different to his usual jovial humour that had always made her laugh. Now that seemed like a world away and the look on the visible area of his face was one of desperation and fear.

'You'll be home in no time Fruity, she said, 'has Elisabeth been to see you?'

Edward said nothing and turned his head slightly away.

'What is it?' said Molly, 'has she been here?'

'No, Molly,' he said, 'Elisabeth won't be coming in, I don't want her here, seeing me like this. She doesn't even know that I'm here. I wrote to her yesterday, or at least one of the nurses did it for me. I told her that it's over between us and to forget about me.' He paused, 'I'll never be the man that I was, Molly - the man that she wanted to marry.'

'Oh Fruity,' said Molly now in tears, 'I think that you underestimate just how strong and loyal Elisabeth is, and most of all, how much she loves you, no matter what condition you're in. She would never turn her back on you Fruity ... never.'

'Can we talk about something else Molly, please,' implored Edward.

'Of course,' she said, wiping away her tears, 'if you feel up to it, please tell me what happened in the desert. I need to know, but only if you're OK talking about it.'

'It's all a bit of a blur actually Molly' ... he paused ... 'I can remember that we were in the desert, west of Tobruk, and moving up for another battle near the Egyptian border ... our tanks were advancing through the scrub, firing continually on Jerry's on-coming tanks. Shells were whistling in from everywhere and exploding all around us ... the noise was deafening ... I saw two tanks hit by a shell exploding between them and the crews scrambled from the turrets ... and one of the tanks erupted in flames ... it was Bernard's tank ... it took a direct hit and I saw it burst into flames. We were moving forward and firing continually so we had to press on. We chased Jerry for miles ... but there was a huge explosion ... and then everything turned red...'

Molly had tears in her eyes again as she reached out her hand to touch Edward but then withdrew it, quickly realising that wherever she placed her hand - and no matter how softly - she would probably cause him extreme pain.

'I had to leave him behind,' he continued, 'I had no choice Molly, and all I could think about was going back for him. I know I told you I would keep an eye on him - but then everything just went blank, and I couldn't feel my legs. I couldn't move. I'm so sorry Molly … but I just couldn't move.'

Tears began to run down Edwards's face and Molly brought a hand up to her mouth to cover it; stifling the sobs that rose up within her. Edward saw that Molly was crying and tried to gather his composure in an effort to calm her.

Molly leant closer to him. 'I am so glad that you're alive, Fruity. You are going to get through this, and you're going to be back on your feet in no time. Thank you for the letter. I know how difficult that was to write.'

'Will you forgive me Molly?'

'Please don't say that. There is nothing to forgive.'

After spending a few more minutes at Edward's bedside, Molly left the ward and after wandering aimlessly around the corridors for several minutes, managed to find her way to the hospital lobby.

She felt utterly empty and drained of emotion. Her eyes were drowsy and she could barely lift her feet, as if every ounce of energy had dissipated. As she walked out of the hospital door and into the street, the fresh air almost knocked her over and she had to steady herself against a wall. It took some minutes for Molly to get her bearings and to remember where the coffee shop was and that her sister was waiting for her.

After a few minutes of navigating around the streets of war-torn Millbank, Molly entered the coffee shop and Mary quickly stood up from the table and walked over to meet her.

'Oh my gosh Molly,' said Mary, 'you look terrible, come and sit down. I'll order you some sweet tea.'

'I may need something stronger,' said Molly, as she sat down.

'Well it's only tea or coffee here, I'm afraid,' said Mary, 'and it's far too early in the afternoon, so will you settle for strong tea with honey?

'Fine,' said Molly.

'How is Edward?', said Mary.

'It's worse than I thought, and on so many levels Mary. He's in a bad way and God only knows how long it will take for him to get back to normal…I mean…' Molly faltered '…a semblance of normal…' She gazed down at the table, the image of Fruity lying in bed seared onto her mind. 'He's so frightened, and that was the saddest thing to see.' Molly paused. 'He told me about Bernard. It's all too horrible to even talk about Mary, and in one way I wish that I hadn't heard it ... poor Bunny.'

The waitress brought over a tray of tea, and the sisters sat and chatted, mostly about Edward and Bernard and then about the family, and then Molly's work at the ATA. It was the first time in over a year that Molly had the chance to spend time alone with her beloved sister, reinforcing in Molly's mind the importance of family; not only to help her through this awful situation but also in the years ahead, whatever they may bring.

'Are you coming back to Cambridge with me?' asked Mary.

'I can't,' said Molly, 'I'll make my way back to Hamble this evening, but before that, I need to visit someone in London.'

***

Molly and Mary parted company in the early evening, and after a tearful farewell, Molly walked north along the River Thames and then down Horse Guards Avenue to the junction with Whitehall. There on the corner was a large and somewhat oddly shaped neo-Baroque building with four distinctive domes; a later addition that creatively disguised the unusual trapezium shape of this most famous landmark. The War Office was a Department of the British Government, and responsible for the administration of the British Army. It was also the place of work of one of Molly's closest friends, Elisabeth Hemsworth, the fiancée of Edward Egerton-Reed.

Earlier that afternoon, Molly had surprised Elisabeth with a phone call and a request to meet for tea after Elisabeth had finished her work. Elisabeth was delighted to hear from Molly and was unaware of any news regarding Edward and the situation soon to confront her. When Elisabeth finally finished at her work, they met outside the War Office entrance, which was heavily secured with guards and barricades. As Molly watched Elisabeth walk towards her, she thought how happy she looked; a huge smile lighting up her pretty face and Molly captured that moment and stored it in her mind, knowing that Elizabeth's life was about to change forever and wondering if she would ever be the same after Molly's words. Elisabeth hugged Molly tightly, but as she released her hold and looked into Molly's eyes, her smile evaporated in an instant, her brow wrinkling into a frown and her mouth opening slightly to form words but hesitating; waiting for Molly to say something.

Molly took her arm and they quickly crossed Whitehall and made their way through the small alley alongside the Horse Guards building, and out into the beautiful green and open space of St. James's Park where they could breathe freely.

'What is it Molly?' said Elisabeth, 'Something is wrong. Please just say it.'

'Two things,' said Molly, but first you need to know that Edward is going to be OK.'

Elisabeth could hardly breathe, and she held Molly's arm as she felt her knees buckle underneath her. Molly helped her down to the grass and they sat in the outer shade of a huge oak as Molly held Elisabeth's hand.

'They were both involved in something quite unfortunate in the desert,' continued Molly, 'and Edward is in the hospital ... but Bernard is gone. His tank was hit and he was killed.'

It took every ounce of courage for Molly to utter those words to her friend, and to elaborate on what had happened to the two men who meant more to them than anyone or anything else in the world.

'Oh my God, Molly,' said Elisabeth, as she sat quietly, tearful and stunned.

Thirty-One

Early the following morning, several pilots entered the Ops Room at Hamble. Molly was among them. The previous evening, Molly had called Margo from a phone box in London and had used every ounce of energy and persuasiveness to convince Margo that she was ready to join her colleagues the following morning.

For most of the conversation, it looked as though Molly's plea would be rejected; Margo explaining that it was too soon after the news about Bernard and asking Molly that she give herself more time to recover. Molly had all but given up when she remembered the words from their conversation outside the sick bay after Molly's plane crash.

'With respect ma'am, you said that I was exactly the type of person that you hoped to find; courage under pressure, a beacon of hope for all females…' Molly went on: 'You said that women are looking to us to change things…How can I let those women down now? Haven't they also suffered losses just as I have and they still have to carry on?…I haven't changed Margo, I'm still the person you were looking for…'

Molly was desperate and could feel her voice beginning to break, which was the last thing she needed. As she breathed deeply and composed herself, there was a long, drawn-out silence at the other end of the line, during which Molly held her breath and shut her eyes.

Then Margo's voice was clear, slow and decisive at the other end: 'Very well Molly. See you in the morning.'

★★★

As the girls assembled in the Ops Room, they could feel the sense of urgency given the frantic pace of the Ops Crew, and the look on Alison King's face.

156

'Today we launch Operation Bowery to replace the Spitfires destroyed in Malta,' said Alison, 'your chits will give you your pick-ups, and the delivery location is once again Renfrew. I'm sure that you already know why you are doing this. The success of this mission is vital to stop Malta from falling into enemy hands. And I don't need to tell you how important Malta is for our chaps in North Africa. Good luck.'

Jane Winstone and another pilot approached Molly.

'We all heard about your husband Molly,' said Jane, 'I am so sorry.'

'Thank you, Jane,' said Molly, 'I've often thought of what you said to me when we first met, but I never thought that it would happen to me. Does it get any easier?'

Jane paused. 'I wish that I could say yes, Molly, but it doesn't. But what we're doing here is good therapy.'

'My condolences,' said the other pilot.

'Thank you,' said Molly, as Jane and the other pilot walked away, passing Mary and Lettice who had both just rushed into the room and were heading in Molly's direction. Molly noticed that Lettice had that "I'm worried about you" look in her eyes and she prepped herself ready to be strong.

'Are you going to be OK?' said Lettice, concerned, 'I'm worried about you'.

'Don't', said Molly, smiling and placing her two hands on Lettice's shoulders, 'I've got this - really I have. I've never been more determined for a task in my entire life'.

'How is Edward?', asked Mary.

'Edward is not so good. He's in a bad way actually - mentally and physically.'

'Are you sure that you're up for this Molly?' said Mary.

'Yes. Of course. I had a good chat with Margo last evening. This is the reason that I joined the ATA … and what else am I going to do? Mope around at home?'

'Everyone seems to be on high alert,' said Lettice, 'the Luftwaffe will anticipate exactly what we're doing, and they'll be all over the sky. I hope that we have enough Spits for this, and that they'll be airborne in Malta before they become targets again.'

'I've been praying for all those other boys in the desert,' said Molly, 'Bunny's comrades and friends are still there you know.'

'And they will be coming home when this is all over,' said Mary, 'Please try not to think of it Molly, and focus on our task. Please be careful.'

'I will', said Molly, 'you too.'

The girls left the Ops Room and ran in different directions towards the waiting taxi Ansons and Fairchilds, which were standing on the apron with engines running. The heightened energy amongst them was palpable; a collective sense that they were about to go into battle; a shared feeling that everything that had gone before – the studying, the training, the work, the elation and the exhaustion - was all in preparation for the task now in front of them. Molly climbed into the Anson and, as usual, Douglas was at the controls.

'Hello old thing,' he said, 'not seen you for a couple of days. I'm so sorry to hear about your husband, and that you've had to go through this. Are you OK?

'Thank you Douglas … 'no, not so OK, if truth be told.'

'It's OK not to be OK,' said Douglas, 'look at you - straight back in. He would be so proud of you.'

Molly could feel the emotion welling up in her and she smiled, took her seat and stared out of the window.

'All strapped in?' said Douglas, 'then Tally-ho and Operation Bowery is underway.'

After a few short hops, where several pilots disembarked to pick up their taskings, the taxi Anson lined up for its landing run at Molly's destination, which by coincidence was RAF Manston on the Kent coast, the same location where Molly had encountered the Buzz-bomb. Molly was now the only passenger on the aircraft and she had passed the last twenty minutes by wondering how Douglas managed to find his way around in thick cloud without even a single glance at a map, or even looking down for that matter. She also thought about the ATA call sign "Lost Child", and how inappropriate that was for a man like Douglas; a pilot for whom navigation was like sixth sense, someone who could be trusted to find the way home when it most counted.

The steel grey clouds were steadily drifting inland; pushed across the Channel by a persistent wind, and Molly was eager to get out of the Anson and into the air for fear of being grounded again. She said goodbye to

Douglas and was out of the Anson and into the cockpit of the Spitfire Mk V so fast that the ground crew barely saw her. She quickly ran through her checks and managed to get off the ground just as the cloud had started to thicken. Visibility was about six-hundred yards and a grey cloud-base of about three-hundred feet hung across the sky. Fog was also starting to appear.

Within a few seconds of take-off, Molly thought that she glimpsed sight of another aircraft in front and she quickly banked left and came around in a 360-degree arc, searching for a gap in the cloud that would give her better vision. Molly was worried as the quick changes of direction resulted in losing the first marker of her plotted route, following roads, railways and part of the coastline. Then within minutes, the cloud density increased, and a squall developed. As the rain began to drum in torrents onto the windscreen, Molly realised that her landmarks had completely disappeared.

'Dammit, Molly - get out of this,' she said.'

As the weather deteriorated further, Molly became disoriented, tapping the glass on her compass as it oscillated wildly. As the altimeter lowered, Molly pulled the aircraft up in an effort to avoid the cloud and rain. The rain had now turned to hail, and the electrical storm battered her little plane with a terrifying din. She tried descending slightly, eventually spotting a small gap in the clouds, but to her horror, she realised that she was flying over water.

'This is not good Molly. This is not good,' she said.

Molly flew for several minutes without knowing where she was, and then she saw a clearing ahead; a patch of beautiful cobalt blue sky. She headed for it, now increasing her altitude. As the cloud fell away behind her, Molly looked to the west to see what looked like five large aircraft heading directly towards her.

'Dammit,' she said.

Molly quickly manoeuvred the agile Spitfire out of their flight path, ascending and banking hard to take a position behind the rear-most aircraft, which suddenly came into focus through the cloud.

'Oh, my goodness, I do believe they're Lancs,' she said, laughing.

Molly noticed that three of them were in bad shape. One had a feathered prop; another had huge jagged tears in its fuselage; a third had wisps of oily black smoke spilling from a gently wind-milling engine. They had clearly been in combat.

'Well you look like you've been in a bit of a scrap and are heading home, so I hope you don't mind if I tag along.'

As Molly throttled back and deployed flaps to slow down to the same speed as the bombers, she manoeuvred her Spitfire to come in behind the tail-end aircraft, planning to follow them to safety. As the visibility continued to clear, her little Spitfire was gradually surrounded by twenty other huge Avro Lancaster four-engine heavy bombers that appeared like a mirage out of the cloud to fly beside, below and behind her; many of them showing signs of damage. Molly had found herself in the middle of a returning raid. She kept the Spitfire tucked in the centre of the group of damaged and lumbering bombers, hoping that they knew she was there, and that she was friendly.

Molly kept her place in the formation and slowly the familiar and joyful sight of the White Cliffs of Dover appeared on the horizon. Molly was surprised at how far across the Channel she had flown. As the group droned painfully towards home, one of the bombers lost height, and flames started licking around two of its engines. It fell towards the sea, hitting the water with a mighty explosion. Molly watched aghast, knowing there was nothing that she could do.

'Oh, you poor boys,' she said.

Powerless to help, Molly scanned the crash site and prayed that there would be survivors. She tore her eyes away from the scene below and thought about their mothers and fathers, sisters and brothers...their sweethearts...

As the journey continued, she looked around and studied the Lancs in the formation. Some of the pilots in the closest aircraft had spotted her and were waving. It felt good, Molly thought; a welcome home like no other for such deserving pilots. It was then that Molly looked up to see the most spectacular sight of all: a thousand feet above, coming straight towards her group was a huge armada of more than 500 bombers in tight formation, flying out from the coast of England, over the White Cliffs of Dover and heading for the continent. Beneath the new out-going raid, Molly's bedraggled formation limped home; the two crossing each other for the briefest moment – a surreal, dream-like juxtaposition.

The noise of the outgoing bombers was deafening as they moved in perfect formation overhead.

'Oh my God,' said Molly as she took a deep breath and struggled to hold in the emotion. Tears welled up in her eyes. She thought it the most beautiful and mesmerising sight that she had ever seen.

'More going out than coming back,' she said, her voice breaking, 'how sad is that – all those brave souls who are no longer with us' … she paused … 'Oh Bunny'.

As Molly reached the coastline, she waggled her wings to say goodbye and left the formation. She checked her fuel gauge, opened the throttle and continued her mission North.

The bombers receded into the distance, becoming small dots on the horizon, and then they were gone.

Thirty-Two

Summer

Diana stepped out of a Bristol Type 156 Beaufighter, often called "the Beau", a long-range heavy fighter, which she had just delivered from the Bristol factory in Filton to RAF Coastal Command. Diana had heard that the Beau was not easy to fly and that good landings were a particular challenge, but after studying the Ferry Pilots Notes and the ATA Pilot's Reminder Book, she confidently brought the large and powerful aircraft in for a perfect landing in front of a number of waiting ground crew and officers. Never missing an opportunity to look glamorous, Diana always enjoyed the astonished reaction from the ground crew when she disembarked any aircraft.

Diana boarded the taxi Anson, a miniature aircraft in comparison to the Beaufighter with the familiar face of Douglas at the controls, cigarette dangling from the corner of his mouth as ever. One other female pilot embarked with Diana for the trip back to Hamble and four passengers were already seated.

'Good afternoon ladies,' said Douglas, 'and welcome aboard this luxurious Anson taxi aircraft. Please take your seats, and the cabin staff will be serving Champagne as soon as we reach cruising altitude.'

Diana looked at the uniformed RAF pilot in the far rear of the aircraft and thought that she recognised him. The officer returned her stare for a brief moment, signifying that he recognised her too. Diana made her way towards the rear and sat in the opposite seat, and the Anson taxied to the runway and took off.

The officer spoke in a broad Glaswegian accent.

'Da ye naw recognise me then?' he asked.

Diana opened her mouth to speak, but before she had a chance to say anything …

'Flight Lieutenant Rory McTavish from 601 Squadron,' he said, 'we met on a train from Scotland ti Southampton. Do you naw remember?

'I do very much remember,' said Diana, thinking how much thinner he was. 'You and your friend very kindly gave us your seats on that god-awful train journey from Scotland. That and his "wee dram" were lifesavers. You're looking very suntanned; been anywhere nice?'

'Aye, I remember that trip too. All that way i the corridor. We shipped oot ti the Med shortly after that. But wee Callum's unfortunately no longer wi us. Aye, very sad, very sad.'

'Oh, I'm so sorry to hear that, he was such a lovely chap'.

'Ah know. Terrible times. Terrible times,' said McTavish.

'You have an excellent memory,' said Diana, 'I remember that you were doing some drills with the Navy, and then off to sunnier climes.'

'Aye. Indeed. Ye may have read aboot it in the newspapers, so ah'm nae speaking out o school. We took a load o' Spitfires ti the Med on a Yank carrier. Flew 'em off the aircraft carrier would ye believe? And intae Malta. Spent the next six weeks keeping the Eyetie and Jerry bombers away. Hell of a task, but we soon got the better of em. Aye, them Spitfires made all the difference. But a few of the chaps didnae make it.'

'Oh my goodness,' exclaimed Diana, 'you went out on the WASP … *you* were in Malta!'

★★★

Later that evening, Diana, Molly, Mary, Joy, Lettice and Jackie walked through the doors of the cinema in Southampton. The once-elegant facade of the old building was now pock-marked with shrapnel scars and had suffered bomb damage, along with most other buildings in the beleaguered city. They entered the lobby area and were excited to see the new American romance film *"This Above All"*. The film was set in the Second World War and told the story of a young, strong-willed, upper-class woman who joins the Women's Auxiliary Air Force and falls in love with a man who resents fighting for the benefit of a British elite that humiliates and oppresses people of his class. The girls anticipated that the film would be a great talking point in the Crew Room over the coming weeks and wondered how the ATA would be portrayed.

They were smartly dressed in their ATA uniforms and as they walked to their seats the girls drew looks from the other cinemagoers, many of whom were also in uniform. As they settled down, smoke filled the air and the curtains to the screen drew open, revealing the Pathé newsreel:

> *"… in the Battle of Malta, a wave of Spitfires takes off from USS Wasp and HMS Eagle and immediately becomes operational, after being rapidly refuelled and rearmed; successfully defending Malta against the air raid intended to destroy them. The aircraft and heroic pilots see off a wave of Italian bombers and forty-seven German aircraft, all of which are destroyed or damaged. The battle abruptly ends daytime bombing of Malta to make a significant turning point in the War and one more step towards victory. Prime Minister Winston Churchill states: "Clearly a wasp can sting twice".*

After watching the film, the girls left the cinema and stood outside chatting; more about the newsreel than the film itself.

'Well, isn't it just splendid that our contribution was recognised.' said Diana, sarcastically.

'Perhaps we should all get medals from the King,' said Jackie.

'Oh, I'm sure we will be covered in medals by the time this is all over,' said Diana. 'Those were *our* Spits from the mission to Scotland. I actually met one of the Malta pilots from that beastly train journey, even though I have tried to wipe every last detail of that horror trip from my memory.'

'That film could have been all about you Diana,' said Joy.

'Yes, I can quite see myself as Joan Fontaine,' said Diana, 'however I'll certainly not be falling in love with anyone who is not perfectly patriotic, even if they do look like Tyrone Power.'

'It's so awful when a film ends without knowing whether the hero survives or not,' said Jackie.

'Right,' said Diana, 'I think that a few drinkies are what we need at this very moment - who's in?'

All the girls were enthusiastic except for Molly. 'Not for me I'm afraid,' she said, 'I just need to get back to the village.'

The other girls were understanding of Molly's circumstances and accepted her refusal without attempting to change her mind. For the past several weeks, Molly had turned her full attention and total focus towards the job at hand and aside from the evening's cinema trip, she had not socialised at all. Her friends understood and respected this; knowing that it was exactly what Molly needed.

'I'll come with you Molly', said Mary.

Molly and Mary walked arm-in-arm through the outskirts of the peaceful Hamble-le-Rice village. The sun was beginning to set and all around was that calm, gentle beauty of an English village, lulled to sleep by the melody of a blackbird on a nearby chimney. It was hard to believe that there was a war on.

'It's good to know for sure that those same Spits we flew to Scotland are the ones that were used to defend Malta,' said Molly.

'Yes,' said Mary, 'and perhaps to save North Africa. The newsreel said it was a major turning point in the war. I feel quite proud to have been a part of it.'

'I want to feel proud too,' said Molly, 'but I can't help feeling that I didn't do enough. I can't have done enough, or Bunny would still be here.'

'Oh, Molly. You can't …'

'I broke my promise to Bernard,' said Molly, interrupting.

'You can't think like that Molly. Everything that you've done since joining the ATA has helped to save so many lives. You can't blame yourself…you mustn't…'

'He broke his promise to me too Mary … a promise to come home. I can't bear the thought of a life without him.'

'War is full of broken promises,' said Mary.

They continued walking in silence until they reached Molly's digs.

'I'll be alright from here Mary.'

'OK. I'm so sorry old thing. I'll see you tomorrow.'

They hugged each other and parted company. Molly continued walking past Mrs Collis' cottage, down the lane and then climbed over a sty into the meadow, where she sat under the canopy of a tall and graceful ash tree. She looked across at the gently rolling hills in the distance and as dusk approached, Molly was filled with trepidation. It seemed that her life was falling apart and for the first time ever, she could not picture her future; it felt as if it had been ripped out from underneath her. Molly wondered if she would be destined for a life of loneliness.

As she sat gazing into the distance, a movement caught her eye. From the hedge at the side of the meadow emerged a hare, its large brown eyes darting around to check for safety as it cautiously moved out onto the grass. Molly sat rigid, not daring to move for fear of frightening it away. She had seen hares once or twice before, but never this close. As it nibbled on some flowers, a second hare appeared; slightly smaller and looking more timid. In an instant they began to play, chasing each other around and jumping into the air, weaving and darting through the meadow in an ecstatic dance as Molly looked on amazed. The magic of these two creatures, so carefree and so wild, so content in each other's company brought tears to Molly's eyes and she found herself crying; tears streaming down her face as the emotions that had built up inside of her for weeks were finally released.

The hares made a final circle before running to the far corner of the meadow and disappearing. Molly reached over and pulled a small leather wallet from her bag and looked at the photo of Bernard.

She wondered to herself if she could ever be truly happy again.

Thirty-Three

Autumn

Molly hurriedly left the Ops Room at Cosford on the second stage of ferrying a 'P1 W' - "Priority 1 - Wait" Spitfire to RAF Bomber Command at RAF Lossiemouth in Moray, Scotland. Under normal circumstances, Molly would have handed the aircraft over to a relay pilot at either Cosford or Prestwick, but this was not always possible. Molly knew "Lossie" well and could not remember having landed there in anything other than awful weather, so she took a small overnight bag with a few essentials. Due to the forecast, the Ops team at Hamble had asked her to stop for a weather check at the ATA Ferry Pool in Prestwick, and not to proceed unless it was clear.

Although trips to the far north of Scotland were fraught with issues such as bad weather, stopovers and the occasional uncomfortable trip back on the train, the stunning scenery more than made up for those hardships. Molly took off from Cosford and in an effort to avoid Liverpool, flew north-east across the Peak District and then across the magnificent Yorkshire Dales and Lake District. The breath-taking scenery and land features in this part of Great Britain were always a source of fascination to Molly. The autumn colours were just starting to appear across the moors and valleys and rushing rivers glittered like diamonds as they meandered past the most picturesque villages. Molly wondered if there was a more beautiful place on earth.

As the familiar sight of the runway at Prestwick came into view, Molly prepared for her landing run just as the weather was closing in, but by the time her wheels touched the ground, the heavens had opened and a torrential rain battered the tiny aircraft. It was a quick reminder of how fast conditions can change, thought Molly. The ground crew were all young lads and as they rushed out to the apron, Molly could see that they were drenched.

'Just in time ma'am', said one of the lads as he helped Molly out of the cockpit; still smiling despite rivulets of water trickling down his face. 'Welcome to Prestwick,' he added.

After thanking the young lads, Molly made a dash for it, but by the time she reached the Ops Room she was soaked through too. She stood in front of the Ops Officer dripping wet as she checked in and was told that due to the storm, everything would be grounded for the rest of the day.

Molly sat by the only oil heater in the room, which was fortunately turned up full and blasting out heat, and she looked around the room noting the similarities to the Ops Room at Hamble. There were a few other male pilots loitering around, most of whom looked thoroughly depressed at being grounded and one in particular who was standing rigid by the window and staring up at the dark grey sky. Despite the predicament, there was something comforting about the sound of the rain, the warmth of the heater and the familiarity of being in an Ops Room environment, and Molly acknowledged in that moment just how much life at the ATA had sharpened the points of her compass.

Molly sat for almost an hour whilst the Ops Team tried to find her accommodation in one of the local villages as there was nothing available at the aerodrome, and when she eventually felt dry enough to pull herself away from the heater, she got up and made her way to the canteen.

The canteen at Prestwick was usually a good social spot for ATA pilots. It was a central hub for relay ferry trips and stopovers to and from Scotland as well as being the home of ATA Ferry Pool No. 4. One never knew who one would bump into, and there was always an air of excitement and anticipation upon entering, somewhat similar to the collecting of a ferry chit first thing in the morning. As Molly entered the room, it was noisy and full of male and female pilots, and she was feeling cold and wet again after making a dash from one building to another. She walked in and quickly looked around to find a seat and to see if there was anyone that she recognised.

'Molly!' called a voice from a table which was tucked away in a corner, next to which was a small oil heater, 'Molly, over here.'

It took Molly a few seconds to realise who it was. The girl stood out from those around her, with a perfectly arranged hairstyle and immaculate uniform; she was made up as though attending a Saturday evening ball. When Molly eventually recognised her, she stood staring for a brief moment, slightly apprehensive before becoming conscious of her own hesitation and then calmly walked over to the table. The person who had stood up from the table and was smiling at her was Jackie Cochran.

'Great to see you again, honey!' she said standing up and, to Molly's great surprise, gave her the warmest hug. As she had been sitting next to the only heater in the canteen, her body was radiating heat.

'Wow you're wet,' said Jackie, 'switch places with me as I'm hogging all the heat'.

'Gosh, you are lovely and warm,' said Molly, as she reluctantly let go of Jackie's warm embrace, and then moved the chair even closer to the heater before sitting down.

'Such horrid weather,' said Molly, 'and my timing was awful.'

'I know, I arrived in a Spit just before it hammered down.' said Jackie, 'Where are you heading?'

'It was supposed to be Lossie, but it's unlikely that I'll get there today given the weather and so they're finding me accommodation.'

'Well that's a coincidence.' said Jackie, 'Me too. I came up from Eastleigh this morning but apparently Scotland is like a Louisiana swamp and it's all "persona non grata" until tomorrow at least. To be honest, after the week I've had, I'll be happy to chill out here for the evening in the peace and quiet of a nice British village. Maybe we can do something together?'

'Yes, that would be nice.' said Molly, as she wondered what she was committing herself to. Molly was nervous at the thought of spending any time alone with the notorious Jackie Cochran. They were completely opposite in many ways, yet despite this, a mutual fascination had arisen between the two girls, each curious as to every aspect of the other's life. Molly had heard all the stories and whilst there was no doubt that Jackie was one of the most capable pilots in the organisation, it was often said that she could be extremely hard and critical. Molly had heard her described as a "man's woman" and she wondered if this was why Jackie did not seem to have many close female friends.

Thirty-six-year-old Jackie was born in Florida and had amassed an incredible number of hours as a pilot. A little over a year before, she was the first woman to fly a bomber across the Atlantic having piloted a Hudson V from Newfoundland; a feat which generated much publicity in the newspapers and newsreels. Before joining the ATA, she had been part of

169

"Wings for Britain", ferrying American built aircraft to Britain in the early part of the war.

Jackie was married to Floyd Bostwick Odlum, founder and head of RKO Pictures, one of Hollywood's biggest film production and distribution companies. Rumoured to be one of the ten richest men in the world, Odlum adored Jackie, helping her to establish her own cosmetics company called "Wings to Beauty". The incredible success of her business, together with Jackie's relentless drive and determination, had made her independently wealthy and a well-known face in the American society pages. That same tenacity was inevitably channelled into her career as a pilot, and Jackie delighted in flying her own aircraft across the USA to promote the company.

Jackie had been made an honorary Flight Captain at the ATA and despite being viewed with scepticism by some, she was well-respected by the ATA's twenty-five American pilots who looked upon her as guardian and protector; much like their very own American "Queen Bee". Attractive and always impeccably dressed, it was even rumoured that on occasion Jackie arrived at the base in a chauffeur-driven Rolls-Royce. Molly had never seen this surreal spectacle herself but found it amusing to picture the reaction of the young security lads at the entrance to the base.

Jackie thrived in the predominantly male atmosphere and although she was comfortable in that environment - a reciprocal understanding having been reached early on - she could turn on the femininity and charm at the drop of a hat. Possessing an inherently competitive streak, in Jackie's world second place did not exist. She positively had to be first, always on her own terms and conditions in the process, and heaven help anyone who crossed her. This fierce determination came across most of all in her flying which was professional, methodical and confident. She had mastered every manoeuvre, be it standard operational, emergency or aerobatic procedure – she could do them all and do them well.

It was little wonder that the naturally modest and somewhat shy Molly, despite being one of the most experienced pilots in the organisation, was slightly intimidated.

As the heat from the oil burner radiated out from the small corner of the room, Molly started to feel warm at last and it was heavenly. Seeing that Molly had stopped shivering, Jackie offered to get her something to eat and when Molly asked for soup, Jackie was up, gone and back in no time at all

170

with a bowl of warm vegetable soup and armed with a pot of steaming coffee. "Efficient" was the first word that passed through Molly's thoughts as she began to eat and feel better.

'You look as though you needed that,' observed Jackie, smiling.

'I most certainly do', said Molly, laughing and looking as though she had not eaten for days.

'I've been here too many times before,' said Jackie, 'Prestwick was the main stop for the North Atlantic air ferry routes in my "Wings for Britain" days. I flew all sorts from the States and Canada, and I brought a few interesting characters over in the process ... you know, diplomats and VIPs and such.'

'That must have been fun,' replied Molly, 'I saw a newsreel about you bringing the bomber across the Atlantic. It was quite something'.

'It sure was,' said Jackie, 'and a major step for the States to involve women pilots in non-combat wartime flying. That's been a challenge for me from Day One and you Brits have got it sorted over here. Things are moving in the right direction though, and that's why I'm going back.'

'Going back?' Molly was surprised and felt suddenly disappointed; she wanted Jackie to stay longer so that she could get to know her better. 'When will you leave?'

'Next week, but no-one knows yet, only Gower and Pops, so keep it under your hat.'

Molly was about to ask Jackie more on the subject when one of the Ops Officers approached the table.

'We have accommodation for you both in Irvine,' he said, 'and a car is ready if you are?'

'Swell,' said Jackie as Molly quickly finished eating her soup, They both stood up and gathered their things before following the Ops Office out to a waiting Hillman RAF staff car.

It took only a short time for the driver to reach Irvine Harbour, and the journey was an opportunity for Molly and Jackie to chat further about their experiences in the air. As the car came closer to the harbour area, they noticed a large number of tank landing craft, some in the water and others in various stages of production in the busy shipyard; a mass of brilliant arcs from the soldering irons reflected like stars in the murky water. The car pulled up outside The Ship Inn which stood on the quayside and before

171

Molly and Jackie walked into the quaint old building, they noticed army troops and military vehicles everywhere.

They entered the inn and registered with the proprietor and were each shown to their small but comfortable room after agreeing to meet in the bar at 18:30 for dinner.

Molly had been desperate to jump into a hot bath, and as she lay there in a tub filled with perhaps a little more water that was officially allowed, she thought about the unusual and daunting evening that lay before her. After her bath, during which time she almost fell asleep, it took only a few minutes for Molly to get dressed and ready.

As Molly entered the bar area, Jackie was already seated and stood up as Molly approached. Both girls had changed out of their uniforms and Molly was surprised to see Jackie wearing denim jeans and a sweater, with slightly wet hair and no make-up. It was a complete contrast to the look she had seen only an hour before. Molly had dressed in a simple chequered blouse and comfortable cardigan atop wide-leg palazzo pants; worrying only moments before in front of a mirror that she might look too casual in comparison to her glamourous dining companion; a thought which now seemed silly after seeing Jackie. Both girls were inconspicuous amid their surroundings and after ordering food and drinks, the first glimmer of mutual relaxation began to set both girls at ease.

'I don't do this very often,' said Jackie, 'especially lately as I've been spending more time on administrative work than in the cockpit, but it's good training I guess, for when I get back.'

'Yes, you mentioned that you'll be leaving,' said Molly, 'that's sad'.

'Sad in one way, yes, but you may know that the OK has been given to form the Women's Auxiliary Ferrying Squadron in the States, which is something that I've been pushing for since I don't know when, but there's still a lot of talk about how it will all work. My vision is for military training and a variety of aviation roles above and beyond ferrying, and that's part of the reason that I've been here, you know, to see what you do and such. Now that it's about to get serious in the States I want to be the person running it, and I can't do that from jolly old England.'

'Will your girls go with you?' asked Molly.

'Some are planning to, and more will travel to Britain to replace them, but quite a few of the girls love their lives here and will hopefully stick it out until

172

the end of the war. It's been tough for a few of them, and none of us expected that they would need more training and testing, because a few of the girls didn't pass which caused a few issues. I do understand though, and I appreciate that your weather is a lot worse than ours, well most of the time anyway, and this whole barrage balloon thing has been a new experience to say the least. Flying in general is a different proposition in Britain than in America.'

'I thought that you handled that whole incident with the doctor quite well,' said Molly, 'stripping naked for tests is quite unnecessary.'

'Stripping naked for eye tests is even worse,' said Jackie with a grin,' but I soon put a stop to all of that.'

'Well done to you - I quite agree,' said Molly.

The food arrived at the table and Molly was surprised at the biggest plate of fish and chips that she had ever seen.

'Wow!' said Jackie, picking up her knife and fork to get started.

'You must be missing your husband?' asked Molly tentatively.

'I do actually. I know what people say, you know, that he's older than me and that I married him for money and all that, but he adores me, and I love him for that, and so yes, I can't wait to see him. I told him yesterday actually that I'm coming back.'

Molly was surprised at her frankness and tried to hide her thoughts as they drifted towards Bernard, but Jackie saw straight through it.

'Aside from all the great stories I hear about you, the one I like most is that you refused to take time away after your husband died. I'm so sorry to hear about what happened Molly. When push comes to shove, and despite all the other things, that alone is the sign of a real character. "True Grit" we call it in the States.'

'Thank you, and yes it was the hardest thing that I have ever done. What do you mean about all the stories – what have you heard?' Molly asked anxiously.

"Are you serious Molly? German Messerschmitts shooting at you; tennis clothes instead of a flying jacket; tipping a V-1 off course; caught in amongst a sortie of bombers; and I'm sure there is even more … you're famous. Are all those stories true?'

"Now I'm embarrassed!' said Molly laughing … 'Yes, I suppose they are really, but I don't actually think about any of it. Nothing is unusual at the ATA.'

When I get back to the States and they ask me about English female pilots, you'll be the one that I tell them about.'

'Golly, that's sweet of you, but please don't. Tell them about someone else.'

Molly covered her face with her hands and then both of them laughed.

Thirty-Four

The ongoing, flawless job carried out by the female pilots of the ATA slowly chipped away at the initial prejudices, each pilot in her own way achieving unparalleled merit, surprising perhaps even themselves. One pilot in particular was the epitome of professionalism; laying the path for others to follow, continually pushing herself to excel, and usually the first to graduate to the more advanced and demanding aircraft. That pilot was Lettice.

The tall, blue-eyed blonde had recently set the bar high by becoming the first woman to be trained by the RAF to fly the Handley Page Halifax, a four-engine heavy bomber, which had become a major component of Bomber Command, performing routine strategic bombing missions against the Axis Powers. Due to its sheer size, the Halifax was always a conversation starter in the Crew Room for any pilot that was fortunate enough to be trusted with one.

Lettice had also previously been introduced to the American President's wife Mrs Eleanor Roosevelt as 'the first woman to fly a four-engine bomber'. Mrs Roosevelt had accompanied Mrs Clementine Churchill during a visit to the ATA to meet the women pilots. The media naturally picked up the story and once again, the 'glamorous' life of female ATA pilots was featured in the national press, with one headline reading: "Mrs Roosevelt meets Halifax girl pilot". Shortly after, Lettice was cleared to ferry additional types of heavy bombers, including the US B-17 Flying Fortress but her greatest achievement, and much to the glory of the ATA, was as the first woman pilot to deliver an Avro Lancaster heavy bomber.

The huge and definitive four-engine Avro Lancaster, or the "Lanc" as it was colloquially known, was the mainstay of RAF Bomber Command for the strategic bombing offensive over Europe, and it carried the largest bombs in use by the RAF. Lettice had become the most experienced and formidable of all the female pilots, with a log book that read like an A-Z of British aircraft of the Second World War.

Her sporty and competitive nature was formed in her early years when she captained the women's lawn tennis team, the Lacrosse team and the fencing team as a triple blue, as well as being a skilled county tennis and squash player. To Lettice, anything other than the best was unacceptable and this became a lifelong adage.

Her privileged upbringing as the daughter of Lord Denbury did not dissuade her from her goal to be a pilot, but only a precious few succeeded in becoming commercial pilots at that time and certainly none were accepted into the Royal Air Force. After studying Mathematics at Oxford she was undeterred and worked hard on her flying, thereafter gaining her commercial B license. Lettice then secured a job flying a Puss Moth fitted with an aerial survey camera, becoming proficient in photographing areas of England for the production of Ordnance Survey maps.

Lettice had been a solid rock for her closest friends including Molly, who admired her directness and no-nonsense approach together with her lack of tolerance for fools. Unfortunately, this particular trait ensured that Lettice was not the most popular person with other pilots, but her friends always trusted her frank and truthful opinion. She was also one of the few people that could keep Diana in check and had a natural and easy way of bringing Diana back down to reality, albeit temporarily; away from the glamour and glitz to which Diana was naturally inclined, especially when Diana was around some of the girls who did not have access to such privileges.

Lettice had been instrumental in shaping Molly's professional career and Molly respected her advice and opinions, even though on occasion their views differed. Molly had noticed that Lettice was not the most welcoming person to the American pilots; she didn't get on with Pauline Gower and she was not the friendliest towards Jackie Cochran, but Molly always tried to understand her dear friend and to see both sides. By contrast, Molly was the most forgiving person without a bad word to say about anyone; always seeing the good side of those she met and oblivious to any character flaws or deficiencies. The personalities of Lettice and Molly, although different, strangely complemented one another and their friendship was dear to them both.

Molly knew Lettice's strengths, weaknesses and idiosyncrasies – she could read in her face immediately if something was troubling her. As Molly disembarked a taxi Fairchild at the Hamble airbase late one evening after a string of ferry tasks, tired and hoping that there would be no more requests waiting for her in the Ops Room, she saw Lettice standing by the apron. Before Molly even left the aircraft, she knew that something was wrong. Lettice stood away from the ground crew as she coldly watched the Fairchild come to a halt. Molly was the only passenger and she quickly picked up her parachute and bag and moved to disembark.

As the aircraft door opened, Lettice was walking toward Molly who came quickly down to join her friend.

'What is it?' said Molly, 'what's happened?'

Lettice put her arm around Molly's shoulder and before she uttered a word, Molly knew that it was serious.

'It's Jane,' said Lettice, 'Jane Winstone, she's gone'.

Molly dropped her parachute and bag onto the ground and put both hands over her face. She stood silent for a few moments as Lettice squeezed her hand.

'Please no…' said Molly, 'What happened?'

'She was taking off in Spit from Cosford and it seems as though there was an engine problem. Apparently, it was stalling and starting until it gave out completely and spun into the ground quite close to the airfield. I'm so sorry Molly. I know that you were dear friends.'

'Sweet Jane,' said Molly. 'It's so awful. I can't believe it. She was so happy here, especially after losing her fiancée. I can't take any more death Lettice, I really can't…' Molly shook her head dejectedly as the tears came. 'When is it all going to end?'

'I wish that I had the answer to that,' said Lettice, turning Molly gently to look her in the eyes, 'but I don't. I can tell you this though: the war will not get *you* Molly and it won't get *me,* because we're not going to let it. We have to stay strong, focussed, and above all, careful. Will you promise me that Molly? Please.'

'I broke the last promise that I made…' said Molly hopelessly.

Lettice reached down to pick up Molly's parachute and bag.

'Well don't break this one,' she said.

The death of both Jane Winstone and Irene Arckless took its toll on Molly, and indeed on all pilots at the ATA. However, death within the organisation was not uncommon; a consistent reminder of the thin line on which the pilots carefully balanced, always at the mercy of the weather and susceptible to a multitude of dangers that could snatch life away at any moment. With each loss, a dark cloud hung over the base and muted the normally happy, buzzing atmosphere; the Crew Room was quieter, the laughter subdued, people went about their business proficiently but without chat, while groups of close friends huddled together around a table in the bar to reminisce…

There was, however, one tragic loss which occurred shortly after the death of Jane, which deeply affected everyone at Hamble. On 3rd April 1944, Douglas Fairweather was killed in a weather-related air incident over the Irish Sea whilst flying the air ambulance. He and a nurse who was travelling on the same flight died instantly. His death was made worse by the fact that his wife Margie gave birth to their daughter Elizabeth only a few days later.

Douglas's personality touched everyone at the ATA, most often whilst he piloted a taxi Anson or a Fairchild. His unique and unconventional brand of humour, whilst not always pleasing everyone, was infectious to those who loved his company.

Yet again, Molly was devastated.

Thirty-Five

Summer

Life went on and war continued to dominate Europe, casting its impenetrable shadow over people's lives and stripping them of normality. Death, grief and loss were words that had now become synonymous with everyday living and the war forced many to confront these visceral fears on a daily basis. The fragility of life was ever-present; either up-close and personal, or through sad stories from family, friends and colleagues. The war chipped away at people; slowly and methodically and painfully, week in and week out, year in and year out...

Yet despite this, where there is darkness there is also a need and a resourcefulness to seek light and people began to appreciate the small things in life, realising that everyone was vulnerable and no-one was invincible. What had been taken for granted in peacetime, now became recognised and cherished during wartime and this led to a certain calm and camaraderie; infectious, sought after, and once realised, treasured by those who found it.

As time went by, encouraging signs gradually emerged and people became more hopeful that an end to the conflict may soon be in sight, although there was still no certainty that Hitler could be defeated.

At the Casablanca Conference, Winston Churchill and Franklin D. Roosevelt had discussed the eventual invasion of mainland Europe, and the concept of "unconditional surrender". For the first time, the Nazi government acknowledged a failure in the war effort after the German 6th Army surrendered at the Battle of Stalingrad, and by 1943, British and American forces had defeated the Italians and Germans in North Africa.

During these turbulent times, the ATA continued to grow requiring the expansion of the Ferry Pools, most of which were mixed with men and women pilots working alongside each other, plus the necessity for more training units. Hamble, Cosford and Hatfield remained as 'all women' Ferry Pools and, in addition to the men, one-hundred-and-eight female pilots were now ferrying aircraft.

England, and especially the aircraft factories, was still sustaining constant aerial attacks. Ferry movements had become even more complicated, as it was essential to get the aircraft to the Maintenance Units and active service squadrons as soon as they were flyable. There was also the continued risk to ATA pilots of flying aircraft that had been damaged in combat. Some were barely airworthy, but it was imperative to deliver them back to the maintenance units or factories for repair.

Due to the ever-increasing number of new recruits from overseas, the ATA had been dubbed "The Foreign Legion of the Air", with pilots from as many as twenty-five nations represented. Even so, there was still a need for more pilots, and the "Ab Initio" programme was created; recruiting and training people with no experience from sources such as the Women's Auxiliary Air Force, non-flying RAF personnel, and the ground staff at the ATA itself. New training schools were set up, resulting in more personnel and more infrastructure. The ATA had become a huge and essential organisation and the ideal way for many pilots, who otherwise would not have had the opportunity to fly, to "do their bit" for the war effort.

Diana had recently married RAF Wing Commander Derek Ronald Walker and still continued her trips to London at the end of each day's ferrying, partying the night away at the most exclusive clubs and gatherings and then returning to Hamble the following morning on the Milk Train. Molly's life had changed little: day-in and day-out she immersed herself in the job. It took some time for Molly to regain her spark after the death of Jane, Douglas and Bernard, who was still very much in her thoughts as he always would be. Molly had no end of offers from potential new suitors but it was of no interest to her despite some of her friends suggesting that it could help Molly to move on with her life.

She had now flown over thirty-eight different types of aircraft from all corners of Great Britain and was familiar with most of the factories, airfields, and Maintenance Units. Even so, new locations were continually being tasked due to the building of new Maintenance Units in hidden locations and pilots of the ATA still had to rely heavily on their navigation skills.

It was a 'rain-out' day and Molly was seated at a table in the library at the ATA Ferry Pool No. 15 at Hamble, along with Mary, Joy and Jackie. Diana and Lettice had finished scouring the bookshelves and ripping out maps from various books. It had become impossible to buy maps due to restrictions, and they were in short supply at the ATA. They walked over to join the others at the table.

'We found one of the West Midlands!' said Lettice triumphantly as they sat down, 'Perfect.'

'Something huge is going on,' said Diana, 'I know it.'

'Yes, it's called a war darling,' said Lettice with an amused exasperation.

'Oh, you *are* hilarious,' retorted Diana, 'but don't you think things are rather more hush-hush than usual? Everyone is being far too quiet, except for the overload of deliveries, most of which are priority. I took two RAF officers to Brize Norton yesterday and they did nothing but whisper for the entire flight ... new balloon barrages are popping up like mushrooms around this airfield ... *and* practically every aircraft has been painted with black and white markings. That has to be a code for something or other.'

'I would feel a lot safer if we had weapons,' said Lettice, ignoring Diana's statement.

'I would feel a lot safer if we had South African sunshine,' added Jackie, 'instead of these horrendous British weather systems - we've had all four seasons in a single day.'

'One of the Polish girls told me about The Nightwitches,' said Molly, 'they're a Russian squadron of female fighter pilots. Now they *do* have weapons. Apparently, one of the most notorious, and with the most kills, is known as The White Rose of Stalingrad.'

'A rose with many thorns no doubt,' said Joy.

'... Think about it,' said Diana, continuing her own conversation, 'new troops arriving all the time. As well as the Americans, I've seen Belgians, Czechs, Dutch, French, Greeks, New Zealanders, Norwegians, and even Rhodesians. Plus, the bottom half of this country is like one big army camp. Whatever it is, it's big ...'

'If it was a choice between weapons and seriously good navigation equipment,' said Mary, also ignoring Diana, 'I would choose the latter. I had to land a Spit at Chattis Hill airbase yesterday and it took me forever to find it. The whole place is rather too-well camouflaged.'

181

'… On the plus side,' continued Diana, now clearly realising that she was talking only to herself, '*so* many lovely American servicemen here since this all began. But something huge *is* happening, and I'm going to find out what the blazes it is …'

The high whine of an aircraft engine broke Diana's sentence, and shouting could be heard from outside.

'What on earth …,' said Jackie, as she jumped up from the table, knocking her chair over in the process.

The air raid warning sounded as a lone Luftwaffe plane appeared from the clouds and flew low over the airfield. It banked steeply, its engine screaming, and with lightning flames flickering from its wing stubs. The staccato rattle of high velocity machine guns followed a few seconds later, and explosive rounds strafed the airfield and hangars.

'My God, we're being attacked,' shouted Lettice, 'get down!'

'You don't say…' said Diana as she dived under a table.

Outside, personnel ran for cover as bullets tore across the airfield and through the hangars. A fuel bowser erupted in flames with a colossal explosion, and the hangar next to it caught fire and burned furiously against the grey sky. The aircraft inside exploded as the flames reached its fuel tanks, enveloping the hangar in a huge wall of flames.

Everyone in the library was taking cover under the tables, and Diana quickly dashed out to drag Lettice away from the window and back under the table with her. Molly and Mary pulled another table in front of themselves as a shield from the shattering glass from the window, which was now scattered across the floor around them. They clung to each other with their eyes closed and then it suddenly became eerily quiet.

Stay where you are,' said Lettice, 'there could be more.'

They heard the sound of approaching Merlin engines overhead, and Lettice jumped up and peered through the remains of the window to see the German aircraft flying away at low level in the distance, with two Spitfires on its tail.

'He's gone,' said Lettice, 'but oh my God, it's a mess.'

A huge black smoke cloud billowed above the burning hangar. In the ensuing confusion, personnel rushed to help the wounded; some running towards the fire as airbase ambulances with clanging bells rushed to the scene. The girls carefully crawled out from under the tables and shook the broken glass from their uniforms; helping each other to pick glass fragments from their hair before walking gingerly from the library. Molly looked in shock towards the burning remains of the aircraft hangar where an ambulance team was pulling two people out on stretchers.

'Sweet Irene always said that this base is too close to the Spitfire factory,' said Molly, 'she always said that we're an easy target for the damned Luftwaffe.'

Molly turned and saw Margo running towards the girls, shouting: 'You all need to get out of here and into the shelter – quickly! There could be more of them. Come with me.'

They followed her immediately, running out of the library, along the corridors and out towards the shelter; hundreds of other people joining them to take refuge underground.

It took several days to clean up the mess and months to rebuild the hangar, which had been completely destroyed. A few people were hurt and the incident was yet another stark reminder of the vulnerability of the airfield given its proximity to the nearby Spitfire factory at Eastleigh, but more importantly, it was now evident that Germany had recognised the importance of the ATA.

Thirty-Six

After the Allies had successfully ended the campaign in North Africa, and had subsequently invaded the Italian mainland, it became necessary to gain a foothold in Europe to bring the war to an end. This was especially urgent as the Allies feared Germany would invade Great Britain, and there was also intelligence regarding German plans to unleash their latest weapon, the V-2 long-range guided ballistic missile.

US President Roosevelt and Winston Churchill agreed in principle that a major confrontation with Germany on the continent would deliver the greatest blow of the war. The alternatives were a negotiated peace with Hitler, which would entail German domination of the rest of the continent. It was therefore decided that a cross-Channel invasion in Northern France would be the quickest route into the heartland of Germany, and after much deliberation, and known only to a handful of people at the highest level, Normandy was chosen as the landing site.

Molly circled to land at Hamble Aerodrome in a Vickers Wellington long-range twin-engine bomber; a whale-like aircraft often dubbed "The Wimpy" after the character from the Popeye cartoons. Molly liked the Wellington as it was known as an extremely tough aircraft that could sustain heavy battle damage and still return its crews home to safety.

As Molly emerged out of cloud to cross the Solent, a naturally-formed narrow waterway that separates the Isle of Wight from the mainland of England, the normally quiet coastal waters were a hive of military activity, crowded by a massive build-up of naval vessels; battleships, cruisers, motor torpedo boats, destroyers, and landing craft of various types. Molly thought that there was more visible iron and steel than there was water.

'Well well well Diana,' she said, 'perhaps you were right after all.'

The huge wheels of the Wellington touched down perfectly on the runway and glided to a smooth stop. Molly disembarked, signed the aircraft in with the ground crew and headed over to the Crew Room. As she entered, she noticed a strange quietness; only a few people were scattered about despite the usual plethora of activities. Diana, Lettice and Margie were seated at a table, and Diana was leaning back with her feet on the table and hands comfortable behind her head. They looked up as Molly approached.

'Did you see the Solent? asked Molly, 'There are even more than yesterday - battleships, cruisers, destroyers, and pretty much every other type of vessel, all just sitting there!'

'One could walk from here to the Isle of Wight without getting one's feet wet,' said Diana.

'It must be the invasion, surely?' said Molly, 'Oh my God. All or nothing - liberation of the continent - hopefully?'

'I didn't think that our chaps would be going in from all the way down here,' said Margie, 'I thought that it would be Norfolk or Kent, but maybe it's a small part of something much bigger?'

'I've been hearing rumours about our boys gathering in Scotland for an invasion via Norway,' said Lettice, 'and also that Patton's First U.S. Army troops are ready in Kent.'

'Deception my dear Lettice, deception,' said Diana.

'Churchill would hardly choose Calais for a full-on assault,' said Molly, 'Jerry would be so ready for us at the closest point across the Channel. I've been reading that they've spent months building the Atlantic Wall, over two-thousand miles of obstacles. They have millions of mines, thousands of concrete bunkers and pillboxes with heavy artillery, tank ditches, and all sorts of horrid beach obstacles … *and* Jerry would be dug in on the cliff tops overlooking the landing beaches. Can you imagine? It has to be somewhere out of the ordinary.'

'Ordinary!' said Diana, 'there's no such thing as ordinary anymore. In fact, I think that word should be temporarily removed from the English language and put back when this is all over.'

Margo entered and walked over to where the girls were seated.

'You have no doubt seen the build-up,' she said, 'so no need for me to tell you the obvious. I need you all back in the Ops Room immediately to go over tomorrow's activities. You have a very early start I'm afraid.'

★★★

185

Molly walked slowly through the countryside to her digs in the village. Just before she arrived at Mrs Collis' cottage, she looked at the vast gathering of small ships in the mouth of the River Hamble. One of the elderly ladies from the village saw Molly walk by and hurried out of her cottage.

'Ooh hello there dearie,' she said, 'I've not seen you for a while. Do you know what on earth is going on? I hope those Germans are not landing in the village because you can't be too careful now you know. My husband's dead and my boy's been called away and I'm all on my own now.'

'Everything is going to be fine Mrs Furness,' said Molly, placing a reassuring hand on her shoulder 'please don't worry. And I'm sure your son will be back very soon.'

'I do hope so. I'm glad that you girls are helping out at the base because someone needs to look after our boys. They have such a dangerous job.'

'Yes, we are all very busy, Mrs Furness,' said Molly smiling.

'And what is it that you do again, dearie?'

'I just help around the base and I try to be useful. I do my bit as best I can.'

'Well you shouldn't be out on your own, because you can't be too careful. I'm talking about those Germans you know.'

'Goodnight Mrs Furness,' said Molly as she continued on to the cottage.

***

The sky was pitch black and a crescent moon shone brightly amongst the stars as early the following morning, Molly, Mary, Joy and Jackie walked into the Ops Room. The Ops team were, as always, busy posting new listings on the blackboard.

'It's all a bit uncivilised starting at this ungodly hour,' said Mary.

'Well it must be important, whatever it is,' said Molly.

As the girls walked toward the table to collect their chits, Alison called them over to her desk.

'Ah,' said Alison, 'just the girls that I'm looking for. Molly, Joy, Mary - Three 'P1 W' Spits from Supermarine to Renfrew. No relays, so they're all yours all the way. You can stop off at Cosford but stay together on this one as we want the Spits in at the same time. By the way - they are fitted with the new 80-series Griffon engine, so they're fast - and watch the swing on take-off. There's an Anson waiting for you on the apron.'

'That's nice,' said Jackie, 'you three get to stay together, while I've dragged myself out of bed at the crack of three for nothing.'

'Don't speak too soon Jackie,' said Alison smiling, 'I have something very special for you.

Molly, Joy and Mary disembarked the Anson at the Supermarine factory in Eastleigh and said good-bye to the new pilot. As the sun rose, they walked towards the apron and the Anson taxied out.

'It's so strange not seeing Douglas,' said Molly, thinking of how he always made her smile. 'What was all that about the swing on take-off?'

'It's the new Griffon engine,' said Joy, 'the prop rotates in the opposite direction to that of the Merlin, so it swings to the right on take-off rather than to the left. Compensate by going heavy on the port trim instead of the starboard.'

'And open the throttle slowly or the heavy swing to the right leads to crabbing,' added Mary.

'I love this job,' said Joy, 'no two days are the same, that's for sure.'

Molly, Joy and Mary approached the Spitfires. The aircraft stood against the spectacular backdrop of a golden sun rising over the trees in the distance, infusing everything with a shimmering glow. They stopped and stared at the breath-taking view.

'Golly, look at that,' said Molly, 'how beautiful is the Spitfire.'

'It really is the spirit of freedom,' said Joy.

They approached the aircraft whereupon Mary took out a pen from her bag and with a flourish, wrote her name on the inside of the drop-down door of one of the Spitfires.

'Are you signing your autograph?' asked Molly.

'Maybe a lovely RAF chap out there somewhere will see my name and he will come and find me,' said Mary.

'Spitfires and romance,' said Joy, 'a match made in heaven... surrounded by the hell of war.'

The girls climbed aboard the Spitfires, powered up the engines and taxied to the runway. They took off one by one and quickly moved into airborne formation side by side, with Joy a few feet short of the centre, so that they could clearly see each other in the cockpits. As they approached the Cotswolds, Mary looked across to Joy and then to Molly, and smiled. They sensed what Mary was thinking and smiled back as she twirled her finger and then broke from the formation.

Molly and Joy followed as Mary decreased her altitude and barrel-rolled as the Griffon engine kicked in; its own unique adrenaline touching every part of the small aircraft as it twisted, turned and looped through a series of aerobatic manoeuvres which Joy and Molly followed with perfect precision. The dazzling and alluring combination of pilot skill, British craftsmanship, technology and cutting-edge design merged together in perfection as the three girls revelled in a breath-taking aerial display, like a flock of starlings gracing the sky in one of nature's greatest spectacles.

After a few minutes of exhilarating aerobatics, they broke off and levelled out, coming back into formation. Molly, Jackie and Joy were breathing heavily; their hearts racing and their smiles beaming out across the sky.

Molly contemplated how many more experiences like that she would have.

Thirty-Seven

The past few days had been strangely quiet at Hamble Ferry Pool with only a handful of ferry trips being tasked. For the pilots, this resulted in long periods of sitting around and waiting, as they filled their time by drinking tea, playing cards and listening to wild predictions about the future course of the war. The shared feeling was that history was about to take a dramatic turn, and they eagerly awaited news connected with the persistent rumours of an invasion. Molly used what she considered to be a temporary reprieve to wind down and relax; looking forward to jumping into bed every evening with a good book after listening to the daily escapades of her ever-more-eccentric landlady.

Mrs Collis had indeed kept her promise, purchasing a dairy cow which she quickly installed at the bottom of the garden and set about making it work for her, milking and bottling the produce using methods which were all completely new to Molly, but which Mrs Collis had done many times before. Molly took a keen interest and named the cow "Beau", primarily after the Beaufighter aircraft, but more so because she thought the cow pretty, and Molly looked forward to returning to the cottage in the evenings to see it.

On a beautiful morning in early June, Molly woke late to the sound of a small chiffchaff that was perfectly perched on the windowsill of her room, the scrabbling and scratching of its tiny claws on the wood being the only noise that could be heard in the stillness of the morning. Molly sat up and looked at the little bird, wondering if it had flown in from Africa or the Mediterranean, and whether it had flown more miles than she had during the past few months. She slowly got up from the bed as the book that she had been reading before falling asleep fell noisily onto the floor and the startled little bird flew off. Molly quickly moved to the window and watched

189

the chiffchaff disappear into the distance, staring down into the garden of the cottage as nature slowly unfolded its morning spectacle in the early light.

Molly suddenly remembered the build-up in the Solent and the previous day's conversation, and she quickly rushed over to turn on the radio. After a few minutes of music, the broadcaster announced a news bulletin:

'Here is the news from the BBC in London. D-Day has come. Early this morning the Allies began the assault on the north western face of Hitler's European Fortress. The first official news came just after half-past-nine when Supreme Headquarters of the Allied Expeditionary Force - usually called SHAEF from its initials - issued communiqué number one.

This said: Under the command of General Eisenhower, Allied Naval Forces supported by strong Air Forces, began landing allied armies this morning on the Northern coast of France. It was announced a little later that General Montgomery is in command of the Army Group carrying out the assault. This Army Group includes British, Canadian and United States Forces.

The Allied Commander-in-Chief General Eisenhower has issued an order of the Day addressed to each individual of the Allied Expeditionary Force. In it he said, "Your task will not be an easy one. Your enemy is well trained, well equipped and battle-hardened. He will fight savagely. But this is the year 1944. The tide has turned. The free men of the world are marching together to victory. I have full confidence in your courage, devotion to duty and skill in battle. We will accept nothing less than full victory. Good luck, and let us all beseech the Blessing of Almighty God upon this great and noble undertaking."

Molly sat on the edge of the bed, motionless, her mind whirling as she thought back to the recent flights across the Solent when she looked down at what she now realised was the invasion fleet. She thought about all the pieces of information that Diana had put together during their conversation in the library. Her mind drifted further back to the time at Irvine Harbour with Jackie Cochran and seeing the vast amount of landing craft bobbing about in the water and also being manufactured in the shipyard, and then to the aircraft that she had delivered over the past weeks that had black and white markings. Molly suddenly felt a rush of satisfaction at the realisation that she had been a part of D-Day, albeit in a small way. Her contribution mattered and it was something that no-one could ever take from her.

But then another more frightening thought crossed her mind: 'Was this the beginning of the end... and if so, the end of what?'

On the 6th June 1944, the landings at Normandy constituted the largest seaborne invasion in history and was a major turning point in the war, as over one-hundred-and-fifty-thousand troops crossed the Channel on that day, and over five-thousand landing and assault craft participated. It was the start of the campaign to liberate Europe and to defeat Germany.

Part of the success of D-Day was due to a military deception strategy codenamed "Operation Bodyguard", which misled the German High Command as to the time and place of the invasion. In addition, the Allies were able to achieve and maintain air supremacy, which prohibited the enemy from observing and acting on the invasion preparations underway in Britain. The ATA had been one of the vertebrae in the backbone to Britain's air strategy, and although unrecognised by the mainstream, those who truly understood the structure of the nation's air defence system acknowledged, albeit not publicly, the vital part played by the organisation of "Ancient and Tattered Airmen".

Although the allied forces secured a foothold in northern France, the fight was nowhere close to being over, as the Allies encountered fierce German resistance when attempting to push their way through the Normandy countryside.

Shortly after the D-Day landings, tragedy struck at the heart of the ATA once again. On 4th August 1944, Margie Fairweather died after she force-landed a Percival Proctor single-engine low-wing monoplane in a field in Cheshire following engine failure. The aircraft dropped into a hidden ditch at the end of the field. Margie's sister Kitty, who also worked for the ATA, was in the aircraft along with an official from the Ministry of Aircraft Production and both miraculously survived the accident. Margie was rushed to the Chester Royal Infirmary hospital with serious head injuries, however she failed to regain consciousness. She had only just returned to work after giving birth to a daughter. The technical investigation showed a mechanical problem with the fuel tank.

It was Margo who broke the news to the girls one evening in the Crew Room. Diana, who had been close to Margie for many years, took it badly, especially given that Elizabeth, the child of Margie and Douglas, was now an orphan.

***

After several months, the tide of the war began to turn with Germany now under attack from all sides. Although deadly V-2 rockets were raining on Britain, the end of the war became a tangible prospect. It was business as usual at the ATA Ferry Pool No. 15 at Hamble. Things were changing for ATA pilots as they were now given permission to fly into Europe; ferrying food and supplies to liberated countries and attracting further recognition of their value. As a consequence, the pilots were taught how to use radios and the call sign was changed from "Lost Child" to "Ferdinand"; much to the relief of many and resulting in several taxi Ansons being emblazoned with Disney's "Ferdinand the Bull" character.

Molly, as usual, focussed with utmost dedication on the job at hand and the ferry tasks continued relentlessly. She no longer had to think about the little blue book of Ferry Pilot Notes as Molly had now accumulated a breadth of experience and was more than capable of handling most types of aircraft. She felt trusted to fly anything, and that had become the new unseen stripe on the shoulder flash: the ultimate accolade, and one which only a handful of pilots had achieved.

The invitations from interested male officers continued - parties, cinema trips, group gatherings, quiet dinners for two, all of which Molly rejected without a second thought. Her social life was her friends, and they had become so much more than that over the years. They had been through it all together: the excitement of gaggle trips, the heartbreaks and the jubilations, the deep and meaningful conversations, the advice and counselling, and the unforgettable evenings when they had laughed until they cried, like a family of sisters who could be trusted and relied upon no matter what.

Despite the company of those most precious colleagues and the love of sliding into a cockpit and soaring up into a celestial blue sky, there loomed in the back of Molly's mind that thought of potential emptiness, and the

192

great unknown she would have to face when the day that everyone dreamed of, and wished for, eventually arrived. It was like a great paradox; the joy of Germany's defeat set against the uncharted return to what would be the remnants of Molly's normal life.

The Bugle Pub in Hamble-le-Rice village had become quite the "local" for the ATA pilots, situated a few minutes' walk from where most of the girls were billeted. It was a small and quaint coastal village pub, and its association with the ATA and the RAF resulted in the walls being adorned with photos of aircraft and pilots, among whom were those most familiar to the British public, such as Lettice Curtis, Amy Johnson and Maureen Dunlop.

On a cold evening in December, several officers from the Fleet Air Arm and the RAF were laughing and joking at the bar and drinking beer from tankards as they told their stories of flying. Sometimes the laughter would diminish as someone inadvertently mentioned an incident connected with the loss of a colleague, but then they would quickly bounce back in good spirits. A few of the local villagers were dotted about and the whole pub had a pleasant and cosy ambiance.

Molly, Diana, Lettice, Jackie, Joy and Mary were sitting at a table in the corner and raising a toast. Jackie was drinking orange juice.

'Here's to our being officially cleared to fly to the continent,' said Joy, 'and to the person who made it possible - Diana.'

'To Diana!' they cheered, raising their glasses as Diana beamed.

'Did you actually have permission to fly a Spitfire to Brussels?' said Molly to Diana.

'Of course, darling,' said Diana, 'would I ever do anything without permission?'

'Noooooooooooo,' they said in unison, laughing.

'I was simply following my husband,' continued Diana. 'He had authority for the delivery of two Spitfires and accidentally forgot to mention that I would be the second pilot. It was rather marvellous, I must say. One of my most memorable periods of weekend leave.'

'You were on leave?' said Mary, 'Really Diana, I just don't know how you get away with it. But at least we are flying across the Channel now, so that will spice things up just a little, plus I much prefer "Ferdinand" as a call sign. 'Lost Child' is hardly appropriate if Jerry is listening.'

'I'll be lost when the war ends.' said Jackie wistfully, 'Have you ever thought about what we'll do when this is all over?'

'We've been so busy that I haven't actually had a chance to properly think about it yet,' said Joy, 'but I'd like to carry on flying.'

'Me too,' said Mary, 'but it may be a devil of a job finding space for us girls once all the chaps come home.'

'We're all experienced and capable pilots,' said Diana, 'We can make the space I'm sure.'

'We'll spend a lot of time remembering those we loved - and lost,' said Molly, as everyone at the table became quiet. 'I don't just mean Bernard. I'm thinking about the lovely Jane Winstone … and the beautiful and vivacious Margie Fairweather.'

'Poor Jane,' said Diana, 'it seems an age ago when we first met her in Austin Reed; do you remember? She had just arrived from New Zealand and was trying to get over the loss of her husband.'

'Yes,' said Molly, 'and dearest Douglas as well. Oh my gosh - wasn't he a larger than life character?'

'Yes, he was rather wonderful,' said Mary, 'as long as you didn't mind sitting in a fug of cigarette smoke.' They laughed.

'That's true,' said Diana, 'did you know the secret of his navigation? Did you ever wonder how he managed to come out of fog or clouds, and right there in front of him would be the middle of his destination airfield - no maps, no looking down for landmarks - it would always be right there.'

'Yes, he was rather good at that,' said Joy, 'a lot of experience and practice I suppose.'

'It was those cigarettes,' said Diana, 'he knew exactly how long it would take him to smoke each cigarette, and so a quick time and speed calculation times the number of cigarettes gave him the distance; he used it as a measure!'

'I asked him once if he was ever worried about being dismissed for smoking in the cockpit,' said Joy, 'and do you know what he said? He told me that was the reason he loved flying in fog - because with the side window open when he landed, no-one could tell the difference between his smoke and the fog!'

The girls were laughing, but at the same time trying to hold back their tears.

'I miss him terribly,' said Lettice, 'and lovely Margie too. Their little one is a year old now; it's all so desperately sad. The poor little mite never met her father and will never remember her mother; both killed within a few months of each other. It's just too cruel.'

Lettice raised her glass and the other girls followed.

'To our wonderful friends,' she said, 'great aviators one and all.'

'Our wonderful friends,' they repeated, 'great aviators one and all.'

'Do you think our days as professional aviators are numbered?' asked Jackie, clearing her throat.

'Well there will be a huge surplus of pilots at the end of the war,' replied Joy, 'so our opportunities will most certainly be more limited - to say the least.'

'And it will all start again no doubt, said Mary, 'women taking jobs away from men!'

'Oh, I don't know about that,' said Joy, 'I have a feeling that I'll be flying for the rest of my life.'

Thirty-Eight

On an afternoon in May, Molly landed a Spitfire Mk XIV at Hamble airfield and noticed a large number of personnel running towards the Crew Room. Her first thought was that something bad had happened; her usual 'go-to' reaction over the past few years. 'Where on earth is the ground crew?' asked Molly to herself, looking around to see if she had missed them in her line of vision. She guided the Spitfire in by herself, drew back the canopy, quickly unstrapped, and hopped onto the wing and down on to the ground.

Confused, Molly threw her parachute over her shoulder and was about to cross the airfield when Mary sprang out of the crowd and ran up to Molly.

'Mary, what on earth is going on?' asked Molly, 'Where is everyone going?'

'Oh Molly, haven't you heard? It's over,' cried Mary, 'the war is over!'

Mary gave a little jump into the air and then turned excitedly and ran toward the Crew Room leaving Molly standing rigid; her face expressionless, her mind racing at a thousand miles an hour. It seemed to Molly as if time had frozen in that instant, her peripheral vision picking up the movement and excitement all around her, yet she was rooted to the spot, her mind trying frantically to process the news and everything that it entailed. Molly had suddenly realised that her entire life was about to change - again.

People were shouting and hugging each other or running in different directions, mostly heading to the Crew Room, so Molly followed. As she entered, there was a huge celebration unfolding. People were standing on the tables and on the bar, corks were popping and beer, wine and Champagne was flowing as people cheered, kissed each other, or caught hold of each other and spun round. Molly appeared to others as though in a mild, euphoric shock with no outward display of reaction or emotion. People were running up to her and hugging her, many of whom she knew, and many she did not. She barely reciprocated their hugs but instead looked lost and faraway. Mary spotted Molly from the side of the room and moved into the crowd to pull her out of the arms of one of the ground crew, who had perhaps taken the opportunity to fulfil an ambition. Molly seemed to be oblivious.

'Come over here,' said Mary, as she took Molly by the hand, 'the girls are by the bar.'

Just as they reached Lettice, Joy, Jackie, and Diana, who was busy popping a bottle of Champagne, Gerard d'Erlanger entered, and the room erupted into a deafening roar. There were shouts and applause, and cheering seemed to be coming from all corners of the room. Dennis Lead, the former taxi driver from outside the Savoy Hotel, was at the front of the crowd in his ATA pilot's uniform.

'Speech, speech!' he shouted, climbing on a chair and holding his drink in the air.

Everyone joined in and started banging the tables ... 'Speech! Speech!'

Gerard d'Erlanger stood on a table and the whole room suddenly became quiet. He looked around for a few seconds before speaking, taking in the proud faces of the hundreds of people who were hanging on his every word.

'We have just heard that the Russians have taken Berlin,' said d'Erlanger, 'Germany has unconditionally surrendered.'

A roar went up that threatened to lift the roof off as everyone banged the tables.

He waited for hush and then continued: 'In these great days of the magnificent victory of our fighting forces in Europe, I congratulate you all and thank you all for a fantastic job, superbly carried through to the end. We've had our own battles to keep this organisation alive, to do what it was born to do, and to do that thing to the best of its ability... to *fly*, and to be a real and essential part of this war.'

The jubilant crowd cheered again and several of the men and women were in tears.

D'Erlanger continued: 'There have been many casualties in the ranks of the ATA, and today we remember with pride the many male and female pilots and ground staff, who gave their lives in the service of our great country. It is our duty to ensure that their sacrifice has not been in vain.'

D'Erlanger raised his glass as the crowd fell silent.

'To our friends,' he said, 'gone but never forgotten.'

'To our friends,' they repeated, 'gone but never forgotten.'

Molly pulled the photo of Bernard from her breast pocket where she had always kept it, close to her heart and only a touch away, and as she looked down at it, Mary put her arms around her and hugged her tightly.

'It will be OK, old thing', said Mary.

'One final thing,' said d'Erlanger, 'when you walk out of those gates for the last time, and you look at the fields; the villages, the trees, the people in their cars and on their bikes, remember that this is *our* country. Every one of you helped to ensure that it will always be *our* country, and anyone in the future who thinks about taking it away from us – *let them think again!*' He raised his glass, 'Aetheris Avidi, Eager for the air.'

The whole room erupted again in loud cheers and applause.

'I don't want my life here to change,' said an emotional Joy.

Molly was so happy, yet at the same time so immensely sad. She clutched the photo of Bernard and the full impact of going back to normal life as a widow hit her with the utmost force. She managed to hold back her tears and then she heard Diana's voice in her head: *"Get a grip old thing. Feelings are for peacetime"*.

Thirty-Nine

During the first few weeks of peacetime, the western world erupted in a celebration like no other; almost six hard years of war was finally at an end. Over a million people gathered in the streets across the United Kingdom, with London the particular focus as crowds gathered in and around Trafalgar Square, Leicester Square and Buckingham Palace, where the King and Queen appeared on the balcony alongside Winston Churchill.

The new freedom finally meant the end of restrictions and some rationing. Blackouts, air-raid warnings and bombings were now to become things of the past; although the scars of war would take time to heal, and the experiences would stay with people until the end of their lives. The journeys home to families and loved ones commenced, and villages and towns across the country were adorned with bunting and flags. Church bells rang out proclaiming peace and their news drifted across villages and fields, towns and cities. For most, those sounds were joyous and life-affirming, but for many they were a deafening, relentless reminder of their own loss and sadness: an altogether different kind of celebration, and a sombre recognition of those who had bravely given their lives for their country.

Peace was here, but for many people it also brought the reality of their loss, now to be processed and understood in times of quiet reflection during those first days and weeks in the immediate aftermath of war. For many that loss was huge and all-engulfing, like the crater left behind in a city street where once had stood a house and where a family had lived and loved. The void was immense and the pain unbearable, and it would echo long into their futures.

The reality of the situation also began to set in at the ATA Ferry Pool No.15 at Hamble, and indeed at many of the other Ferry Pools; all of which were in the throes of closing down. The majority of pilots had been released from their duties and some were commissioned into the RAF, whilst others were planning to return to their native countries. Much of the ATA's work was transferred to active service squadrons within the RAF as many aircraft needed to be flown to scrapyards.

The ATA offered assistance to pilots who wished to secure their licenses for a career in the commercial sector, however quite a few were at a loss as to what to do and were hesitant to face the new world. The Crew Room became a sanctuary for those who did not want to, or simply could not let go, and several sat and watched, disheartened as the aerodrome disintegrated around them.

Vehicles of all types buzzed across the airbase as leftover supplies in boxes of all shapes and sizes were prepared and packed. A few stationary aircraft were still scattered around haphazardly, looking slightly lost and lonely. Cars arrived to pick up personnel who had packed and were ready to leave, many of whom were still in uniform, and the occasional ambulance arrived to transport those patients from the sick bay who were too injured to travel by car.

Molly was still dressed in uniform, and gathering her things from the locker room, pulling out clothes and various memorabilia that she had collected over the past few years and throwing everything into a large canvas bag. Mary entered, bright-eyed and radiant and wearing a polka-dot summer dress, and with sunglasses holding back her hair.

'I hoped that I would find you here,' said Mary, 'I cleared mine out yesterday.'

'I feel so depressed,' said Molly, removing the photographs and magazine clippings stuck to the inside of her locker door, 'but I feel guilty for being depressed. This should be the most joyous of times.'

'I know old thing,' said Mary, as she took Molly by the arm. 'Do you remember what Diana said about temporarily removing the word 'ordinary' from the English language, and putting it back when it's all over? Well I don't feel that anything will ever be ordinary again.'

'I have no idea what I'll do now that it's all over,' said Molly, 'anyway … sorry … I'm being a terrible bore. I've already said my goodbyes but I promised Lettice that I would pop in to the Crew Room before I go. Are you going over?'

'Yes,' said Mary, 'the others are just coming. Finish packing up and I'll see you there.'

Mary promptly disappeared as quickly as she had arrived, and Molly could smell Mary's perfume in the air. Molly thought that everything about her friend looked different, and she was happy to see her in such good spirits. 'Mary deserves that', thought Molly as she closed her bag and walked out of the locker room and turned into the corridor.

The door to one of the offices flew open, and Margo Gore quickly came out. Both girls jumped when they almost ran into each other. Margo was carrying a clipboard and she had a pile of papers under one arm, and a pen between her teeth, which she struggled to remove so that she could speak to Molly.

'Ah Molly,' said Margo, 'sorry, I know you're busy, but Ops has just been on and they want someone to meet a Flamingo transporter coming in, and to direct two of the passengers to the sick bay. They haven't got anyone available with all this hubbub, and we're nearby, so, could you kindly do the honours? It'll just be a couple of ticks. Thanks Molly.'

'Yes ma'am' said Molly, happy to be doing something that took her mind off of things.

'Oh, I almost forgot,' said Margo, 'here's a letter for you'.

'Thanks,' said Molly, as she quickly tore open the envelope and pulled out a wedding invitation to the marriage of Elisabeth Allesandra Hemsworth and Edward Egerton-Reed on Saturday 25th August 1945 at St Eadburgha's Church in Snowshill in the Cotswolds. Elisabeth had written on the back of the invitation: *"Darling Molly, Thank you for everything. You may remember that there is something that I was supposed to ask you about my wedding, however I didn't get the chance. I'll see you soon. Love, Elisabeth"*.

Molly smiled and made her way out to the apron as a de Havilland DH.95 Flamingo transporter taxied in and came to a standstill. The twin engines of the huge aircraft cut and the props slowed to a halt, and Molly could see the two pilots seated side by side in the cockpit with a radio operator behind them. The aircraft could carry up to seventeen passengers and Molly thought about how much she enjoyed flying them, and how she may not see one again.

Molly walked across the grass towards the aircraft as the door opened, and she watched two nurses help two fragile men alight. Both men were bandaged, and one had bandages over his eyes. The nurses supported the men as they slowly and carefully took the few steps down to the ground. As Molly walked further towards the group, another figure stepped out of the aircraft unassisted - a tall, gaunt, sun-ravaged man in an officer's uniform, and he stood for a moment looking around at the airfield.

Molly stopped in her tracks and stared. She could not believe what was in front of her eyes and for a brief moment she swayed on her feet, thinking that she may faint.

'It can't...be...' she said, 'surely... it can't be...'

Captain Bernard Rose was standing by the door of the aircraft. Molly burst into tears, crying out his name over and over 'Bunny! Bunny! Bunny!' as she ran towards him faster than she had ever run for anything in her entire life. Bernard spotted her and limped painfully down the stairs to the ground and towards her. They fell into each other's arms.

Oh my god - Bunny; is it really you?' said Molly in floods of tears, 'I thought you were dead - I have a letter - two letters - saying you were dead. I thought that you were gone forever.'

'Molly, oh my sweet Molly,' he said, tearfully, 'Yes, my darling, it's really me, yes. You mean they didn't tell you that I was on my way back? Oh Molly, I've missed you so much. It's the thought of you that has kept me going.'

'But I don't understand. How? What happened?'

'My tank took a hit,' he said, 'and we all bailed out, and then I tried to get someone else out of a burning tank just before ours went up in flames. It was such a mess and we were all separated; they must have assumed the worst for me.'

'But poor Fruity got back - what happened to you?' said Molly, wiping tears from her eyes.

'That bugger Fruity left me in the desert,' said Bernard, smiling, 'I need to have a serious word with him. We were found by a German patrol that night; marched for days from one camp to another for months on end. We were pretty much done in when the Yanks arrived and flew us back to Europe; and then the RAF brought us home. It's been utter chaos.'

'Oh Bunny, I can't believe you survived all that. My poor darling.'

Molly threw her arms around Bernard again.

'It was all pretty ghastly,' he said, smiling, 'I did however manage to compose some music; I couldn't exactly form a chamber orchestra, but it did keep me sane. That and thinking of coming home to you my darling.'

'You did keep your promise after all.' said Molly.

'And you kept yours.'

'Let's go home Bunny.'

The couple walked away arm-in-arm towards the main gates. Margo, Diana, Jackie, Joy, Lettice, Alison and Mary were standing outside one of the office buildings watching them.

As Molly and Bernard walked through the gates, a lone female figure in uniform lowered the ATA flag from the main flagpole, and Molly looked up to see a solitary Spitfire flying overhead.

Forty

November 2015

Molly is standing on the lectern in St Paul's Cathedral, and in her mind's eye she is flying, looking down from the dome with a smile on her face, she reaches up to her lapel and gently touches the broach of golden wings.

'To quote Laurence Binyon,' says Molly:

'They shall grow not old, as we that are left grow old:

Age shall not weary them, nor the years condemn.

At the going down of the sun and in the morning,

We will remember them.

The hymn Jerusalem begins to play as Molly is assisted down from the lectern by her son, and together with Joy and Mary, they walk towards the exit of St Paul's and out onto the steps, under the canopy of an endless blue sky.

Epilogue

During the Second World War, 1,250 men and women from 25 countries ferried over 309,000 aircraft of 147 different types. In total 173 ATA aircrew died in ATA service. They are commemorated on a special memorial plaque in St Paul's Cathedral, London. As is quoted on the plaque: "Remember then that also we in a moon's course are history".

The Battle of Malta, which could not have taken place without the efforts of the ATA, abruptly ended the daytime bombing of Malta, and in effect secured North Africa to alter the course of the war.

After the war, Molly and Bernard were together for a further 51 years until Bernard died on 21st November 1996 (aged 80). Molly lived until the age of 95 and died on 16th October 2016 in Cupar, Fife in Scotland. Molly's ashes are buried beside Bernard's in the graveyard of St Mary's Church, Bampton in Oxfordshire.